Lake Miskatonic

Jeff Pollet

For Lauren

Prelude

August 1924
Oakland, California

He felt the power of the crowd, the force of the chanting resonating in his spine, his bowels, the bones of his face. He felt the moment growing close now, the culmination of all of his hard work, decades spent gathering his power, unrooting enough rubes to forfeit their power without even knowing they were doing so. And he had waited for so long, just as he waited now. Waited for the power to build within the auditorium, to expand toward the water and the city outside. It all came down to this one night. He shook his head slowly as he removed his ridiculous white hood, a sly smile on his lips. He still couldn't quite believe that It had all led to this little city, on the wrong coast, to a swamp the locals called a lake. He looked around at the crowd, moving as one creature, undulating with hate they felt as joy, with words escaping their throats as if a benediction. Many had on their tall white hats and hooded robes, decorated with new religion symbols, mostly the crosses that were still in favor. They wouldn't be in favor for much longer, he thought. And these men would soon be dead.

There were flames in the auditorium, rising from four 10-foot tall burning crosses in the stands. A thousand people, perhaps more, ignorant of the death that was about to come to them, cheered their new inductees at the center of the auditorium. All were unaware of what was coming, he knew, completely unaware, and that was fitting. Their hate was irrelevant in the coming world, and would soon be barely a memory. He would remember them as just another tool to get him what he desired, to broker the arrival of a Being whose power would turn their petty beliefs to wet ash. The hate in their eyes, the revelry in that hate, would give him the last bit of power he lacked to bring his Master into being here.

And then he felt the silent call. It was unmistakable to him, though none of the Klan members around him could feel it. His heart felt it, the blood in its chambers turning hot, his mouth filling with his own salty spit, tasting of copper and brine. The call pulled at him. It was time. He made his way through the back of the crowd on the auditorium floor, to a small alcove, and approached a locked door. The pull was strong, and he felt an impossible compulsion to throw himself against the door, but this wasn't his first dance with this particular devil, and he resisted. He took one last look back at the crowd. In a few minutes, they would all be gone, fuel for the eternal fires his Master would bring. He reached into a pocket on the inside of his robe, removing a small piece of rough stone, hard won decades ago, feeling it pulse in his hand like a living thing. Shedding his robe now like a snake sheds skin, he unlocked the door, opened it, and walked out into the crisp night, smiling at the thought of his dark dreams finally coming true.

In the lake, something stirred.

1

Oakland, California.
Now.

The birds have come back to the lake, and the bodies. The birds never really left completely, of course. Oakland's pretty much always had a bird sanctuary. "Oldest wildlife refuge in the country", point of fact. Nobody ever believes that when I tell them, even Oaklanders. I know a bit about the lake though. And about bodies.

I still walk the lake most mornings. Gets me out and about, keeps my old bones from getting too stiff. There's a regular crew of folks running, walking, going to work. Some of us say casual hellos to each other, the regulars. I walk along slowly, sure, but I make up in consistency what I lose in speed. Been doing it for close to 50 years now. Not sure how much longer I can keep it up. Life is a thickening haze into history at this point, but I still love the lake.

Never loved the bodies. It's always a bit shocking, to see a dead body, even after you've seen a few dozen. Sometimes I think it's more shocking now, since I'm closer to being a dead body myself than ever before. My associates don't like it when I talk like that, but it's true. No use avoiding the truth, and dark humor has always been in my wheelhouse. Now it's a friend, a confidante. Some friends will never leave you, though most do, especially at my age. I'm grateful the humor hasn't left me, even through the hardest days. Where was I? Oh yes, bodies. I try to stay out of the business of bodies these days, though they used to be my main business. Lately I stick with cheating spouses, petty white collar thieves, that sort of thing. Most of that stuff doesn't even require much footwork these days. That's why we have the series of tubes, now, right? A few well-placed clicks and I've got more information than I could want. It's the sifting through that takes time. And I have Darya for that. She wouldn't want me saying that, even though she's very good at it, and it's hard to teach that part of the job. She likes being out and about just as much, talking with people, which will serve her well, though the sifting is most of the job now, as I said.

Still, two bodies in the lake in just two months. Even now, as the population here shifts and shimmies, folks are on edge when bodies show up in the lake. Some people call that shimmy "gentrification". That's another word for "fucking over poor people", which is pretty obvious if you've lived in a city for any length of time. I try not to get involved in all of that. Darya says I'm lazy to not get involved. If she's in a mood, she says I'm full of white privilege. Or full of shit. She's probably right, but I'm too old to think about that crap now. And now I'm thinking about the bodies anyway. I figure I can do more good for Oakland thinking about bodies than I can spending time on anything else. But maybe I am just lazy.

I see Frank up ahead in his usual mussel-eating spot. I think of Frank as something of an acquaintance, since I see him most days. Frank is a seagull. Frank might be a bunch of different seagulls, I guess, but I usually see him around this spot, sitting on the edge of the lake this time of the morning, working on a mussel he's ripped from the lake, trying to get to the good stuff inside. "Hi Frank," I say to him as I slow briefly to greet him. He looks at me for a moment,

2

seems to recognize me. At least he recognizes I'm no threat, and he goes back to work on the mussel. Another daily ritual for both of us, ever since the mussels returned full force in the last few years to the lake. Technically it's a 'tidal lagoon'. As I get closer I see maybe Frank has injured himself, with blood on his beak. Maybe it's mussel blood? Do mussels bleed? He stops and looks at me again, side-eyeing me in that bird-like way, pausing from his work. "I'm not going to take your food, Frank," I say as I get within a couple of feet of the bird. I do want a closer look suddenly, because if he's hurt maybe I can let the folks at the bird sanctuary know. It is blood, glistening a dark red against the bland yellow-white of his beak. I take another slow step toward him. Frank seems frozen now, staring at me, a bit of mussel hanging from his lower beak. Maybe it's not blood. Looks like it might be green. Maybe muck from Frank digging around at the bottom of the lake. No, looks like blood. Huh. Dark green-red blood. I take out my phone to get a picture when Frank looks startled, and a skinny white guy running by nearly kicks him into the lake.

"Look out old man, fuck!" says the runner when he's past us. Frank has flown off, flipping his quarry back into the lake. "Have a nice day, douchebag," I say, under my breath. When people ask me if Oakland is a safe place to live, I tell them that you really mostly have to watch out for the runners around the lake. Those people will run you down and smile while they do it. I see a bit of the muck on the ground still, and take a picture of it. Green and red, for sure. Do mussels bleed? I'll have to ask Darya later. Or Google. I resume my walk, knowing I'll probably see Frank tomorrow anyway. Hope he's ok.

It is nice to see the birds come back. There are fish in the lake again, now that they're letting more water in more regularly, ever since they took out the big underwater screens linking the estuary and the lake proper. Not just gulls, either. A family of pelicans was here last year. They should be back soon. A handful of ink-black cormorants, who I see here and there around the lake, wings spread, worshiping the sun in their own little way. Egrets. It used to be that the lake had no "r-egrets". Ha. Funny old man. I'll try that one on Darya. I can kind of lose myself to the morning light, the sameness of the bustle around the lake. I know it's good for me, the walking, but I am tired already. The lake is vaguely shaped like a mutated "U", with lots to do within the "inside" of the "U"--parts of the park include places to barbeque, a playground, bocce ball, a fountain. Children's Fairyland, a neat little miniature amusement park for little tykes lives near the peak of one side of the "U". The bird sanctuary lives in the water near the inside of the bottom of the curve. So, walking the whole lake takes me a good long while, an hour or so depending on how I'm feeling. Today I'm feeling tired, and walking slowly.

I look up at one of the few skyscrapers on the lake. Huey Newton lived up there for a bit, up in a penthouse, during the days when the Black Panthers seemed to be everywhere in Oakland, everywhere in the country, really. I wonder what he would think of how Oakland has changed, and how it hasn't. I like to think about him up there, looking down at the town I love, keeping an eye on things. I wish I believed in ghosts. If I did, Newton would surely be hanging around Oakland still, doing his part. I read once that he didn't really like living in the penthouse on the lake, but his being there made a statement, and he agreed to do it for that reason. Odd to think of living in a penthouse as a sacrifice, but that man made so many sacrifices, including his life. People walk and job by this place all morning, and I'd guess few of them know any of this history. I wonder if Newton knew the history even further back--the Ohlone used to fish here when it was just a part of the larger bay, before they were 'relocated' to San Jose. I love my town. Most of its history, like most towns, are built on bones and blood. It's a good thing to remember for me, as I walk.

Today I have a destination. A little coffee shop on the lake. There are about a million of them now that money's come back to Oakland. That's a benefit for me. You can learn a lot talking to baristas, customers, spending time in a cafe, listening to people talk. Today I'm meeting Detective Harks. Knew her dad when he was a detective. When he was alive. She doesn't call me often, so I know the investigation involving the bodies must have hit a wall somehow. She knows I know things, she knows I know Oakland. She also knows I don't have much of a relationship with the Oakland PD any longer, so she'll be buying.

I see her at her usual corner table, saving me a seat. She's got my drink on the table already. Chalk that up to one of the advantages to being an old man who is needed. The place has an early-morning bustle about it, and I notice yet again how many more young people, really young people, dressed in business casual seem to be sprouting up from the muck in the lake. Pop! Pop! Pop! More kids with 50's haircuts and electric scooters. They're mostly harmless, I suppose, but it takes getting used to. I make my way to the table, invisible to most of those younger folks, and sit. That invisibility comes in handy sometimes, too, the filter that people under 40 seem to have for not seeing anybody over 40.

"You can't smoke in here, Walt," Harks says to me, like she always does. I take the stub of a cigar, which hasn't been lit in a few days, out of the corner of my mouth and set it on the edge of the table, leaving the well-chewed end hanging in space. "And that is disgusting, Walt. Just. Disgusting." She smiles when she says it, but I know she also kind of means it. I also don't care much. I've lost track of what I do that's because of my age, and what's just my lifelong rudeness. Where does the cigar fit in? Not sure.

"Yeah, well, you're not supposed to talk cases to civilians, but here we are." I smile too. She's one of the good ones. I take the plastic lid off the paper cup, checking the contents. To-go cup. That means Harks is in a hurry for answers, and doesn't just want to gab today. Do people in their thirties gab? I take a sip. Sweet spicy chai with oat milk. Tasty.

"I can't believe you drink that stuff," Harks says, sipping her black coffee, with sixty-two or so sugars. "You're an old man, can't you act like one?"

"Well, we can't all be walking clichés all of the time, Detective. Did you already eat your donut?"

"Har har. Funny old man."

I pick up a little flier sitting on the table, asking people to come out to the lake next Saturday, and join the yearly vigil, where local folks surround the lake, pay respects for the people killed by police around Oakland, around the country. "You organizing vigils now, Harks? Your dad would be proud."

"Guy was handing these out. I took one. I might go. I didn't go to the one last year. Not sure how welcome I am there, really."

"Well, I'll go with you, if you want a non-police escort. People who know you know you belong there as much as anybody."

"Not everybody knows me," she laughs. "I'm not some weird old man who walks the lake every morning. I have a job."

"Which reminds me," I say, "you got another body last night, I saw."

"Business talk already, huh?"

4

"Well, I have to finish my morning walk, and you already look like you have been here too long." And she did. Eyes darting around, nervous in a way that might just be a cop on a case, or just a police being a police, but in my experience with Harks it's something else. Fixing her jacket lapel that didn't need fixing, brushing off slacks that didn't need brushing off, removing her glasses briefly to push her hand against her eyes as if fighting off a headache that keeps coming back.

"Right as usual, Nostradamus. Usually I just want to see your pretty face, but today, we have another body." Her deep voice lowered to almost a whisper now. "Found in the lake, like the one last month. She takes a breath, and sighs. She really is worn out. "I really could use your help on this one. Between you and me, we have nothing to go on yet. On either of them. Have you heard anything?"

"You mean on my super secret PI network? No. But I'll take a look and ask around," I say and hold out my hand, palm up. She places a small thumb drive in it.

"Same deal, right? Destroy this."

"Of course, Officer Harks," I say with mock official tone, though she knows I would never get her into trouble. Her dad got me out of trouble far too often. She knows that I will always owe her, in a way, because I will always owe him. And she knows that I like to help. Mostly, though, she knows I *can* help. I sip my chai, glancing up at her, noticing something worrisome there that I haven't seen before. "I'll take a look Monica, don't worry. We'll figure this shit out together. We always do." And then less seriously, as I take my drink, pick up my cigar and get up, pocketing the thumb drive, "getting tired of all those bodies ruining my morning constitutional, anyway." I get a hint of a smile from her as I leave her with her coffee, the tech-bro bees still buzzing around the cafe.

***

I work my way around the lake, headed south toward the estuary now, fingering the thumb drive in my pocket. I have a feeling. Maybe I'll take a look at the data before I hand it over to Darya this time. Not that I can't trust her. Just a feeling. I speed up slightly. One more stop before I can head back to the office. I already know that the body was found near the estuary, near the spot where the intake from the bay is controlled so that the lake doesn't flood. That's what makes it a lake instead of just part of the bay. It's also the best place around the lake to drop a body, especially now that the lake has more people around it, especially now after they've cleaned it up quite a bit and paved nice paths all around it. The estuary is back behind the community college, and, while there is still a paved path, it's full of potholes and not as well traveled or maintained. I like it back there, even though it's a little detour from my way back to the office. Fewer people, more geese. This time of year there are even a few goslings, sometimes.

Just a few years ago, even the main lake path wasn't a place you could walk around at night and feel safe, though it wasn't as dangerous as folks might have thought. I had quite a few midnight walks even during some of Oakland's more gritty days, though of course I always brought a revolver, or something else. These days I have mace and a taser on me at night. They're harder for somebody to take from me and shoot me with. But in these days, even after midnight, the runners are the most dangerous part of the lake.

5

Or they were. Rounding a corner high with reeds I see the remains of the police tape tied to some small trees, flapping in the breeze. Here the estuary is fairly wide, but I could still throw a rock across it if I tried. Well, maybe not today, but if I were still 50. Or maybe 40. The reeds are matted down where the body was dragged ashore. Approaching, most of what I can see is cop footprints in the muddy weeds, but yeah, there's where the body lay once they brought it out of the water. I take a breath, dead cigar in my hand, and kneel down. I'm not in horrible shape, but I feel the age in my knees these days, and kneeling isn't always the best idea. I need a closer look though.

As I approach, what I notice first is the smell. Not dead body smell exactly, though there is a remnant of that. It's the brine. The lake is saltwater, and it gets stinky in that briny way depending on the weather, and the tides. But this is stronger. Sharper. Odd. I poke around with a pen I always carry in my jacket pocket, but I don't find much. A bit of muck, no blood. The water, and then the mud, have erased most of what I could have seen. There are a lot more empty mussel shells than I would have expected to see here--the mussels are more in the rest of the lake, which has a rockier bottom than the estuary. Maybe the gulls are hoarding them here now? Hopefully the thumb drive will have some good pictures. Never know what you're going to get with Oakland PD. It takes me a while to stand back up, which is lucky, because it's then that I see that it's not just goop from the lake bottom dragged up with the body. There *is* a bit of blood. Dark red blood mixed with that green muck from the lake bottom, shiny in the sun like the slime a snail leaves behind. For a moment I wonder if Frank came by this way.

Huh.

"If you're hungry, you'll have to look somewhere else. They took the body away already, Walt," I hear a throaty growl of a laugh from behind me, and he adds: "you need some help getting up old man?" I rise as quickly as I can manage, but I already know it's Stoney.

"I'm good, Stoney. How you doing?" I walk a few steps across the path to where he's standing, beer in a paper bag in hand. He's setting down a plastic milk crate upside-down, one he carries with him a good deal of the time, and sits down on it. I notice Stoney's tent sits a few feet off the trail in the weeds. A joke about drinking so early in the morning is on the tip of my tongue before I decide to swallow it. Stoney lives pretty rough. I shouldn't begrudge him a beer in the morning. I'm not sure how long he's been living outside around Oakland, but it's been at least a decade, the whole time I've known him. He sticks to the lake, mostly, when the cops let him. Or, rather, when the new people in Oakland stop themselves from calling the cops on Stoney. The tent is newish--a slight step up for him, since the last one I saw. He's a veteran, but he won't talk about that. He'll talk about almost anything else, in fact. I've never asked him his age, but he's always called me "old man", and I suspect he is younger than the 45-50 he appears to be. Morning beers, while comforting, don't lead to looking young, I guess. Everybody who is a regular on the lake knows Stoney, and any regular worth a damn likes him. He's a nice guy, and he keeps a lookout for folks, keeps an eye on things.

"Good, good, Walt. Can't complain," he sips his beer.

"You see them haul this body out, Stoney?"

"What body?" he says, smiling, playing coy.

"Mhmmmm. What body. Maybe you were too busy sleeping in your fancy tent last night?"

"Oh, that?" he turns, looking at it as if he's never seen it before. "That's the hot new trend for urbanites, Walt! Keeps the homeless more hidden, so everybody wins." Chuckles to himself.

6

"C'mon Stoney. What did you see? Help an old man out."

"Walt," he looks at me in mock anger, "I am not your Magical Negro."

"My what?"

"The magical black man who solves the white protagonist's problems. Bagger Vance? Red Redding? What, you never watch movies?"

"I stick to trashy novels, mostly. So you have no magic for me today, then, is what you're saying?"

He begins a reply, then looks at the ground, shakes his head and laughs a deep, quiet laugh, almost to himself. "Nope. No magic today, no. But yeah, I did see them pull the body out. They already asked me all about it."

"Anything...odd about it?" I ask him. I want some answers, but I don't even really have the questions yet. Stoney looks up at me now, as I sip my chai. "Are you fucking kidding me?" he asks, a look of honest wondering on his face.

"What? You know I don't kid." His face breaks a bit now, and he shakes his head again.

"Well, you almost always kid, but you're not kidding now, are you. It looks like they haven't told you nothing yet huh? Anything weird...fuck," he continues to chuckle to himself.

"Not much, no. I guess it's need to know. You know, and I need to know." I wait for a response, which is not forthcoming. He's holding back in a way that is a little concerning. This is a guy who loves to talk. "Stoney, what the hell did you see."

"That body must have been down there for a long time, Walt. I've seen bodies before. Hell, I've even see a body in the lake before. That girl and her abusive boyfriend a few years back, remember that? I saw them pulled out in the middle of the night. But this was pretty fucked up. They really didn't tell you?"

I try to keep it light, to no avail, "Well, you know, I'm old. They don't tell me everything at once. They're afraid they might kill me." I'm only half joking.

"They said it was a fresh body, Walt, but there's no way. No way in hell."

"Why do you keep saying that?"

"It was covered with shells. The little mussel shells, y'know? Head to toe. They must have grown there, over years and years, like they grow on the rocks on the bottom of the lake. It was shaped like a body, but..." he hesitates, and I give him time to take a sip, and continue, "it was just smothered with them, couldn't see a thing. Couldn't even tell if it was a man or a woman. Shaped like a body, but just shells, just mussels, oozing this green bloody crap. I'm not talking lake muck, Walt. It was like. I don't know. I'm not fishing out of the lake for a while. Something weird going on in that water."

I can't help but glance at the beer, and back into Stoney's eyes.

"Fuck you with that, Walt. I saw it. I don't know why they didn't tell you."

"No, I believe you, Stoney. I believe you. I wouldn't be here if it wasn't something weird happening." Stoney had gone quiet, and stared at the ground. "Hey, didn't you used to park yourself over by the old auditorium with some of your friends?" I point down the pathway.

That seemed to wake him up a bit, "Oh, yeah. Yeah I did, but we got cleared out of there. It was a good setup. One guy even had a little stove that he let us all use. But yeah, they cleared us out."

"The cops ran you out?" I knew that OPD had actually been avoiding clearing them out of the parking lot behind the permanently closed concert hall. It was an ad hoc solution in a town that didn't have real solutions for folks who weren't getting by. Better to have folks there, a bit out of sight, than hanging around where the new residents would see them.

"Nope. It was the people renovating it. I guess they're getting it all fixed up or something? Anyway, they are always going in and out of the building at all hours anyway, so it wasn't the best place to sleep, and then they started hasslin' us directly. Kicking over tents, even starting a fire. They were mean people, Walt. I didn't want to mess with them, y'know?"

"Well, you made the right choice there, obviously. Better to be down this way, with the dead bodies."

"Ha! Yeah, you're right there. I have to work on my Magical Negro things down this way for you," he waved his fingers around in front of his face, playing at invisible piano keys.

"I'll watch Bagger Vance once this case is over, because I still have no idea what you're on about. None."

"Don't I know it," his smile is back now, the fear gone.

"I appreciate your help, Stoney," I say, as I approach him with a five and slap it into his empty hand.

"Five dollars? You cheap old man," he says, laughing. "This will hardly buy a beer in Oakland anymore, Walt! You want me to starve."

"I'm almost retired. I have to put my money into my 401k."

"That there's my 401K," he says, indicating his tent.

I fish out my wallet for my emergency 20. I don't carry much cash these days, but always an emergency twenty dollar bill. "Here. That's prepayment. Keep an eye out for me? I think you're right. There is something weird going on here." He nods, looking at the twenty. "But it's not the lake, right? It's the people. Always the people. The lake is sacred."

"That it is. That it is," he responds and, holding up the twenty in a mock salute, "will do." He takes a drink, and I move on.

***

I'm not sure how to take Stoney's story. He's pretty reliable for information, usually. He's helped me on several divorce cases--it's amazing how many people think walking around the lake with the person you're cheating with is a good idea. He's a vet, so I'm pretty sure dead bodies don't freak him out the way they might freak out a civilian. On the other hand, he's a self-acknowledged drunk, and I'd bet he's been hassled a lot more recently by cops. Rich folks can't afford to live in San Francisco any longer, so they're coming to Oakland in droves, and with them come different attitudes about how their new home ought to look. I have to suffer through the computer-backpack kids in the cafe, but Stoney has to suffer those same kids calling the cops because he's a black guy living in a tent near the lake. Things like that can cause some extra stress in a person's life. Not sure it could make him see a dead body covered in shells being hauled out of the lake though. All of which makes me want to get the thumb drive back to the office and have a closer look at what Harks gave me. I can put Darya to work figuring out what those people Stoney mentioned are up to at the auditorium. Doesn't seem right Stoney being moved from there, and I had thought the city owned that property. "Put Darya to work" is a funny way to think about it, since she pretty much runs the place these days. I guess I think of it that way because it would piss her off. I can't help but smile.

2

Had to install a ramp to my office a decade ago, something about being compliant for the wheelchair folks. I'm often pretty non-compliant, but I figured I'd give in--it takes a lot of effort to fight the city of Oakland. Gotta pick your battles and all of that. I was ticked off at the time, but honestly I'm grateful for it now, at the end of my walk around the lake. The last half-mile was on autopilot as I thought about Harks and Stoney. About what they said, sure, but more about the looks on their faces as they said it. Harks doesn't scare easily. She's a Black cop in Oakland, and a woman to boot, and that means she has already pretty much seen it all. Her father was kind of famous police around here, and he was also kind of infamous with his colleagues. He was a reformer, a man who moved up the ladder through hard, honest work. But he was also a Black man. That didn't sit well with everybody, and Harks decided to follow in his footsteps as a police, and to do it in Oakland, which sort of makes her infamous by proxy. Her father wasn't the sort to use his rank to help her succeed, and people were looking too closely at her for that anyway. Instead of smoothing things over for her, he looked the other way and let her handle the bullshit herself more often than he would have with any other police. I suspect she loved him pretty hard for that. But all of this means that a dead body (or two) wouldn't normally phase her much. She cared, sure, but she was all about the job, getting it done, figuring it all out, stopping the people who needed stopping. I hadn't seen fear on her face very often.

Stoney, too, has been around. Told me once that he had people who had been in the Black Panthers in Oakland, that he had received some breakfasts through their breakfast program. His father went to prison, for something he didn't do, or for something small that they made into something big. His mom raised him during a dangerous time in Oakland. Well, if I'm being honest, being a Black kid in Oakland, has always been dangerous. So, he was a pretty tough guy. He didn't scare easily. I think his biggest fear lately is that he won't be able to live around the lake much longer, which would be a shame.

Point is, they were both spooked, which meant I was spooked. As I walked up the ramp to my office by the lake, my brain felt a little itchy. I wanted to see what they had seen, or I wouldn't be able to start putting the puzzle pieces together. The door was locked. I had told Darya that she could leave it unlocked once she got in, that maybe we'd get a walk-in from time to time, but she wouldn't have it. "They. Can. Ring. The. Bell." she'd tell me. Probably smart. My keys in hand, the sun was just right for me to see my reflection in the grid of glass on the door. Faded lettering was reflected there too, "Walter Denin Investigations." I'd had that lettering redone too many times over the years, something about the salty lake and the direct sun for a few hours during the afternoon wasn't kind to advertising my business. I took my cigar out of my mouth to get a good look at my face. Used to be handsome, I guess, in that hounddog way, I have been told. People often thought I was from the Midwest for some reason. Must have been my family roots showing through. Those bags under my eyes sure aren't getting any smaller. Many mornings now I think maybe it's time to hang it all up. The business, yes, but maybe all of it. Get out of Oakland. Out of California. Head to Idaho like lots of folks from here do when they retire. Or Montana. We'll see. I think about it a lot now, but the lake always comes back into my field of vision, and back into my mind. I just don't see how I could go on without the lake now.

Been my neighbor, my friend, for far too long. Maybe I'll stick around as long as she does. We'll see.

"Walt," Darya says, opening the door in front of me, surprising me out of my trance. "You have a call, Walt. Want to take it? It's some cop."

"I..uh. Hmmm" I say, dropping my keys back into my jacket pocket.

"I'll tell him you'll call him back," she says, making my decision for me, holding the door open for me and then turning around and heading into the office.

"No, no, I'll take it. Who is it, again?"

"Some cop."

"We may have to work on your phone skills," I say as I take off my jacket and head toward my desk.

"Oh, you know, they all sound the same to me. Except Harks. When are you going to bring her by again? She's a cutie."

"Don't you have a girlfriend?"

"Like I would date a cop anyway. I just like to window-shop. To browse," she lets that last word flow slowly off of her tongue. Then she hands me the phone, presses a button.

"This is Walter Denin."

"Hey Walt, this is Curtis." I groan, looking at Darya, who I'm certain knows who is on the other line. Curtis was Harks' partner-in-work. Not my favorite person, or hers, which Darya knows. She stands in front of me, barely containing her joy at having tricked me.

"What can I do for you, Detective Prak?" Prak always used my first name. He didn't seem to catch on that I never used his.

"Hi Walt," he repeated, "I just wanted to ask you if you've talked to Tonya this morning? We were supposed to meet up, and if she's goofing off, it's usually you she's goofing off with!" Prack was trying to be light and funny, but coming off as his usual self, which is not ever really very funny.

"Sorry Detective, I can't keep track of your partner for you. Maybe you should track her phone?"

"Tried that. She kills it when she's goofing off."

"Well, I hope you find her. Give her my best when you do," and I hang up before he can continue. Right now that's the best I can do to keep Harks out of trouble.

"I could have used an assist, there, Darya. Have you ever screened a call for me?"

"Oh, I save you from lots of cold calls, and of course all of those ex-girlfriends calling to harass you. But I don't want to ever keep Prak away from you. If I have to talk to him, you have to talk to him."

"Who works for who again here?"

"It's an open question," Darya is sipping her coffee from a ceramic cup that says "Male Tears". "Hand it over," she says.

"Darya, I'd like you to do some research on the Oakland auditorium, please. Who owns it now? Does Oakland still own it? And if not, we need to find out who. And who is hanging out there, kicking the homeless folks out from the parking lot."

She ignores everything I've said. "Hand it over, old man," she holds out her hand, palm up.

"What is with the 'old man' stuff today. You 'whippersnappers' are on my lawn again." I do my best old man impression, which is undercut considerably by the fact that I'm actually an old man.

"Harks already called. She likes me. She knows you save all of the fun stuff for yourself, so she let me know you'd be coming by with a present for me. Thumb drive, please."

"Suit yourself," I say, giving in and placing it in her hand. "But I want that auditorium research today, please. After you're done looking at the fun stuff."

"Mhmmm," she says, heading toward her desk.

"Hey, Darya," I try for my best serious tone. "Let's use the air-gapped laptop for that." I point at the thumb drive in her hand.

She stops mid-sit and stands back up. "Reeeeeaaally. Ok. Now I'm definitely in charge of this case." She rolls her chair over to the locked filing cabinet, she holds her hand out again. "Keys."

"You have your own."

"Yes, but they are way over there," she indicates her desk, still almost within arm's reach.

I shake my head, but walk over and hand them to her, then get settled in at my desk. Inside the filing cabinet is a laptop I keep around for more sensitive data work. She opens it, plugs it in, and holds it up, keyboard facing me. "You also have the password for this," I say.

"Yeah, I don't remember it. You don't let me play with the fun toys often enough."

I type in my passphrase and head over to the fridge. "We have any of that chai left?"

She ignores me, already bent over the laptop, deep-diving into whatever is on the thumb drive.

***

I let Darya go to work for a while, and hear her making little excited noises under her breath, typing, taking notes. I find it's best to let her do her thing. She gives me fresh eyes on things, and sometimes spots things I don't spot, makes connections I don't make. She's not the first part-time grad student I've had working for me--really, there's been a string of them--but she's definitely the best. Shows up on time, knows how to handle troublesome people on the phone (with, perhaps, the exception of Prak), is good with details. But she also really enjoys a puzzle, which is half of the job here, even on the simple who-is-cheating-on-who cases. I was hoping at some point she might just take over the business for me, keep doing the work I do here, maybe even do it better. She's been with me for two years, and it feels like I have yet to convince her that might be even remotely a good idea. Her degree will be finished up soon, I think, and then she'll head out just like the others. Which is a shame, because she's good at this, and she seems to enjoy it. Plus her girlfriend works at city hall, which is a great connection to have in this business. I sip microwaved chai and check my email, wondering again about the future. Maybe this will be my last case. Maybe I'll make it my last. Darya can finish her thesis and move on, and I can close up shop. I close my eyes for a few moments, resting body and brain.

When I open my eyes, my gaze rests on the little carved pelican sitting on the edge of my desk. I reach out and move it away from the edge. Never really did finish this piece. It's still rough even though the last time I took my whittling knife to it was years ago now. A doctor had told me to take up something that used my hands, something to keep them moving in different ways, and limber, to stave off losing motion to arthritis. I don't remember why I picked whittling, really, just that it felt nice. I think part of the reason I let it fade from my habits was that I was a little embarrassed doing it. I mean, is there anything more cliché than an old man whittling? Maybe I'll do more when I retire. It's only a few seconds before I'm distracted by my screen.

Nothing much in my email, but one subject line catches my eye, from one of the neighborhood listserv websites. I still call it a listserv, but I guess it's 'social media' now? I like to see what people are saying about the neighborhood. Mostly it's people complaining about somebody's dog, or some racist who doesn't think they're a racist complaining about a "suspicious black person", but sometimes I do learn some things. You can tell a lot from the comments there, even though they are soul-crushing. Just like Yelp comments often tell more about the commenter than about the thing being reviewed, people unknowingly let themselves show in listserv comments. The one that I click on stands out only because of my morning walk:

@marty_guy
Subject: THE BIRDS
What the hell is going on with the birds at the lake? Has anybody else noticed this? I mean, there are a lot more of them, which is fine, ok, the bird sanctuary is nice and all that, but THREE TIMES now I've seen birds eating what looked like bloody seaweed or something? Like that crap at the bottom of the lake is bleeding? I know there have been two murders by the lake but should the birds be eating blood like that? It's freaking weird. Once over by the estuary, and once right near the library! I might start running somewhere else. Also: What's with all the electric scooters around the lake. Pissing me off.

@finding_peace
Subject: Re: THE BIRDS
I saw that twice too! It is a little weird. Maybe all the fish coming back to the lake means the birds are catching fish?

@only_the_lonely
Subject: Re: THE BIRDS
I've seen it a bunch too. I bet the mayor and city council are in on it. We have to vote those bastards out!

@love_the_craft
Subject: Re: THE BIRDS
Please do not worry about it. It's just nature doing what nature does. It only disturbs you because it's not what you're used to. The Lake does what The Lake wants. The Lake will take care of herself.

@EatTheRich
Subject: Re: THE BIRDS
Yeah, f*ck those f*ckers on the scooters. Push THEM in the lake.

I add the original post and the comment from @love_the_craft to my case notes. Just a gut feeling, but something seems a little off here. I know some people who know about the ecology of the lake. Maybe I should check in with Dennis. Haven't seen him for a while. He might know why the blood. Probably unrelated to the case, but it's odd enough that I want to rule it out. I shoot him a quick text asking if he knows what's up with the odd things birds are eating around the lake and return to my light research. Nothing more on NextDoor about the lake, except people understandably freaking out about two dead bodies in two months.

I switch over to a few police blogs and listservs that I'm part of to see what they're all talking about, and it's uncharacteristically silent about the new bodies. Police keep it professional on the public forums but will sometimes let important things slip on the listservs. There doesn't seem to be anything about the bodies, which tells me that this body, and the one before it, may involve something out of the ordinary this time.

"Walt! What the fuck. You have to see this," Darya sips her coffee but stands up and away from her desk, away from the laptop. She points at it like it will jump up and bite her. "That's...just...wrong," she says. I wander over and take a seat. She's looking at some pictures and video of the autopsy of the body that was found, and I don't blame her for freaking out. It's just like Stoney said. It's a body, but it's covered with shells. Not shells--actual mussels, as if the body were carved from rock and left at the bottom of the lake. I look at Darya for a second to make sure she's ok, and reach out to tap the spacebar, playing the video.

It's standard procedure to record autopsies these days, video and audio usually. The camera is mounted over the autopsy table, so, over the body. Almost a kind of god's-eye-view. If you're not used to it, it's kind of creepy. Darya and I are relatively used to it, but this body is special, and the recording just feels off, since the body is so odd. There's no sound at the moment, but I don't need the sound yet. I see the medical examiner staring at the body, and Detective Harks standing a foot or so away, looking on. That's not usual, to have the detective right there during the examination of the body. If it's a body. The M.E. is Cindy this time, and I'm glad. She's on the ball, and has done this work for quite a while. I can see that she's talking, making verbal notes, but I still don't need the sound yet. All I can focus on now is that mass of mussels, because she's already removed a few of them from where the face of our victim should be, and I can see an open eye there. Cindy moves to remove another shell, and as she nears the mussel with her scalpel, it opens, and it squirts an ooze of some sort, green and red again, reminding me vaguely of some sort of alien Christmas. And then Cindy shouts at Harks, and they both run out of the room quickly, Cindy with her scalpel still in hand. Ten or so seconds go by, and the video stops.

"What. The. Fuck. Walt. What the hell was that?" Darya says with a mix of fascination and fear.

I hesitate, and then, "There must be some explanation. Nature is weird, right? The lake has been through a lot over the years. Maybe this is a new kind of mussel."

"No. Not that, Walt. That I can handle. Evolution, sure. Whatever. But that. You didn't see it, did you?" I look at her helplessly.

"I don't know what you're talking about, Darya. Honestly."

She gives me an impatient look and bends over the laptop, moving the video back a bit, and plays the last part again. She's touching the computer like it's diseased, and she steps back a

14

few steps again when she's through. "Here. Just before they run out. Watch the body. Watch the face."

I humor her, and watch. My attention is drawn to the missing patch of mussels, at that dead eye staring out blindly. The camera is above the body, to the side a bit, but I can see the sheen on the mussels, still wet from the lake water, I suppose. I'm staring closely, trying to catch whatever Darya saw on her first viewing. Watching this, it's difficult to not imagine myself covered with the creatures, sitting at the bottom of the lake, encrusted with muck and mollusks. I'm drawn into the video again to the point where I can almost smell the briny lake. And that eye, still open.

It blinks.

***

I watch it a few more times. Darya is pacing the room behind me, glancing at it but not really watching it. For some reason the video ends ten seconds or so after Harks and Cindy abruptly leave the room in an odd flurry of interference fuzz, I notice this time. Darya has a moment of inspiration, and leans over my shoulder, putting her hand on the desk. "Wait! She's fucking with you, Walt. That has got to be it. Fucking Harks."

"That's an elaborate prank."

"Well, yeah, but what the hell else could it be, right?" Darya is laughing and nodding in the way that people do when they hope that they're right and want you to agree with them.

"Hmmm," I look up at her seriously. "Does Harks strike you as a practical joker?"

Undeterred, Darya responds: "That's the best kind of practical joke. The one you never see coming."

"I don't think it's a joke. I think it's..." I look back at the screen, and play the video again, "...something else."

She picks up the laptop, unplugs it from the wall, and walks it over to my desk, setting it down there. "Ok, you knock yourself out, sir, and I'll take a look at the history of the auditorium, and who owns it. Maybe there will still be a case when you and Harks are done with your little games."

Darya doesn't fool me for a second. She's doing that thing she does to calm herself, where she dives into work. I do it too. I used to call it "monkey work" until I hired somebody to do so much of it for me. The dry detail work, now often done on the internet, but also done by knocking on doors and talking to folks. The nuts and bolts of the job are comforting. Used to be I'd spend time in the darkroom, developing pictures of people cheating, or people not cheating. Something to take your mind off of the larger problems of life. I guess in this case to take your mind off of seeing something that isn't quite...natural. At my desk now, I set the video to play on repeat, hoping to see something less disturbing and more helpful. I pull out an old cigar from my desk drawer and place it in the corner of my mouth. I don't smoke them much these days, but it's an old habit, and it calms my nerves even without the actual tobacco smoke. It's a disgusting habit, I've been told by Harks and others, but if there is any advantage to my age, it's that the number of fucks I give has decreased exponentially with every year.

As the video plays, I pick up my phone and scroll through to Dr. Cindy Malto, medical examiner. We're not close, but Cindy knows me enough to call me Walt and not bother me by doing it. I don't think Harks is playing tricks, but it doesn't hurt to cross that off of my list of

15

possibilities. I usually get her voicemail--like most county employees she's busier than she ought to be--but she picks up after one ring.

"Hey Walt, I bet I know what you're calling about."

"Cindy Malto, you're a mind-reader now too? That's not going to creep anybody out down in the morgue, I guess."

"Detective Harks needed my help to get your help, so yeah, doesn't take a mind-reader. You watched it?"

"I watched it. My assistant thinks Harks is playing a hilarious joke on us."

"I wish that were true, Walt." I know she doesn't want to say much. It probably wouldn't happen, but she could lose her job letting out evidence like she and Harks have done.

"Any chance I could come down and take a look at the body? I don't want to get in your way, Cindy, but it might help figure out what's going on."

"How about we meet for lunch instead. Noon? I'll fill you in."

"And then maybe a peek at the body?"

"I can't do that, Walt, sorry," she is more quiet now, and I hear how tired she is in her voice.

"No pressure Cindy, I know it's sensitive. Can I ask why though? I'm discreet. In and out, no fuss, no muss."

"It's not that I don't want to. It's that I can't. The body is missing."

3

Cindy won't tell me anything more on the phone. We agree to meet a little later in the day, not far from my office. Cindy says she'll bring Harks along if she can. They're both in a little bit of hot water, having a difficult time explaining why they ran from the room in the first place like a couple of cadets, and unable to explain why the medical examiner's camera, as well as morgue security cameras, were on the fritz when the body disappeared.

My brain itches again. Too many dependable people are freaking out around me. I feel like the connective tissue between all of the freak-outs, and I can't quite breathe right. Seeing a seemingly dead body look around a morgue while covered with shells isn't helping my state of mind. A dead body blinking, looking around. And cameras going out? I'm reconsidering Darya's practical joke theory, because any other explanation is too uncomfortable for me to think about. I need a change of scenery, even if it's just my living room ceiling.

"Hey Darya, you doing ok on that research?"

"Yep." One-word answers from Darya mean I should leave her alone to work. We're alike in more than a few ways.

"I'm going to go take a mid-morning nap," I tell her, heading toward the back door of the office that leads to my apartment.

"Mhmmmm." She's not surprised. I wear out more easily these days, and I have never shied away from a good nap, even when I was younger.

The office has its own little kitchen, a couple of desks, books and such, but not much else, partly because I live behind it in a full apartment. Lots of live-work spaces in Oakland, which I appreciate. I suppose the way my space is arranged has encouraged my workaholic tendencies over the years, which accounts in part for the whole no-wife, no-kids thing, but these days I'm more addicted to napping than I am to working, so the arrangement suits me just fine. I close the door behind me and I'm home, though I can still just barely hear Darya away at the keyboard. Taking out my phone and setting it on the table, I tell it to wake me up in an hour. I probably shouldn't nap that long--makes me groggy, but I'm worn out. Not from my walk, but from all of the thinking this morning. My brain is tired and itchy and I scratch the back of my head as I lay down slowly on couch, rub my hands over my face. Old leather man on the old leather couch, I think. I drape one arm over my eyes to keep out the wan light, and quickly I fall asleep.

***

When I wake up it's not because of my alarm, but because something else has startled me. My heart is beating fast, as if I've just woken up from a nightmare. I've obviously overslept. It's dark, except for the weak light of downtown coming through my windows. Sometimes Darya will let me sleep away the day, but I can't remember the last time I went down for a nap and woke up at night. Maybe I was more worn out than I had thought. Some days I enjoy this feeling, the disorienting feeling of being displaced in time and space as my brain grinds awake, but I'm not enjoying it right now. Sitting up, I don't see my phone where I left it on the coffee table. Don't hear Darya clicking away any longer--she's probably gone home hours ago. I shuffle back into the office on unsteady legs. My bones are hurting tonight. The office is dark, and I notice the air-gapped laptop has been left out on my desk. That's not like Darya. Usually she covers my tracks for me when I do crap like leaving the laptop out.

A sound from outside startles me, a deep screeching: "Wrrrrar!". A cat crying out? A seagull? Sounds like a seagull, but they're usually holed up for the evening by dark. I can't see much out of these windows even if I were to draw the blinds, though they face the lake. Years ago I had them covered with a dark, milky plastic film to protect the office from the harsh direct sunlight. Opening the office door to look outside, I smell the lake even before I see it. Brine. It gets that way sometimes, but this is stronger than I've ever smelled it, strong enough that I cover my nose and mouth with my shirtsleeve. They may have let all of the water out today with the tide--sometimes they do that to...I realize I don't' really know why they do that. That can stink up the area, but this seems different. I hear the sound again, louder with the door open, "WRRRRRRAR", and it startles me even though I am now sort of ready for it. That's definitely a bird. At least I think it's a bird. I'm still foggy from my long nap. Sounds like it might be in pain. Well, I've still got my shoes on, so even though it's a little chilly out, I walk outside, and head across the street toward the path by the lake. There are some reeds there, and some low-growing olive trees that I know hold resting birds sometimes. I wonder if a gull has left behind a baby gull. I feel a thumping in my chest that's not my own body. Probably a car going by with some late night heavy bass. It's rhythmic, and I've grown used to the particular sounds and feel of it over the years. It's sort of the heartbeat of Oakland now, different cars playing different songs with the same bass line, keeping all of our chests thumping. This one is loud. The briny smell is even worse now, and I suddenly want to be back inside, on my couch.

The animal--is it a bird?--calls out a few more times as I cross the street and approach the lake. The lake is reflecting a lot of moonlight tonight. The streets seem empty, despite the rhythmic bass beating in my bones. No cars, no people, which is rare. Must be three or four in the morning, when the young folks finally go home and other folks aren't quite getting up yet. "Rrrrrrwar" sounds again, making me stop in my tracks for a moment. There's anguish in that sound, I'm certain of it. I'm no saint when it comes to animals, but the sound pulls at the base of my spine, and in my heart, and I instinctively feel the empathy that comes from hearing another living thing in pain.

And then I see it. It's not a gull, it's one of the geese, and a big one. It's dark out, despite the moon, but I can see it's at the edge of the pathway, which drops off into the lake a foot or so below. The sour, salty smell is even more pungent now, almost overwhelmingly so. I'm walking slowly toward the bird and as it sees me it begins calling out to me repeatedly "Rw'kaw!" It's stuck in some plant matter or something, partly covered in...seaweed maybe? There is a bit of that in the lake from time to time. I know I have to be careful, because these geese can be real mean sometimes. I've been bitten. But I couldn't just leave the poor guy there, and I feel driven forward by the thump-thump I can feel more strongly now in my whole body, and the despairing calling out of the bird.

I'm just a few feet away now, and I can see it's not seaweed. Something has a hold of it, there's a sharp contrast between the whiteness of the goose and an almost absence of white wrapped around it. And whatever it is, it's moving as the bird struggles. A snake maybe, which doesn't make sense, because no big snakes live around this lake. That's what it looks like

18

though, a wet, slimy tether around the goose's body, and though the bird is calling out nearly constantly now, almost matching the thump-thump rhythm that has become part of my own body, it's moving less, struggling to stay on the path, but the--snake?--is trying to drag it into the water. I rush now, not caring that the bird might bite, and I see it's not a snake. *Thump-thump.* It's a tentacle. It's black and glistening with lake water in the moonlight, and writhing around the goose. What I'm seeing just isn't right, but that doesn't matter now as I hear, and feel, the *Thump-Thump. Rkaw!.* I'm on it now, trying to pull it off, while the goose struggles with renewed vigor at my presence, but I can't get a grip on the damn thing, can't get my fingers around it or under it. It's too slick, and the stench almost knocks me off of my feet. It's smells rotten, the smell of death on the water. It's moving, constricting and I glance at the lake and see that more tentacles are coming out now. Some of them are crusted with the shells of different mollusks, gleaming sharply. I try to step back, abandoning the poor bird in my own fight-or-flight now, but there's a tentacle around my ankle, holding me fast, and I fall back hard, landing on the path.

Thump-Thump. Rkaw! I've hit my head hard, and I'm scrambling to keep the thing from dragging me into the lake. I yell, "Fuck! Help! Let go!" looking around, but there's still nobody around, and now I'm losing my footing at the edge of the lake. The thing is strong, and thick, constricting up my calf, and I know I'm not going to win this one. The goose has already been silenced, drawn over the edge, into the water, and the thumping grows louder, stronger as I hear it thrashing. I'm fighting as hard as I can, but it's no use. I'm old and this fucker is strong. I'm going over. I scream as I hit the water, the slimy, salty liquid filling my mouth, forcing itself into my lungs as I'm pulled further down.

***

"Walt! Walt! It's ok, it's ok!!" Darya is standing over me, hands on my shoulders, pinning me against the floor between the coffee table and couch. Daylight is still pouring into the room, and my phone's alarm is vibrating on the table near my head. My assistant is looking at me, concerned, as I try to slow my breathing and tell her I'm ok.

"Sorry. Sorry, sorry," I repeat, like a mantra as I wake. "I guess I was having a bad dream. Sorry if I scared you." I move her hands gently from my shoulders, and she sits back on her heels. She reaches over and turns my alarm off.

"I could hear that thing vibrating against the table all the way in the office. You were on the floor when I came in. You really ok?"

"I think I fell of the couch," I say seriously, before I realize how silly I sound. Darya looks at me for a moment, kindness and concern in her eyes, and then bursts out laughing.

"Really? You think so? Have you ever thought about being a detective? Maybe a private investigator?"

I can't help but laugh along with her as I sit up and move myself back to sitting on the couch. I wince as I feel the back of my head pulse. I hit it pretty hard. I touch it tenderly, and I don't see blood, so that's good. Darya walks behind the couch and takes a look.

"It's not too bad, but why don't you stay sitting up for a little bit for me, old man. Don't want you falling asleep and never waking up."

"No, I don't want that either. Ooof. I'll have to get one of those hospital beds with the side guards, at this rate."

"What were you dreaming about, anyway? Being chased by a mollusk-encrusted zombie?" She gives me a wry look.

"I did dream about the lake. It was an odd one."

"Zombie joggers?"

"I wish the joggers were zombies. They'd move more slowly and carefully," I say as I start to get up. Darya pushes me back down. Her manner is softer still. That's not like her. Can't have her worried about me that way. "I'm ok, darlin', I really am."

She takes a moment, walks over and sits next to me. "I know you hit your head hard if you think I'm going to let you call me 'darlin'. Let me get you some ice for your head."

"Sorry, sorry. Yes, thank you."

I rest sitting up for a while, checking my phone, with a baggie of ice in my hand, resting against the back of my head, thanks to Darya. She goes back to the office, but leaves the door open where she still has line-of-sight on me. My biologist friend hasn't gotten back to me, which is a little weird. I'll give him a call after my visit with the medical examiner. I look at the time and I have a few minutes before I have to head out to that. Shuffling slowly into the office, I sit at my desk and ask Darya if she's found anything interesting about the auditorium.

She looks at me, trying to appraise my ability to listen with a bump on my head, and then begins an information dump for me. This is her standard procedure, and it is something she's really good at: research and distilling important information, which can't be overrated in this business. It's odd to find someone who is as good with the details of research as she is, who also has the people skills. It occurs to me again that she'd be great at this job on her own, when I'm gone. Whatever "gone" means at this point, I think, as I shift the ice bag on my head.

The Oakland Civic Auditorium, redubbed the Kaiser Auditorium in the eighties, turns out to have a fairly interesting history. I knew a bit of it, but Darya fills me in on the basics. Built in 1914. Owned by the city until a few years back, during which time the Grateful Dead played there a million times. Elvis twice. There was even an Oakland Christmas pageant there for almost seventy years, with kids from all of the schools in the area. I remember a few of those, even though I'm more of a humbug about Christmas. Never saw the Dead there, though I may have smoked some pot in the parking lot a few times before their shows. Dr. Martin Luther King, Jr. even spoke there once, a famous speech, though not the "dream" speech. I search my memory for why I missed that speech, but it's foggy. Oakland closed the auditorium down in a decade ago and it has sat empty ever since, though it's parking lot has been used for various book fairs, and, more recently, some homeless encampments. Darya is still researching they why of it being shut down, but she gets more excited as she tells me about the more recent ownership.

"For a few years now it's been owned by Miskatonic Industries, which is one hell of a shell company, I think. I have to look into it more, but I think it boils down to being owned by...get this...Victor Immack!" The name registers but it takes me a moment to place it with a person.

"Ah. Huh. That's a tech millionaire guy, right? Young guy, not from around here?"

"More like tech zillionaire, but yeah. He's from back east, but it looks like he's got his fingers in some pies around the Bay Area, and not just in tech, in real estate and some other holdings.

It will take more time to figure out the intricacies, but for all intents and purposes, Victor Immack has owned that place for years."

"He's eccentric, right? Like that Elon Musk guy?"

"How many billionaires do you know? They're all eccentric. There also seems to be some sort of contractor group or something affiliated with it now, maybe doing some remodeling. I'll need more time to find out about them too. "

She's back to work already, which makes me smile. She really likes this part of the job, which is great for me, since it's not my favorite part any longer. I like walking and talking more, which is what I used to have to do for this sort of information anyway. Don't get me wrong, I love the internet and how it's helped with my job, but I guess I'm a people person, when I'm not a misanthrope. "Well, I'm heading out a little early for my meeting with Cindy and Harks," I say, setting the ice pack into the sink.

"Oh! Yeah. It's almost time. Ok, hang on for a second, I'll just save this and log out."

"I can talk to them, you keep working." I'm putting my jacket back on, taking an old cigar out of the pocket.

But she's already closed her laptop, and getting her things together. I note that she has indeed put the air-gapped laptop away already. "No way, old man. You had a bad fall. Plus, I'm sure Harks would be disappointed if I didn't' show up. I think she has a thing for me."

"You think every pretty lady has a thing for you."

"Yeah, well, sometimes beauty is a curse, Walt. You know what I mean." she says, and we're out the door.

***

It's not a long walk to the restaurant, but my nap didn't recharge my batteries in any way. Drained them a bit, and added a smack on the back of the head for good measure. Maybe I need a nice, napping recliner. Be harder to fall out of that. Darya is texting and googling and silent as we walk, effortlessly navigating us both around other people rushing about during their lunch breaks. She keeps a slow, steady pace, and I have time to muddle over some of that bad dream I had. Bad dream. I've always had them, honestly, few times a week, but not usually in the daytime. And this one felt real, though in the back of my head I think I also knew it might be a dream. That's something I've worked on over the years, noticing when I'm dreaming. It's a good therapy for having nightmares, if you can do it. Take the power back, recognize you're dreaming, slow your heart rate if you can. With good dreams I can even steer them a bit sometimes, turn running dreams into flying dreams. This one, though, had a grip on me, even as I tried to recognize I was dreaming. It was taking me somewhere for some reason, somewhere I didn't really want to go. That is a new feeling. I'm not one for believing in the supernatural, but I try to be open to the fact that I don't know everything, though Darya might argue about that. I can't shake the feeling that somehow the lake itself was trying to tell me something. I take out my phone and make a note to ask my biologist friend if there were ever any octopuses (octopi?) in the lake. Seems unlikely, and they wouldn't reach up for sea birds would they? Another question for him. I just don't know where my brain would have picked that up from, the very idea of it seems bizarre.

21

I've stopped walking to type it down, and Darya stops with me. She's used to this start-stop when walking with me. Sometimes it's just because I get worn out, but most times it's because I'm typing something down. This is where her patience with me shines, really--most folks her age get impatient with "olds" needing to stop, to write things down, to get exact change out of their wallet and the like. Darya looks around at the beautiful almost-spring day, at the folks around the lake.

"Lake smells gross today," she says when I'm done typing, and we've begun moving today. I look at the water, inhale deeply.

"Hmmmm. I can't smell anything much these days. Does it? Briny?"

"Yep. Like low tide on a sunny day." But the lake isn't low today, it's actually quite high with the tide. The birds are busy on it, knowing some folks share a bit of bread from deli lunches, but also going about their normal business, eating the green stuff that grows on the bottom. The gulls are fishing out mussels, opening them up on the path.

Fifteen or twenty years ago, the lake smelled briny more often, and worse than briny. That was when the estuary wasn't opened up as much yet, and the lake water would stagnate more. Plus, everybody knew that there was still waste being dumped into the lake, even though it wasn't legal any longer. Waste that didn't add a pleasant smell, let's just say. Back in the 1930's that was what the lake was used for, a dumping lagoon for the developing city. Back before that it had been a nice little salt-water marsh, and there was even an Ohlone shellmound near it back before that. A spiritual place literally turned into a place where settlers dumped their shit. Not a nice legacy. Lately I was hoping, seeing all the birds coming back, and the marsh-life thriving, that maybe it would become a heart of the city, a place of community for everybody, in the way that it had been a place of community for the Ohlone, but also an expansion of the community it had fostered over the past thirty or forty years. It had been a place of community for the poorer folks who had lived near it for the decades when it was the cheapest place to live, instead of one of the most expensive. But that wasn't really happening, of course. Lots of development, and not of homes for poor folks. San Francisco's tech folks were once again spilling into Oakland in search of "cheaper" places to live, and its culture was changing as people were forced to move away. Still, the lake has potential, I think. People from east and west Oakland come here on the weekends to have picnics and barbecue, to play music, dance, laugh. That can be healing for a city, having folks of different kinds hanging out, if not together, then at least near each other. It's kind of a rallying point for a diverse, thriving Oakland, which is what I love to see, and though a few people would rather it be their private backyard, it seems like Oaklanders aren't about to let that happen.

We'll see. Maybe people are dumping waste into the lake again...maybe that's what my dream was about? I can't help but chuckle to myself: Me and my shitty dreams.

Before I know it, we've arrived at the little hipster diner that Cindy picked out. Folks are milling about out front, but we head in and then out the back to where the medical examiner is already sitting with detective Harks. We exchange pleasantries, Harks asks me to not set my cigar on the edge of the table because it's disgusting, and we all order. This place has a great lox bagel, which I order. At least the hipsters like to eat good stuff sometimes. While we wait for our food I take in Cindy and Harks' constitutions--they're trying for breezy conversation but it's clear they're spooked. Cindy is a god-fearing Christian, I know, somebody who doesn't just go to church on Christmas and Easter, the kind of person who keeps a 'swear jar' in her office just

22

for her own transgressions, so I'm a little surprised when she looks around to gauge how loudly she can talk, leans over toward Darya and me, and says "Walt. I think somebody stole that fucking body."

4

Cindy explains in good detail the behind-the-scenes of the video that we saw. Harks interjects from time to time, while I listen closely and while Darya flirts with Harks. I'd call the flirting inappropriate or unprofessional, except that Harks obviously enjoys it and, hell, we're talking about corpses with open eyes being stolen out of the morgue while we eat our lunch, so what's appropriate behavior, anyway? They woke Cindy up to come into work yesterday morning in the early hours, the body having been discovered around 2:30 a.m. There is an ME on call during that time who wasn't Cindy, but Harks rightly understood that they needed their best person on this, given the oddness of the body itself. So, Cindy came in, and Harks was present for the examination.

Right from the start, of course, it was a weird job for Cindy, but she started the recording and went to work. The usual tools for confirming death--a check for pulse, respiration, and reflexes-- were slightly more complex. Getting a pulse on a body entirely encrusted with shells was problematic. Visual confirmation of lack of lack of respiration was more simple, and Cindy decided to forgo a more thorough confirmation until after she had removed some of the shells. The same went for reflexes. She'd simply have to remove some shells first to do her job. She took a look around the front of the body, looked for spots where the mussels might not be attached as strongly. She decided to start around the eyes, where some of the softest tissue on a body is. Her other option, she told us, was genitals. Her explanation seemed to require a response from Darya about she herself "going for genitals before eyes". She likes making Harks laugh. The M.E., always a professional, ignored her.

Cindy said that she considered waiting until morning to examine the body, only because she had wanted to talk to an expert on water deaths, because she certainly had never seen anything like this, and, in fact, didn't think that mussels could even attach themselves to flesh in this way. Skeletons, yes, but dead flesh itself, not usually. Harks had urged her to begin though, because this was something the department was trying to keep under wraps, and the sooner they ID'd the body, the better. A brief effort to remove mussels on the fingertips was a disaster, with the flesh of the finger being removed as the little creatures held on tight.

"Why not go for the teeth first?" I interrupted. I knew that in the case of severe water damage or severe burns, teeth were sometimes a way to identify a body, though DNA matches were often preferred. You could get lucky and get a quick hit on DNA while the ME was still taking a mold of the teeth.

Cindy paused, looked at Harks for a moment. "Well, that is what I had in mind, eventually. But when I tried to go directly to the mouth, I felt like I was going to rip flesh again. The mouth was sealed shut by the mussels. I thought perhaps I could disengage the little guys from the eyelid without tearing apart the entire eye."

"I see. Start at the eye, get some practice, then go for the teeth."

"Or the rest of the face, yes, that was the idea. I was concerned about getting an uncontaminated DNA sample as well, from the skin at least. The little beasts where just everywhere. There wasn't even any hair on the head of the body."

"Mmmmmmm," Darya took a large bite out of her burger, letting the greasy juice drip down onto the plate. "I just love eating lunch with y'all," she said, getting another guffaw out of Harks.

Cindy continued, explaining that the mussels around the eye seemed to not be attached as stridently, which is what she had hoped. The first one came off without even damaging the eyelid, she said, so she continued until the eye was exposed. In doing this, the eyelid had moved to the "open" position, and she could see the eye intact, not even very waterlogged, as she would have expected. She removed a few more of the small creatures, and then took a few long breaths, getting herself ready to move on to the rest of the face. Harks had looked on without moving any closer.

"And I was right there, staring at the face, planning my next move, when this dead body blinked at me. I've been in this business for a while, and I've seen a lot of things in that morgue. But that blinking? That scared the hell out of me. It went right to my lizard brain, Walt, pure fight-or-flight," Cindy had stopped eating her chicken salad while she talked, and now her hand was shaking a bit as she held her fork. She set the fork down, looked down at her food, and was obviously not hungry any longer. "I've seen bodies sit up, from reflexes. I've seen dead bodies have erections. This person blinked, and then looked around, then looked at me. I'm sure of it. Harks saw it too."

"Yeah, I wasn't that close, but I saw it. It was hard to miss. You saw the tape. When Cindy ran out, I'm not ashamed to say I followed suit."

Even Darya had stopped eating at this point, and she was uncharacteristically quiet. I was done eating, so I popped my cigar back into my mouth and had a little chew on it while everybody at the table moved to regain a bit of composure.

I started the conversation back up: "So, tell me what happened with the cameras, and with the body going missing."

Cindy explained that they had locked the morgue at that point, and gone to her office down the hall. They had caught their breath, sat down, and talked about what they had seen. Cindy said she was sort of grateful Harks had been there, and grateful for the cameras, because already she was doubting what she had seen. Harks was too, but since they were both doubting the same exact thing, it was harder to rule out that it had actually happened. They spent a half hour talking, deciding what to do, and had decided that they would go back in together, just the two of them. They didn't want to bring anybody else in just in case they had both imagined it. For a moment I was happy that whatever this whole thing was happening on their watch--if Prak had been lead on this case I'm not sure I would have believed him if he had told me the same story, even with video evidence.

When they went back, Harks even drew her stun gun.

"Would a stun gun work on a dead body?" I asked.

"We're well beyond those kinds of questions, I think, Walt," she responded calmly, "mostly I just didn't want to shoot the thing 20 times with my gun, which I was apt to do after what I saw." I don't think I'd ever seen Harks draw her gun, or her taser.

Cindy unlocked the morgue doors, they went in slowly, and the body was already gone. There were a few shells on the table and a small trail of saltwater from the table to the door, but somebody had taken the body. They rushed back to Cindy's office to check the video, which is when they saw there was saltwater there, too, like the body snatchers had dragged the thing, and not been particularly careful. And when they got back to Cindy's computer, from which she could see her recordings, they saw that the camera had failed just where the video I had seen had stopped.

"Not only that, but the hallway cameras, the parking lot cameras, all of them went down. We had an IT person and a hardware person come out--they both said that it was a little odd, the timing, but that "these things happen". They couldn't give us a reason. The cameras will have to be replaced, even. They were broken as if they had just worn out," Harks told us. Sure, these cameras don't get looked at much, being in the morgue, but still, the timing can't be a coincidence."

"So," I said. We've got a weird dead body. And now we've got somebody who wanted that body enough to break some cameras and risk breaking into the police morgue to get it. This case just gets weirder and weirder."

"Or," Darya spoke up quickly, with an almost excitement in her voice, flirting forgotten for the moment, "the body walked out."

***

Walking back to the office, Darya pleaded her case again. "Walt! Cindy herself said it blinked! It looked around! How can you be ok with it doing that, but not at least entertain the idea that the guy got up and left?"

"Well, it is entertaining, you got that part right."

"But you'll believe the eye thing."

"I saw it on the tape, Darya. I did not see a body that had been in the lake for at least a few hours walk out of the morgue, and I don't see how I could believe that until I see it."

"So the blinking and looking around was just a, what, a reflex?"

"Makes more sense than a walking body."

Darya mocked my tone, changing her voice to what she loving calls 'old man voice'. "Makes more sense than blah, blah blah…Walter Denin, nothing makes sense about this. I say if we're talking about a blinking, looking-around-the-room, dead body covered in mollusks, we may as well be talking about a dead body breaking cameras and walking out."

"It would have had to break the cameras before it walked out. It would have had to break the cameras while laying on the slab."

"I didn't say I could explain it all."

"Get back to me when you can," I laughed. "That would make this whole day a lot easier for me. "Ok, ok," I placated a little, noticing her frown, "let's say it did walk out. Where the hell did it go?"

"Well, if I were him. Hmmmm. Back to the lake."

"I'm not doing a stakeout for the entire lake to see a dead body walk back, Darya. And I'm not paying you to do it."

"You're right, yes, you're right. But let's keep the possibility in our heads. One more odd possibility isn't going to break things."

I thought of the autopsy video with a dead man blinking and wondered.

We walk a bit more in silence, when something inspires me. "Let's meander over to the auditorium and take a look. Walk off our lunch a bit."

"Fine by me, if you feel up to it."

I glare at her and chew my cigar, but yeah, I move slowly. The shut-down auditorium isn't that far past the office, and I was just down that way this morning talking to Stoney, but I think it's worth taking a look for myself. There aren't many people about now. People are back at work after lunch, though a few joggers and young folks are usually milling about in the daytime. A few familiar homeless folks lay on the grass, taking in the sun, enjoying the slow turn to spring. Some geese cackle or hiss as we walk past, either asking for a handout or keeping us away from their territory. It's strange to see so many geese already here by the lake. They usually come a bit later in the year. Maybe climate change has hit the geese's lives already. They're big birds, and mean as heck at the best of times. I saw one chase a toddler almost right into the lake once--the kid's parent obviously hadn't been to the lake before and had encouraged her to "feed the geese". Their bites hurt, too, I'm told. Today they're not chasing anybody, just making noise. I mutter a warning to them under my breath, "Watch out for the tentacles, my friends."

As we approach the auditorium, I notice immediately what I hadn't noticed yesterday when I had walked past, deep in thought after having talked to Stoney: I don't see any tents. Tents in the parking lot had started popping up there over a year ago, as the homeless population in Oakland had soared. The cops (and the city) looked the other way--there's nothing most cops like less than moving homeless people from where they've been trying to just live. It reminds me of tales of the Great Depression my father used to tell me, of tent cities and hardship. He'd never had to live in a tent, but it was only luck that made it so. We're not in a depression right now, but that doesn't mean we're taking care of our own.

But the tents are gone, just like Stoney said. The auditorium parking lot abuts the lake path on one side, and the beginning of downtown Oakland on the other. Entrances and exits have been blocked off for probably two years now, and the tents moved in soon after. But now it's cleared out. Clean, even, which is odd because the parking lot itself isn't fenced off and this is a city with a litter problem. Darya notes that it looks weird now, without the tents, and I agree. The building itself is several stories tall, a style of architecture that I recognize, though I don't know the name. Reminds me of old buildings in France. To my layperson's eyes, it's a big rectangular box with lots of huge doors, columns, arches. Like a child took a shoebox and decorated it with doors and arches. Stairs and an entryway lead to the huge auditorium doors on one side, but the stairs are fenced off by a (clean!) chain-link fence. The building has been cleaned up a bit on the outside, but it's still slowly crumbling, which is why the city closed it down over a decade ago. I wonder if the new owner is going to tear it down, or renovate. Why isn't this damn thing a historical landmark, anyway? MLK spoke there, and if Elvis and the Grateful Dead played there, how much more historic could it be?

Darya and I stand on the path looking at the building. She's tapping away at her phone, texting and taking pictures of the building. "I'm going to get some shots around the perimeter, Walt. Just in case you're onto something here. She heads off into the lot, circling the building, stopping to take a shot here and there. I stare at the building, look back toward the lake, which I can also see from here. A jogger moves past me, nods a hello. I take out my phone and make a note to ask Harks if the police checked out this building after the body was found. It's too close to where the body was found to not check it out, and once you remove all of the homeless folks' tents, in the middle of the night, this part of the lake would not be a horrible place to murder somebody without being seen. There are big oak trees here, blocking the city lights, and lots of bushes and undergrowth to sneak around in. I imagine a path from the building's front steps to the lake, a little dotted line that could be used to carry a body to a spot not far from where our body was actually found. Worth checking out, at least, I think to myself.

Then I hear Darya cry out, "Walt! Get over here! Tell this bastard to get the hell away from me!" She's already around the corner of the building so I can't see her. I jog over, which for me isn't an easy thing, really. When I get close to the corner, I'm winded and walking. I round the corner of the building and I see a man behind Darya, his arm around her neck, attempting something like a choke hold. He's dressed in an odd long, straight, red...robe? Some sort of ornamental or religious robe. Briefly I wonder why security would need such an outfit, because others are coming out of the building now, in the same attire, through a small side door, rushing toward the man grappling Darya.

"Walt!" she sees me now. She is not afraid, she's pissed off. "Tell this fucker to get his hands off of me."

One of the red-robed men steps toward Darya and her assailant, is whispering "let her go, man". He's clearly trying to de-escalate the situation. I want that too, but it seems like the stick will work better than the carrot right now.

"You heard her," I say, approaching slowly now, my hands open and out to my sides, my phone in my right hand. "Let the lady go. I have 911 on speed dial." I can tell he's tightening his choke hold despite the entreaties of his friend, and I wince, because I know that Darya isn't going to stand for that. Literally. With one Doc-Marten-clad heel she stomps on his right foot hard. His security outfit doesn't include hard boots, apparently, because he yelps both in surprise and pain. Darya quickly drops down, bending over as his arm grip loosens slightly. She reaches between her own legs and grabs his ankle and calf, and pulls it up to the level of her waist, easily putting him on his ass. His buddy has backed away now. I'm still catching my breath, but I can't help but laugh. Before I can say anything else, she's turned on him, and taken out her taser. All of the other folks dressed in red have stopped in their tracks as if she's pulled a gun. "What the hell, people!" Darya yells. I was just taking a few pictures. You can't assault somebody for taking pictures!" She brandishes the taser and I'm glad it's not a gun. The man on the ground is scurrying backward as he stands up, trying to get away from her, and the six men and women begin to form a semi-circle around Darya, and around me as I approach.

I hold up my phone again, and speak at the red-robed people: "Do I need to call the cops?" I ask them, calmly holding up the phone, my thumb ready to dial. Then I look at Darya and repeat myself to her: "Do I need to call the cops?"

"Ask them," she responds, calm already settling in on her face. "Would you like us to call the cops?"

One of the women in red robes holds her hand up to her friends, giving them a kind of stand-down signal. "No," she says, "No. but you're trespassing. Please give me the phone so I can delete those pictures." She's clearly in charge, and used to being in charge. She's telling us, not asking us. I almost feel bad for her when Darya responds, "Why don't you come here and try to take my phone, little red riding hood? I'd like to see that. I really would." The woman quickly assesses the situation, while her peers shift their feet, clearly uncomfortable with confrontation.

"There's no need for violence," she says.

"Tell that to fucking Hulk Hogan over there," Darya says, pointing at the man who grabbed her, who is now trying to get the dirt off of his robes.

"I apologize for my colleague. He was just doing his job."

"Oh, great, the Nazi Cop defense, that's always a good one" Darya retorts. "We're leaving, and if you're lucky we won't file charges." I notice for the first time that all of the red-robed people are indeed white. It's probably nothing, but what with neo-Nazi's actually coming out of the woodwork these days, I have to wonder if Darya might have a point.

"And if you're lucky," Little Red says, "we won't file charges. But I'd like your phone, please," she says, intensely, with the confidence of a CEO, or, yeah, a Nazi Cop. Darya actually moves a step closer to her now, before saying, "What, you think you're some sort of Jedi?"

"We're not the droids you're looking for," I say, as I gently take Darya's arm and begin ushering her back toward the path. "We're leaving. We're leaving. I would advise you to not accost people who accidentally stumble onto your property. This is Oakland, not Florida. Put up a fence if you don't want people taking shortcuts, for Christ's sake." I make a mental note that, sure enough, nobody really is cutting through this parking lot, which would be a pretty good shortcut for some paths.

Red-robes stand down, and we begin to move off, not quite turning our backs on them. Darya puts her taser away, grumbling. They stand in place, watching us go. When we're almost back on the lake path, I just can't help myself. I do a little of my Columbo impression, taking a few steps back toward them, "Oh, hey, just one more thing. Is this a church now? What's going on with the robes?"

"Goodbye, sir," Little Red responds almost cordially.

I take one more stab: "Be careful around here at night. The cops found a dead body right over there," I say as I point toward the lake. It's just a moment, but I note hesitation and surprise in Little Red's face, just around her eyes. The rest of the robed people can't help but glance toward one another.

"Thank you for the...warning. Please go."

We go.

5

I don't like turning my back on those folks, but I do it anyway, and with my body language urge Darya to do it too. I'm grateful that she follows my lead even in the face of being bodily harassed. She's calmer now, but still fuming, understandably angry, talking at me through gritted teeth.

"That was wrong, Walt. They can't do that. We're going to call Harks at least, aren't we?"

"Keep walking, please," I say. I'm relatively spry for my age, but I'm not going to be jogging away from the auditorium. I move as quickly as I can, helping Darya to resist the urge to stop and talk before we are out of sight of the harassers.

"Well, I can't let it slide, Walt. You may be able to, but I can't. I'll grab Harks and come back and have a little talk with those...those people. And if Harks won't, I know some people who will, and we'll have more than a little talk."

She's not lying. She does know some folks who would be willing to go back and rough some robed wizards or whatever those people are. People paid under the table, or even just friends who normally would get paid for it, but who would do it for free for Darya. Darya grew up in Oakland, and as the daughter of Iranian immigrants, has faced down worse people than whatever those cosplaying thugs think they are. I don't think she would actually go back and hurt people, and normally I would try to dissuade her from such things. Muscle has its place, sure, and you have to defend yourself.

"You know that I think about that, Darya. Mind beats muscle in almost every fight."

"Says the man who has been in countless bar fights."

"Well, learn from my mistakes."

"You could learn a thing or two from me, old man," she says. "Old White Man."

"I hear you. I do. I think you should go back. Tonight."

"What? Really?"

It's not often that I can surprise Darya with anything I say, so I take a few moments of joy in her speechlessness, the look of confusion on her face, as we start to walk less hurriedly toward the office, away from the auditorium, not looking back.

"Yes. I want you to be careful, but I want you to go back tonight. Actually, probably three or four in the morning, if you're ok with that. You don't get paid for overtime, but I'll make coffee."

"YES. I knew you had it in you, Walt. You're always telling me, 'A fight you walk away from beforehand is a win' and all that stuff, but you know what's what. Who should I get? Harks? Some people you don't really want to know who they are? I can't really do both. They won't get along with each other."

"I think you should go alone," I say, trying not to smile. That gives her pause.

"Well. Huh. Ok. That actually sounds kind of satisfying. I'll need both tasers. And I'll have my phone dialed up to you for backup. You're just going to stay home, old man, while I defend myself? Who says chivalry is dead?"

"No tasers. And yes, I'm staying home. You can handle it. But I don't want you to engage them."

"Walt. I'm not following you," she's run out of steam, and the look on her face tells me she thinks I need another nap. "I'm really not following you," She stops walking, and I stop with her.

We're safely out of sight of the robed folks now. "You want me to go back, but not engage? I'm not doing a stakeout at three in the morning by the lake, alone. That's isn't my idea of a good time."

"You're nimble and fast, I'm sure you can handle a quick in and out."

"I'm not going in that auditorium alone after what just happened. No."

"Don't need to go in, I just need you to retrieve my camera."

It takes a few moments, but she starts to chuckle. "You bastard."

"Why do you always have to bring my mother into this?"

"You BASTARD," she's laughing harder now, as we go further around the bend.

"Where? When? I didn't even see you plant the camera."

"Well, good, that's the idea. If you didn't see it, hopefully they didn't either. I put it in the tree I was leaning on. First big branch, right in the nook. Hopefully it's pointed at the building properly. I didn't have much time."

"What, you just carry that thing around with you just in case you need to plant it?"

I pull a small, cube-shaped camera out of my pocket, holding it up. "Nope. I carry a few."

***

It's not a camera that transmits--I could get some of those, some that are even as small as this one, but they're too expensive for an operation like mine. So, we need to get the camera back, or at least the SD card that's in it, in order to watch the video. It's set to record 24/7 right now (the motion-detecting cameras are a little too big for my tastes still, at least the ones I can afford), but we'll only get 20 hours of black and white night-vision video. I just want to see if anything odd goes on there at night. We already know they're kicking out homeless folks from the parking lot to keep it empty, so we'll at least see them doing that, see if they use some strong-arm tactics like they tried to use on Darya. If we see anything incriminating, I'll make an anonymous tip to Oakland PD, but technically leaving a camera in a private parking lot is in a gray area legally, so I can't really bring Harks in on it unless we find something juicy.

Darya is still giggling to herself when we get to the office. My camera antics have helped diffuse her anger. She's young, has a temper. I used to have a temper, but that was a long time ago. I've learned at least that in life--my temper almost never got me what I wanted. It feels good, to let anger fly, but it rarely has helped me, and I've lost a lot because of it. I don't miss it.

I take care of some housekeeping chores when we get back, some emailing, a quick check-in with my biologist friend about our upcoming call. We have a more official relationship than I do with folks like Stoney, or Harks. I actually pay her by the hour when it's related to a case, even though we also just go out for a walk around the lake sometimes. She loves the lake almost as much as I do, perhaps for slightly different reasons, but still, we're kindred spirits in that way. She has to pay the rent, so I pay her. Which makes me think, not for the first time, why am I doing this case? Nobody is paying me for this, not in cash anyway. Harks and I have helped each other in countless ways over the years, so much that I've lost track of who's back might need scratching this time around. She'll pay me back with information or help in the not too distant future. And she knows she's paying me in other ways--she knows I like an actual mystery, where there's something I haven't seen before, something that I don't already know the outcome right from the very start. It's a problem when you're old. Everything begins to look the same, people slide easily into categories that are full of other people you've encountered in your life. Cheating spouses. Angry business partners. Stalking men thinking that unrequited love means they are the victim. Something really new is a jolt to the system, a welcome surge of strange reality that makes me feel a few years younger.

I work on my two other cases a bit, work I can do from the desk, tying up loose ends on what somebody thought was a missing persons case, but which was a somebody-who-didn't-really-want-to-be-found case (as they often are). Normally I'd meet the client in person, but Hark's case is too important, I think, to worry about these niceties. Darya works behind me at her desk. I wonder if she'll be working on her thesis tonight.

I notice again (did I notice this today already? I've forgotten) that we're out of my chai in the office. I stopped with coffee a while back, enjoying the caffeine from chai more. It's smoother, and not as hard on my stomach. A few clicks and I've ordered a case of it, should be here tomorrow. I know I'm never going to make it to three am without some help, but I'm not sure I want to lay down again. My gull dream is still spinning slowly in the back of my mind, spitting out dark thoughts. Ah well, I'm tired again. A short nap now will help me stay up tonight. It's late afternoon now, so just a half-hour should do. Still lots more research I could be doing, but my eyes feel heavy, and maybe if I sleep now it could even help the dark thoughts. Get some rest. It's more helpful than most people remember.

Darya is busily researching the auditorium's new occupants, deep in her focused mode. I decide not to bother her when I walk toward my apartment door. Without looking up, she says, "Why don't you just start out on the floor, so you don't hit your head again." I know what she really means is "I'll check on you in a bit."

"Yeah, yeah. Sure thing," I respond. I do think twice about the couch this time though, and head into my bedroom. It's risky--my bed is expensive and comfortable, and it could lead to a longer nap, but I set my alarm for an hour with a loud tone, setting it under my pillow just in case. I wonder what I used to do without a smartphone. Probably had better naps, honestly. Kicking my shoes off, settling in on my back, hands clasped over my chest, I close my eyes. I wonder if this is what I'll look like in my casket. It's a thought I've had a lot in life, even when I was younger. I like to think about who would come out to see this old wrinkled face one last time. As I fade into sleep, I see people coming up to take a look, looking up at them somehow even though my eyes are closed, I see them sad, relieved, horrified, calm, peaceful and angry. I've met a lot of people in my life. A few exes come by for a peek, still youthful, even the ones who have already passed in waking life. I'm not sure it's bad to have people still angry at me, as much as people are also sad about my passing. Either way I'm remembered. I sleep.

***

This time it's a Cormorant that comes to visit me in my dream, and I'm solidly aware that I'm dreaming. She's big, at first a black silhouette against a blood moon which seems to be rising from the lake itself. She's standing on a small outcropping of rock near the shore of the lake, the rock barely piercing the surface of the still water. On a normal day Cormorants will sit on rocks like this, or sometimes on the shore, stretch out their wings and point their chests at the sun, elegant heads turned to the side, soaking up the sunlight. When they do this, they look like a living family crest, and they stand so still for so long, it's easy to think of them as statues. In my dream, she is alone, and larger than life, standing mostly still, her back to the moon. I know I'm dreaming, but my mind is muddled, cloudy as I walk toward the edge of the lake, nearer to her. This dream is so different. The lake is so calm, undisturbed by any breeze, but I can still feel the cool air coming off of the surface. She moves now, slightly, keeping her wings spread, her head moving slowly from side to side, an ecstatic movement, a ritualized movement that I've seen a hundred times in the waking world, in the daylight, but never like this. I know I can wake up at any moment of my own choosing.

I take my time walking toward Her, toward the edge of the lake, and gaze at Her. This is what the lake is to me, deep down, this natural beauty, a calm, living thing in the center of the city I love. I feel the breeze, though it doesn't seem to disturb the surface of the lake. I enjoy my dream. Her feathers are a deep black, have a healthy sheen. Her outline glows ever so slightly red-orange from the light of the blood moon behind Her, showing wisps of small feathers that look like small flames coursing through her body, emanating randomly, displaying the potential power stirring within Her. It's a kind of ecstasy for me, too, that calm-yet-energetic feeling. Her head turns slowly to center, then right, and left again, as she looks at me from one eye, then the other. I find myself turning my head to look at her similarly, even though part of me knows my eyes are different from Hers, my body structured strangely compared to Hers. She is gazing at me in the way that birds can, taking my measure first from one perspective, then another. I feel her mind for a moment, feel the differences there. She's able to see differently, but also know the world from different perspectives, by virtue of her biology. I find myself wishing I could think like Her, find different ways of looking, at least one more perspective that for now feels deeply out of my reach, unknowable to my kind.

She dips her head and brings her wings in for a moment. It feels like a salute, and a goodbye, and my heart beats faster, stronger. My hand reaches out toward her, falling back to my side when she spreads her wings and flies straight up in one giant movement, her graceful neck splitting the sky above Her. As she does this, the lake's surface swirls, and a wave crests the rock she had been on, disappearing it. She flies up, with a few more strokes of her powerful black wings as the surface of the lake roils with movement. The moon is dark red now, and I see there is something huge under the surface, almost as if the water itself were a creature coming alive. And yet, I am not afraid. I know I can wake up if I need to. I know I'm dreaming. I know She's got this under control, despite the chaos of the water now.

She hits a high point, then dives at a slight angle, plunging with almost no splash into the water, just like her waking-life kin do when hunting their dinner. Moments later the lake stops roiling as she breaks the surface and takes flight, coming toward me. She's as large as I am. No, larger, twice as large, and I stand still as she lands near me. I feel the wind created by the beat of her wings, and see the water flow off of her, and off of the thing she has brought to me. It's a dying thing already, plucked from the lake, which is still now. It squirms in her thin beak as she lowers her head and places it in front of me. It's slick with oily wetness, squirming tentacles of some sort of creature. More than ten arms, a gaping maw with shells for teeth, and eyes. So many eyes. Different sizes, different colors, some with no eyelids at all, some with several, like fish have. It looks around, dazed. It's dying and it knows it. As she looks back toward the lake the creature stops squirming, but instead of dying limply it has solidified into an obsidian totem, a fist-sized chunk of shiny black stone representing the creature that had been alive moments ago. She leaves it with me, flying into the sky, across the lake, and into the tree line across the lake, her form coalescing from the dream-Goddess into the little Cormorant version of herself as she goes, until I can't see her any longer. The peacefulness I've felt the entire dream leaves me suddenly, like a wave having crested and water moving back into the ocean across the sand. I am afraid, but not yet ready to wake.

I squat, and look at the small icon now and notice that, though it isn't moving around any longer, it blinks at me. Its eyes move, looking in all directions. I reach down to pick it up and then the moon goes out. I'm in darkness within my dream.

Frightened now, I will myself awake.

***

My bedroom is dark, and I pull my phone out from under my pillow. I see that it's almost morning, just after 5 a.m. I feel well-rested, and I don't feel the aches I often do when I sleep too long. I don't even think about how long it's been since I had a full night's sleep. Plus I slept in my clothes. I guess I really am worn out from thinking about this case, and what with all of the excitement at the auditorium.

The auditorium. Darya.

I move to text her as I sit up and swing my legs over the side of the bed, but there's already a text from here waiting for me: "I'm back. Letting you sleep because you're snoring like my girlfriend's pug does at home. Coffee's ready when you are."

I really lucked out when I hired Darya. Not only is she great at her job, she's a rarity in various ways--foremost of which, she's kind. Angry, yes, a lot of the time, but there's a kindness underneath that I haven't run into much in life. She's taught me a bit of it, but just getting older has also taught me the importance of kindness. It seems like people take one of two paths as we get older. Some of us accept, even maybe welcome, that death isn't so far away any longer, and are able to look at the world, look at the rest of our fellow humans through that lens. We see even the worst asshole in that light, knowing they, too, are just going to be dust someday, and somehow it softens us, lets us give room to people to fuck up, to be horrible sometimes. Other people see the train coming down the tracks, know they're tied to the tracks, and they panic. They lash out all around them. They're really angry at the finality of death coming their way, choo-choo-ing down the tracks, inevitable, but they find anything else to get angry at--their ex, their spouse, some group of people different from them in some way, their neighbors, kids, whatever. Take it out on them. And it's tempting, sure. I slip up and go down that road sometimes. Which is another reason it's helpful to have a person like Darya around, who has both anger and kindness as her defaults. There are definitely things to be angry about in this world.

I realize that I've drifted again, sitting on my bed, in my dirty clothes. My mind does that more and more. But I do feel some anger. I'm angry that my coworker, my friend, was harassed yesterday, but I'm more angry that there's a dead body, two, that I can't explain, and I have a gut feeling that the two things have something to do with each other.

I take a shower to clean up, but to clear my mind a little bit too, let the fog of a good night's sleep wash away. The hot water feels refreshing today. I think about that little statue from my dream, and it makes me want to scrub a little harder. I think about the Cormorant from my dream, and what it might mean, and I feel strangely calm again. I have to wonder why my

34

subconscious made me dream all of that, and why it felt so real, even though I knew the whole time I was dreaming. The Cormorant I can understand--I love watching the them sun themselves on the lake. But the little relic, the...totem? I have no idea where that came from. Monsters living in a lake aren't really in my wheelhouse, but I can't ignore the fact that I had two dreams yesterday, and they both included some...sort of creature. Tentacles. Long arms. Teeth made of shell. Too many eyes. Maybe my dreams are just feeding off of each other.

I'll have to ask somebody what that might have been. I can't think of anybody I know who would know. Then a memory bubbles up from deep down in my sketchy little sieve of a memory box. There is somebody from a long time ago. Not sure she'll want to talk to me, but I might have to find a way, swallow what little pride I might have in the matter and get some information from her. I start to reach for my phone, but it's too much to think about just now. I make a note to remind me to reach out to her.

Once I'm dressed, shaved and presentable, I shuffle into the office. Darya is perched at her desk, the cube-camera sitting on the corner. She's looking intently at her screen, and looks up when I come in, picks up her coffee and takes a sip.

"Morning, Walt," she says. She looks tired, but alert.

"Were you up all night?"

"Pretty much. I slept on your couch for an hour or so. Hope that's ok."

"As long as you're careful. That couch is dangerous. It'll throw you."

"You slept through the night, didn't you? I can tell. You were out."

"Yeah. I had a good dream, but yeah, I feel good. I feel like I'm sixty again," I joke as I move around to her side of her desk to get a glimpse.

She gestures at the screen with her cup. "I think we have to call Harks now. It took everything I have to not wake you up earlier. Take a look."

I'm seeing a fuzzy, paused video, fisheye lens distorting things across the horizontal, night vision changing things a bit too, but I can still see clearly what Darya's concerned about. Right at the back door of the auditorium, the one the robed jerks had come out of, is a person, standing with his back to the camera, his fist raised. Darya taps the space bar and the video continues. The man is slowly, methodically, almost rhythmically pounding on the door, clearly wanting in. After a thirty seconds or so of his strange knocking, I lean in more closely, almost entranced, though of course there is no sound. The door opens a crack, then more, and then it's opened enough to let him in. Before he enters, he turns and looks behind him, and I briefly see one eye uncovered. The rest of his body is covered in shells. The door shuts.

35

6

I want to see it again. Just like the autopsy tape, it's difficult for me to process what I'm seeing. Despite all of the zombie television shows that are streaming these days, I'm finding it difficult to believe that a body got up off of the autopsy slab, walked out of the morgue, and headed back home to the Oakland auditorium. It just doesn't fucking compute.

"Darya," I say slowly, "Can you play that again for me please."

"Mhmmm. But you saw what you saw, it's him. It's that same guy, same shells, same beady little open eye." She reaches for the keyboard, scans back over a minute and lets me watch a bit more than I had before. I see the man come from the trees along the lake path into view of the camera. It's grainy, sure, but there's no doubt that's him. He knows where he's going, too, not wandering around happening upon the place. He walks right to the door, right up to it as if he's not covered in shells, as if he doesn't only have one eye open. I can see, too, that he's wet, dripping wet, as if he had come out of the lake. The body disappeared from the morgue in the early hours of the morning...could he have been somehow hiding in the lake the whole day? Breathing through a reed or something? None of this makes sense.

He knocks with a heavy fist, with that creepy rhythm we saw before. Same rhythm, but harder and harder, swinging his arm back over his head further and further, until the door is opened. "I guess they aren't walking around guarding it 24/7," Darya says.

"Yes, but people are staying there 24/7, looks like." I tap the spacebar, go back, watch again. I try to stop it right when the door opens, to see if I can see who opened it, but it's too grainy. I think I might see some long hair, so maybe the Little Red Lady from our little confrontation? Seems odd though, since she looked to me to be in charge, and people in charge don't usually keep the midnight to six am watch.

"So, do you want to call Harks, or should I?"

"Well. Hmmm," I'm pulling out my cigar, chomping on it a little. "Let me think for a second."

"Walt, I've been watching that thing for an hour. There's nothing more to think about. The cops need to check that place out."

"Give me a minute to think. Let's think of the long game, first." That's one of the things about being a private investigator, instead of a cop. There's more of a gray area, and sometimes we can use that gray area to get some things done. "We will get the police involved, but let's think it through, first. "You're not usually so keen on calling OPD right in," I say, remembering the times she's taught me not to call the cops because of the damage they can do in various communities, in her community.

"Yeah, well, as far as I can tell, those are all white people being funded by some tech billionaire, so I'm not as worried about any shoot-first-happy cops. And unless you missed it, a dead body just walked into that building. If that happened in my neighborhood, even I would call the cops."

"Did it? I mean, was it dead. Seems unlikely."

"Unlikely?" she's losing patience with me now. "You growing a brain at this moment is unlikely, I guess."

"Darya, we call the cops right now, they go out there and raid the place, what happens? Maybe we need another look around first."

"WALT," she says sarcastically, mocking my name-naming tone, "what if those people killed that guy, and they kill somebody else?"

I nod. "Is there more on the tape?"

"Uh, I think so. I didn't watch much more after that. Yeah," she checks the memory card, "it looks like there is some more. Want to speed through it?"

"Sure," I say, hopeful to continue distracting her from calling the police right this moment. I don't think anybody else is in much danger in the next hour from these people. I could be wrong, but I'm going to risk it to give myself some time to think. Police can sometimes trample down clues, both literally and figuratively, and I'd like to get a better picture of what the hell is going on with the lake before that happens.

Darya speeds through the next half hour, and we see no activity at the auditorium. Then we both see it--the door opens again and somebody new comes out, a man in the robes. Darya slows it down to normal speed, backs it up a bit, and we watch him come out. He is closing the door carefully.

"He's sneaking out," Darya says with surprise in her voice.

I nod, "looks like it."

Once the door has been carefully closed, he looks around, and quickly removes the robe he's wearing, revealing a t-shirt and jeans underneath. Now I notice he's actually carrying his shoes, which he starts to put on, standing first on one leg, then the other. He's leaving his robes there on the ground, looking around, and looks like he's about to jog off when the door opens, and the woman I've taken to calling Little Red rushes out, takes him by the arm. She's wearing normal clothes, maybe even sweats for sleeping in. I look at Darya and she smiles. There is sometimes still a little voyeuristic thrill in PI work. These people are doing something not quite right, right next to the lake, and they think they're doing it without anybody noticing. We are noticing, and sometimes that's a good feeling.

Though we don't have sound on this camera, It's clear that Little Red is entreating the man to not leave. It doesn't look like a lover's quarrel to me--she is smaller than he is but he's acting as though she's an imposing physical force. He's almost cowering, even. Shaking his head. His shoulders slump. She points down, and he picks up the robe. She opens the door again, holds it open for him to go inside. I'm fascinated by the fact that she's somehow bullied him into going back in.

But then he throws the robe at her and runs. He doesn't jog away. He runs right past our camera, right toward the outer parking lot around the auditorium. She makes no move to stop him this time, and his robes fall to the ground. She watches him go, takes out a cigarette, lights it with a lighter from her pocket, and quickly smokes it, holding the door open the whole time. Waiting for him to return? He doesn't. She finishes her smoke, tosses it on the ground at her feet, and steps on the butt. Kicking his robes through the doorway, she goes back inside.

Darya says, "See, Walt, maybe those people aren't there of their own free will. We have to call Harks, at least."

I nod, look at her, but reach down to the keyboard again, backing the video up to where I can see the man's face. It's blurry, but I recognize him. "Before we do, let's try to pay him a visit."

"Oh, sure, I'll just check our drone cam footage to see where he went," Darya snarks. "And after that I'll have our robot dog sniff him out. Let me get on that," she continues, cartoonishly miming typing on her keyboard.

I gently move her out of the way with my hip against her desk chair, and open up a tab on her browser. "You were too busy antagonizing the cultists to notice the parking lot, I guess," I say, bringing up the site I want.

"So we're just going to call them cultists now? Good. I didn't want to be the first to say it, but those robes are creepy, right?"

"Yup." I type a few keystrokes and Darya sees where I'm going.

"The truck," she says. "I did notice the one truck parked in the parking lot. It stood out, since it was the only vehicle in an otherwise empty lot--I remember thinking, what, the cultists all take rideshares to church?"

"Did you note the license plate?"

"Why, yes, Walt, I did. I remember all of the license plates I see, don't you? No! Of course I didn't. You did?"

"It was memorable," I point at the screen, where I've brought up our reverse-find license plate site.

Darya reads it out loud, "JOHN GLT"? Who the hell is John, and what's 'GLT'? Guacamole, lettuce and tomato sandwich? Yum."

"Ok, it was memorable *to me*. I take it you didn't go through an Ayn Rand phase in college?"

"I thought I was going through that once, but I went to the health center and it cleared up. What is an Ayn Rand?"

"It's not important. I remembered it, is all that matters.. And that guy in our video stalked off to the parking lot when Little Red finally let go of him. There's nowhere to go, really, over there, unless you're going to that truck, so I say we check him out and maybe go talk to him." I get his name and address from the reverse lookup. His name is John (of course) Trier, and he's in Oakland. Downtown, in one of the new buildings.

"He's in the techbro dorm," Darya says, referring to a new high rise near the BART station, mostly build for this tech boom, for the workers from San Francisco who can't find housing where they work, even with six-figure salaries.

"Yes. You can ask around when we go there. I'm sure somebody can tell you who John Galt is. Find out what you can about him in the next few minutes. I'm going to make a call, and then we'll head over there."

"You're sure we shouldn't call Harks?"

"Not just yet. If we do, she'll have to try to raid the auditorium. I'd like to talk to this guy firs if we can. But we want to be quick about it. From that video, it's possible he's in danger. Looked like he thought he was, anyway.."

Darya dives in to researching Mr. Trier, and I go into my apartment. I want a bit of privacy for this call. It's been...too long since I've talked to Susan, but I need her help on this. My regular biologist friend hasn't been responding to me, and Susan can help me with that. But she can also help me with...the more odd parts of this whole thing. I'm not sure why I know this. I can feel it in my gut, in the back of my mind, the back of my throat. She may not talk to me, but I have to try. I get her voicemail, which isn't too surprising. I leave my message: "Hey Susan, it's...well, you know who it is I guess. I know we haven't talked in a while, but I have a case I need your help on, if you'll help me. It's about the lake. And some possible murders. But mostly about the lake, and, well, a couple of dreams I've had." I sigh, unsure of what to say. "I'd say more about it but I'd rather talk face-to-face, if you don't mind. Just tell me a time and place and I'll make it work. I can buy you lunch. Or, not. Ok. Ok. Thanks, Susan. Take care." I shake my head at myself. I'm like a teenager when it comes to her. She may not return my call. She was fairly clear that she didn't need to see me again after the last time we talked, but she didn't say don't call her, so. So. Why are calls like that still so much more difficult than seeing a dead body? Maybe even more difficult than seeing a shell-encrusted not-quite-dead body walking around. I head back into the office.

"You got anything?"

"Not much," Darya responds. "He's young, he's a programmer, and he owns that truck. But I'm pretty sure that address is correct."

"Let's go see him then," I say. "You drive."

***

Darya finds some close parking, which is a win for us, since part of Oakland's changing landscape is fewer places to park, and more traffic. Rents are higher, so people are doubling up in their housing, and that means more cars with the same number of parking spots. That's why I walk where I can. My assistant suggested I get a tricycle at some point, and she meant it as a joke, but I kind of like the idea. Cigar in my mouth, riding along slowly in the bicycle lane, pissing off the spandex-wearers and joggers-in-the-bike-lane alike. I'm not a bitter old man, but I do take my simple pleasures in some bitter places, I guess. The saying 'Youth is wasted on the young' isn't really true, but sometimes it feels true. I wonder about my encouraging Darya into the kind of life I've led, about how maybe it's selfish of me. She might be much happier being a professor or some such. She'd be good at being a P.I., sure, but being good at something doesn't mean you enjoy it. One of the odd truths of life.

"How do you want to play this one?" Darya asks me as we get out of the car. We're about half a block away from the entrance. "Should I sneak you in as my elderly grandfather who really needs a restroom?" These new places often have a security desk, which is why she's asking. We'll need a way in, and I suspect Mr. Trier isn't going to buzz us up.

"I know you like to go with the route that is most humiliating for me, but let's see what's what first. If we have to, I'd rather go with me distracting the guard with my quick wit while you sneak by."

"Your wit? We'll never get in."

We're at the glass door and sure enough, we can see the short security counter, and a uniformed guard sitting behind the desk. We stop and I smile my best smile, wave. I recognize the guard. There are only a few good security guard companies these days, and their employees often work at various places, so even though this is a new building and I've never been here before, I recognize Nancy from a building near Jack London Square. She recognizes me, it seems, and buzzes us in.

"Walt! What are you doing over in these parts? A little fancy these days for a man like you, isn't it?" Nancy is in her early fifties, always friendly, and probably doesn't get paid enough for how good she is at her job.

"I just came to say hi to you, Nancy. Everybody is talking about how you're moving up in the world," I say. "This is my workmate, Darya. She's all right."

"Darya, it's a pleasure," Nancy says. "I'm sorry you have to work with this guy, though. What did you do to deserve such things in life?" Nancy has always had an interesting way of putting things.

I point toward Nancy while I look at Darya. "Nancy is really good at doing that thing to people where she's making fun of you while making you think she's on your side. Be careful."

Smiling calmly, Nancy responds with, "I don't know what you could possibly mean, Walter. I was raised right, if that's what you mean. Don't say anything if you can't say anything nice."

"Or say whatever you want to say nicely, and they'll swallow it whole," Darya chimes in.

"I like her," Nancy looks approvingly at me.

"Yeah, well, hide your daughters, Nancy."

"They're both married already, Walt. You know that."

"Then make certain you hide them," I whisper conspiratorially, which makes Nancy chuckle. Darya isn't quite as amused. "Are you two about done?"

"Just about," I say. "Nancy, you know anything about a resident here? John Trier?"

Nancy glances at her monitors and looks around toward the elevators. "Trier. Maybe. It's difficult to tell these young kids apart, Walt, you know that."

"I do. He drives a bright green truck. Douchey license plate?"

"Sadly, you'll have to narrow it down. The John Galt guy?"

"That's him."

"That's so weird, that you'd ask about him right now. I had to ask him to move his truck early this morning. He pulled into the parking garage and was using not only his space, but the one next to it. He wasn't happy to hear from me. Seemed flustered."

"Was that about 3am? Darya asks.

"It was indeed," Nancy looked a little surprised. "Did he do something...bad?" Nancy looks back at me.

"Not at all. We think he may be in some danger, actually." I try to calm things down a bit, by adding, "Nothing that serious, but we'd like a word with him, to warn him." I don't like misleading Nancy at all, but I don't want her notifying any authorities.

"Well Walt, you know I can't help you there. I mean, the guy lives all the way in the top floor, in 6P, and we take our security very seriously here. I mean, the only way you could get up there is if I were to go on rounds right now, and somehow I didn't notice that you were heading up in the elevator." Nancy props up a small sign on the counter, "Back in 10 minutes", grabs a clipboard, and heads toward a the door to the parking garage behind her. "Sorry I can't help you, Walt. See you around. Nice to meet you, Darya," she holds up her clipboard in a goodbye gesture, and is gone.

"No charm, huh?" I say to Darya, heading toward the elevators.

"That lady had more charm in her little finger than you do."

"I can't argue with that," I say, and hit the elevator button. The doors open immediately, and we head up to the top floor. "6P. P is for penthouse, right?" I ask her.

"You need to get out more, boss. Yes. P is for penthouse."

"Fancy."

40

We get out on the 15th floor, and it is fancy, sort of. Modern decor, lots of glass and metal. I wonder how much they pay their cleaning crews. That's a lot of glass to clean. The hallway heads in two directions, and he find our way to unit six. The building is quiet. I wonder how quiet it is, really, living here, with the BART trains going by every few minutes. It feels soundproofed, which is nice. I wonder if I could sleep if it was this quiet. I need the sounds of the city as my lullaby.

I hesitate outside of his door.

"Why don't you let me knock. How do I put this? He seemed like the kind of young man who might be afraid of people who aren't lily white."

She shakes her head slowly, smiling, but she moves out of range of the peephole. "Seems to me white people are his main problem right now," Darya chimes in with a whisper. I nod.

I knock. There is no answer. Nancy mentioned his truck was here, so I suspect he's home. I listen for any movement inside, watch the peephole from the wrong side to see if it goes dark. I knock again, just a little louder. I see and hear him look through the peephole, but he doesn't answer the door. He's scared, which is a kind of relief, honestly. I'm starting to think he should be, the more I think about the cultists.

I call out to him. "Mr. Trier, I only want to help you, and to ask a few questions. I won't take long." There is a pause, and then I hear him through the door. "Who are you?" he asks, his voice almost cracking.

"My name is Walt, but you can call me Howard Roark if you'd like," I say, knowing he'll get the reference, and hoping it calms him down a little. Darya looks at me from the side of the door, skeptical and a little confused.

He opens the door and I see he is afraid. He's been crying. His shirt is rumpled in a way that shows he's been sleeping in his clothes. He glances down the hall, sees Darya, and starts.

"Mr. Trier, may we come in? I think we can help you."

Trier heaves a sigh, catching his breath, and turns around, leaving the door open, as if he's decided to trust me to help keep him safe. I hope he's right.

41

7

John Trier's apartment is a continuation of the building's styling, all glass and lacquered black wood and silver trim. It makes me want to stay away from all of the furnishings, almost like you feel when you're in a museum, or a hospital. He's pacing in his living room area, which is also sort of his kitchen area, and his bedroom area, all combined. I'm hoping there's at least a separate bathroom. These days, folks like John are paying high prices for small spaces, especially if they are near transit that goes to San Francisco; thus, Darya's reference to "dorms". He's got a television on one wall that is larger than his windows, with cables draining out from behind it like dead snakes. Several video game consoles and a PC are attached to it. Scattered around his black leather-ish couch are empty cans of energy drinks and paper to-go containers. The "bro-grammers" often work long hours. He's probably not home much. I wonder how he has time for a cult. Against one wall next to his mattress on the floor are several other mattresses, leaning against each other, each from a different online mattress seller. I want to ask about it, but I don't.

I follow John in, and Darya comes in behind me, shutting and locking the door. I know she's casing the place in a more detailed way than I am, checking for any hints at what this guy is about. It's another of the things she's good at, sussing out what makes people tick from a few looks around their environment, from watching them move through the world. It's almost Sherlock-esque the way she does it. She says it has to do with all of the schooling she's had, but I think it's mostly something she's always been good at, perhaps deep intuitions augmented by her schooling. I've slowly taught myself to listen to my gut feelings, and they are right more often than not, but I suspect she has more natural talent in that way than I have.

It's clear to me that John hasn't slept, or hasn't slept much. Ironic, given how many mattresses he owns. "Mr. Trier, thank you for seeing us," I begin. Sometimes a bit of formality calms people down, especially when it's coming from an old man. He looks startled, as if he's noticing for the first time that I didn't come in alone. He stops his pacing for just a few beats, then begins again, avoiding eye contact. Looking inward, perhaps?

Darya tries a different tack. "Mr. Trier. John. Have you slept? Are you ok?" She has picked up an empty energy drink can, holding it up, encouraging him to take a look at his surroundings.

He stops again for a moment, looking at Darya briefly, then continues pacing, "You're the people from the auditorium. The ones looking around. I remember."

I let Darya keep going, as he seems to be responding to her more than he does to me. Not surprising. Yes, Darya is an attractive young woman, but that may not be all it is. With age comes some invisibility. It's almost like a kind of magic sometimes, like a spell has been cast that helps people's gaze slide off of me. At first it only irritated me, but I do find it useful from time to time. I take a look around John's place while he talks with Darya. It's small enough that he's never really out of my line of sight, much less hearing range.

"That's right, John. Can I call you John, is that all right? I'm Darya, this is Walt."

"Sure, sure. I'm John." He nods at me, doesn't seem to care that I'm looking around.

"And I remember you, John. From early this morning. You were the man who objected to my being manhandled. I should thank you," Darya kept her voice calm and measured, almost soothing. Even though she was only a handful of years older than him, it felt like a mother's voice to me, and I could see John calming down a little, responding to that. I'd seen her do this before, and it was sort of a guilty pleasure of mine to watch.

"No. No, don't thank me. I don't know what they were thinking. That was just the last straw, you know?"

He seems to have crested some sort of wave now, and pours himself into the couch, faux-leather creaking with newness. He's laying down on it now, with two strangers in his home. I wonder if he's having some sort of nervous breakdown. I continue looking through his house, checking out his kitchen cabinets (mostly empty) and his fridge (energy drinks and leftovers). Darya leans, then sits on the arm of his couch near his feet, and instantly creates a psychologist and patient dynamic. She's good. Maybe I should bring her with me to meet up with Susan, if Susan agrees to meet me. Nope. These Jedi mind tricks won't work on her, I know.

Darya gently urges him to continue, repeating the last thing he said: "The last straw…?" I see she's fingering her phone in her hoodie pocket, probably recording him. That's another one of the gray areas we have as PIs. It's nothing that would be admissible in court, but sometimes it's good to have recordings anyway.

John begins to shake, wanting to cry perhaps, but not quite able to. Unfortunately, trying to not cry also means not talking much. Darya talks him down a little. "It's all right John. You're ok now. Try to breathe. Deep breaths." He does as he's told, and calms down moderately, though he's still fidgeting like a little kid with too much sugar in his system, which, I suppose, he sort of is. "If you can tell us what you mean, we might be able to help you."

He bursts out laughing in surprise. "No. Nope! I don't think there's anything anybody can do. I just want to make it through the next few weeks, and then maybe I'll move. Seattle, maybe. Or Portland. Portland is supposed to be good." He's off on his own again, oblivious to us in the room. Darya brings him back.

"It sounds like you don't want to be here any longer. Can you tell me why you left the," she pauses, and I know she's trying to not say 'cult'. "The auditorium? You were staying there, right?" He nods. I wonder how she knew that.

"I'll tell you, just because you're being nice, Darya," he says. I'm shocked he remembered her name, in his state. I find a stack of books. Lots of Ayn Rand, no surprise there. Lots of self-help books, which is another irony, I think. A whole bunch of books I recognize as near-right-wingnuttery, even though I've never heard of them before. Steve Jobs biography. As they talk I meander over to his bedroom area, checking to see if he's bothered by my wanderings. Seems not.

"Those people, Debra from work told me about them. She and I were talking about real estate, about not being able to buy anything around here where we work, all of that," he reaches down for an energy drink can, finds it empty, reaches for another, swigs down the remnants as he sits up a little, his feet on the couch still. Darya stays put. "She told me this group of investors was going to do something about it. They were going to 'disrupt' real estate in the area around the lake, and then buy up a bunch of property cheap. Did I want in. I said yes. I went to a few meetings in the city near work, and it seemed a little shady, but maybe could work."

"How are they going to disrupt things?" Darya prompted.

His voice is quiet, almost too quiet for me to hear: "They are going to kill the lake."

***

43

That perks my ears up, for sure. John spills everything he can. He's at that place in life that we sometimes get into, where we're in way over our heads, have been keeping big secrets, and finally, suddenly, just need to let it out. To tell someone. To tell everyone. As he talks he starts to wind down, the caffeine and adrenaline finally overcome by the necessities of the body. His body calms, his fidgeting lessens and then stops. His voice grows quieter. Darya keeps him talking, keeps gently pushing for more information, and he wants to tell her, wants to let somebody else to know what he's been through. It's mostly a selfish act for him, but toward the end he also takes a turn to warning us to stay away from the folks in the cult. And from what he tells us, I don't think his warnings are exaggerations. These sound like dangerous people, despite the hokey getups, in the same way that just about any kind of zealot can be dangerous.

He's sinking further into his couch as he finally relaxes, and sleep can't be kept at bay any longer. I'm torn--his own warnings apply to him as well, but I don't quite think these folks would harm him now that he's clearly not wanting to be involved. Also, there's the craziness of what he thinks happened to him. Even given what we've seen already that is out of the ordinary, I'm not quite ready to believe he actually experienced what he thinks he did. I suspect a combination of caffeine overdoses mixed with being young and impressionable. And maybe some microdosing of LSD or something? I hear that's popular with the tech crowd these days. But I don't know. I just don't know. John is fast asleep now, and he will likely be out for a while. We leave, making sure the door locks behind us, but we stop by to talk to Nancy again. I don't give her enough details for her liking, but I put her on alert. The next people who come to visit John may be dangerous. She's seen dangerous before, and she takes it seriously, and actually thanks us. I tell her to call me sometime and we'll catch up. She pretends that she will.

Darya and I walk silently back to the car, lost in our thoughts, yet still keeping a paranoid eye on our surroundings. We've been up there for over an hour. Darya starts her car and looks at me. "Yes," I say, answering her unspoken question. "Let's get back to the office and we'll call Harks from there." She drives.

***

Back at the office, I set my phone on my desk and Darya and I tell Harks the details of John's story, after we tell her about our interactions with the cultists at the auditorium. I don't leave out any details. I don't see a way around letting Harks know about my camera, so I just leave those details in as well, and move past them as quickly as I can. Harks listens, only interrupting a few times to get a detail she missed the first time.

John had gone to a meeting with his friend from work, a meeting in a hotel conference room in San Francisco, with the intention of learning about a potential real estate deal he might invest in. Young people with high-paying jobs are often ripe for the picking for scammers. The meeting sounded like a TED crossed with a Scientology class, with a notion of "disrupting" the real estate market in Oakland. Oakland is already the new place for tech folks to live, given San Francisco has too many Zuckerbergs who buy a huge house and then buy a circle of houses around that house to wall themselves off from the masses. Real estate around the lake had already skyrocketed, but these folks had a secret plan, one that you could learn more about if you came to a meeting in Oakland. After several meetings, John's friend from work dropped out, thinking it was too weird, a sort of scam, or maybe even illegal. John liked the idea that it might be shady. That's what "disruption" is all about! Yet when he figured out that the group was going to do something *to* the lake, something serious that maybe crossed the line from disruption to destructive, he began having his doubts about the whole thing.

Still, a lot of money could be made. And they way they told it, the lake would be back to normal in a few years--they would do things to it for just enough time to give them a window to buy and then flip some property. He decided to give them some money, a substantial amount, is how he put it, and wouldn't tell us just how much. This was a guy who probably paid three or four times for rent what I did, so I guessed 'substantial' was at least high enough to explain why I wasn't invited to the party. The next step for him was a special ceremony with other investors, one where they treated everybody like they were part of a secret society, "like Masons or something" John said. He thought it was a lark when they put on some robes. He thought it was interesting and fun when they did some chanting--it had reminded him of corporate events, call-and-response sorts of things where the CEO would yell "What Do We Want?" and the tech folks would yell back "Synergy" or something. Only this chanting was Secret Society Bullshit chanting, words that weren't even in English, or any language John understood. They were given the words on little sheets of paper, and chanted them not knowing what they meant. He thought it was kind of fun. It became a weekly thing, for over two months now, but he didn't get to know the other people at all, really. They were asked to not talk about it outside of the group, so that nobody got wind of the huge real estate deal they were about to make. John had paid his money and thought the meetings were goofy fun enough to keep going.

They would chant in a circle of fifteen or twenty people, Little Red leading them on. They never learned her name, everybody just called her Sir, oddly enough. In that group, with what they were doing, it was the least strange thing about those evenings. John said he was an atheist, but it felt like an almost religious experience. He felt part of a group for the first time ever, really. They chanted, talked about the progress of the plan (of which only very vague details were given to the investors), and then went home. He mentioned those nights were the best nights of sleep he had ever had, though he felt like he had a hangover the next day. He kept telling Darya "it just seemed like fun". Expensive fun, maybe, but fun.

Until it wasn't.

Three nights ago they met up in the Auditorium. They chanted as normal, but then Little Red told them tonight was the night that "It" would begin. The lake would change, and in a few more days the property they all wanted to buy on the cheap would be theirs for the taking. The group grew excited, but she calmed them down quickly. Because that night was a special night, she said, one of them would have a chance to be a bigger part of it all. For a bigger sacrifice, they would get a much bigger piece of the pie. John, and the others, assumed this meant more money paid, more money returned on the investment. A few people raised their hands enthusiastically. John wasn't so sure. He had enjoyed thinking about maybe making some money, and the chanting and good nights' sleep, but he wasn't going to put more money into it. A young man was chosen to give a "larger sacrifice". But instead of signing some papers or something like that, he was taken to the center of their circle. A box was brought out for him to lay down in, the exact size of a simple wooden coffin. The chanting died down to a murmur, prompting Little Red to prime the pump and get them chanting again. It was starting to not feel quite as fun to John, but looking around, everybody else seemed into it, so he kept at it. It wasn't him going into the box.

And the man lay down in the box enthusiastically, still chanting himself. Inside was salty, briny lake water, they could all see and smell it as they continued their call and response. It was like some odd baptism, John realized, and that had somehow calmed him. More rituals he didn't understand, but whatever.

"What did any of that have to do with real estate," I had interrupted. I couldn't help myself.

Startled a little out of his memory, John had responded, "It made sense at the time. I can't explain it. It fucking sounds crazy, I know, it sounds crazy just saying it now. But it felt really right at the time. Like something crazy happening in a dream, but it feels right, y'know?"

I did know.

More salt-water was poured into the coffin, and the volunteer was given a small plastic pipe to breathe through, a Do-It-Yourself snorkel. Lake water was poured in from odd vases, and the circle began to close in, the group all unconsciously wanting a closer look. Little Red increased the volume of her calls, and the responses upped their volume as well, and the speed. John remembered the volunteer was told to keep his eyes open, even though the water was lake water, salty and silt-filled. And he did. The chanting built as the box filled, to a crescendo. John remembers thinking that maybe this was a little bit much for him, but looking around, everybody was so into it. He had kept repeating that to us: "so into it".

Suddenly John's explanation had broken off. He didn't remember any more of that evening. He didn't even remember driving home. His truck was there, he was in his bed without his robes on, in his clothes, with no memory of leaving.

Then, yesterday, he was contacted for an emergency meeting of the group. That was the first time they had done that--everything had been scheduled and methodical up until that point. He took a day off of work, went to Oakland, and the group was in the middle of being told there was a problem to be solved. They were broken up into smaller groups, each given a different task. John was in a group that was to keep a lookout around the Auditorium. He didn't know what others were told to do, just that some of them left and came back a few times. And then last night when Darya and I had run into John and his crew, and he was starting to feel in over his head. He talked with another of the cultists about leaving, but was convinced to stay, just see how it played out. After the altercation with Darya, he really wanted to leave, but after mustering up the courage to talk to Little Red about it, he somehow just...didn't leave. His memory is muddled on that point, and that frustrates him as he tells us more.

And then, in the early hours of the morning, the knocking had started. They had been told to guard the place, so they had been sitting around, patrolling a little outside, then coming in to play cards, then going back out. When the knocking came, they weren't sure what to do--people coming here should either have had a key or knew to just knock once to get in. This was different, the pounding that stayed hard and constant. Finally Little Red answered the door, and they let in what John recognized as the man who had volunteered, horrifically covered in mussel shells, smelling like death. A while later, freaking out now, John had made his move to leave. We had seen the rest.

After Darya and I went over John's story, and ours, with Harks, she told us they would have to go officially check out the folks in the auditorium. First they would go talk to John. I thought that was a good idea in any case, even though John probably wouldn't like that much. If he was

46

in danger at all, some police presence around his building might deter the cultists from causing him harm. Harks thought they might also get some more information out of John, some info that could help with her warrant, though the camera footage of the "dead" body would likely be enough. I'd send it to her through an anonymous channel we've had set up for a while now, TOR-based, relatively anonymous, of course. Unless some people did real digging, they won't trace it back to me. Of course, John will likely mention us to the police, but we'll deal with that when it comes.

"I'm almost sorry I got you involved in this, Walt, but I appreciate your help. You're looking in directions we haven't been looking," Harks tells me.

"Almost sorry? You know, you aren't the first person to say that to me."

"I really don't want to hear about your love life, Walt."

Darya interjects, since we're still on speakerphone, "You really don't. But I'd like to hear about yours, Detective Harks."

A pause. And then Harks continued: "I bet you would. Maybe we could have dinner sometime and I'll tell you all about it. Just you, me, and your girlfriend."

"Ouch. I'll see if she's available, detective," Darya laughed.

"If you two are done, I have to make another call, speaking of my love life," I said, ready to hang up. "Keep us posted on how it goes with Trier and the auditorium."

"Will do. Talk to you soon Walt. Darya."

I hang up, and mock-glare at Darya. "You really are insufferable. What if I talked to Harks like that?"

"That would be creepy. Creepy old man. When I do it, it's charming."

"I hope you're right."

"Go make your call. Say 'Hi' to Susan for me," Darya goes to her desk and begins to do some work. "I'm going to try to get some more information on Tech Billionaire and see how he relates to those people in the auditorium. Seems weird he'd rent it to them, right? Or do Tech Billionaires own so much of Oakland that they can't keep track of cultists coming out of the woodwork?"

"Good point. Find out what you can. Wish me luck," I sigh, and head into my apartment.

I sit on the couch, gather my wits, and make the call. Susan picks up on the third ring, "I know why you're calling me."

8

It's a short call. She agrees to talk to me, but only in person. I'm fine with that. If I'm honest with myself, it will be good to see her again, after what is it, five, maybe six years? Time slides together these days, and I can usually add a few years on to any estimates I have about how-long-it's-been-since. She's still in West Oakland, in the same house a house we shared briefly. Very briefly. I'm both surprised and not surprised that she hasn't moved. That home was such a solace for her, even if it was also salted with some bitterness given all of the battles she has always fought, continues to fight. Battles against the city, against oppression, against Old White Men. Men like me. And yet, West Oakland has changed in recent years, more than any time in my lifetime. Housing prices have doubled, tripled, so people are finally selling, getting out. Some of them have tried to hold out, but are being driven out, and not by the promise of some money, but by the cultural shift that comes when rich people move in. There goes the neighborhood.

As I head out of the office, I see Darya has finally succumbed to the aftereffects of her sleepless night, head on her desk, snoring. I gently wake her just enough to move her to my couch, put a pillow under her head. I make certain the office door is locked on my way out--I guess I'm coming around to her way of thinking now that I know we might have a murderous cult living around the bend. Taking a moment to look at the lake in the noontime sunlight, wanting to remember why I love this town so much, even in the midst of some...horrors like the bodies and whatever craziness is going on around them. I see a few herons perched nearby on the lake, keeping an eye on things, black-crowned night herons that always look to me like Alfred Hitchcock morphed into bird form.

People are out on their lunch breaks, enjoying the cool spring weather, the sunshine. The lake draws people from all over town, and I see not only workers on lunch breaks, but some parents with their kids walking around. The lakeside kid's place, Children's Fairyland, is closed right now for some remodeling, but the kids don't seem to mind at the moment, chasing geese around the lake, and sometimes getting chased back. A flash of the shell-covered body hits me hard, and I check my phone to see if my rideshare is getting close. I don't drive much these days. I have a car, but it sits in the garage most of the time, unless I want to get out of town. There was a time with a taxi wouldn't even take me to west Oakland from downtown, when that neighborhood was thought of as too dangerous. Like most change, it makes me uncomfortable, even though it's supposed to be a kind of progress.

The ride out does spark some memories for me. The rideshare driver is mercifully quiet. Susan and I haven't been a romantic item for decades, and we were only together for a few years, but it was an intense relationship, and the intensity stays with me. Seeing streets we used to drive down together, places we used to go together, I find myself thinking about what-if's and if-only's. Sentimental old man, though I've been this way since I was young. The work has hardened me some, sure, but catching so many cheaters, as well as just working for folks who are already in a bad place, a place where they think they need a person like me to follow their partner around, it makes me appreciate what Susan and I did have. Even if it was troubled, and brief. We never worried about cheating, that was not our concern. It was the rest of the world that fucked us up, really.

We pull up at the house and stop, stirring me from my memories.

Standing outside as the car pulls away, phone-tipping my driver, I take in the smell of the place. Susan's got an amazing flower garden out front, still, and the lavender overwhelms my senses for a moment. They say smell is one of the most memory-inducing senses. I can't smell much these days--another consequence of aging, and the cigars don't help. I wonder if fading memory and fading sense of smell are related. Susan opens her door, pushing the screen door out. "Come on in Walt. I don't want my neighbors seeing you skulking around. They might call the cops." She laughs quietly at her own joke.

Susan looks the same to me as the last time I saw her, six or seven years ago, but I also see her through lenses that hide the vagaries of time. I'll always be a little shocked to see her as an old lady, much like I'm still shocked at seeing my own face in the mirror, some old man staring back at me. She smiles, which is a good sign. I wasn't even sure I'd get that. She's got green eyes that still mess with my heart, and her long, dark hair greyer now than the last time I saw her. "Come in, c'mon," she encourages me out of my stupor.

"Hi. Thanks for meeting with me," I say, walking up the few steps to her porch.

"Well, you still know how to push my buttons, Mr. Denin. A marine biology question and a spiritual question?. I believe you knew that would be difficult for me to resist." She takes my hand for a moment, squeezing it, and leads me into her living room. "No cigar today?" she adds.

"Didn't want to push my luck."

"Well, you were never dumb. I almost miss being cranky about it with you. Almost."

We sit in her living room. There's no television, but I see books everywhere. I'd worry that she was hoarding if she didn't have such an organized system. This stack is clearly a mix of feminism and Native struggle against oppression. This one is perhaps recent books on, what, mollusks? How can there be that many books on mollusks? I have never met anyone who reads as much as Susan reads. On her walls are Native paintings mixed in with photos of the many protests and other gatherings of the movements she's been involved in. One picture has her standing next to Huey Newton, both of them laughing. I know it's one of her favorites. Another has her standing as a young woman next to then-Governor of California, Ronald Reagan. Unbeknownst to Reagan, Susan is flipping the bird to the camera. It's maybe my favorite. I wonder if she'd mind if I took a picture of it.

She's staring at me now, on a chair facing the sofa I'm on. I can tell she's having some of the same thoughts that I had upon seeing her. "I look old, huh?" I try to jostle her.

"I was thinking the opposite. You look pretty good. Must be whatever case you're working on. You always did look more chipper when you had an interesting case."

"Chipper? Nobody has ever accused me of that, especially you!" I can't help but laugh. We laughed a lot when we were together.

"I won't argue with that. But it does look good on you. You're here about the bodies on the lake." It's not a question.

"I can't even pretend to know how you would know that, Susan. Do you have a spy in my office?"

"No, I read the paper. I saw there was a body in the lake last month, and I read online there was one more the other night. On some local news site, I think. Doesn't take a detective to guess it might be related to why you called me up after eight years."

I smile. I tend to forget that Susan's smarter than me. Probably my vanity that does that forgetfulness. "I was respecting your privacy, like you asked."

"And I appreciate that. What has made you violate it now?" I begin to stutter a defense of my actions, and she holds up her hand, "Don't worry about it, Walt. I'm ok. I wouldn't have responded if I weren't. I'm glad to see you. Kind of."

"Kind of? Well, I'll take that."

"It's all you're going to get at the moment. So tell me what you need a retired biologist for?"

"Well, before I talk to the biologist, I have a more delicate matter to discuss. I want you to promise not to tease me about it."

"I will make no such promise."

"Fair enough." Now that I'm here, talking to perhaps the one person I can talk with about my dream, I hesitate. It's not easy. One of the things that split us up was my not being able to understand how her mind worked around, well, spiritual things. I'm not a spiritual man, I don't believe in ghosts, and anything unknown can be known if we try hard enough. I find no joy in vague mysteries of the afterlife, the way some folks do. I love a good sunset, but I don't think god sent it to me. Susan understood that about me, part of her did at least. But only a part. She is a scientist, but she is also, well, a shaman. There's no other word for it, it's the word she uses, and the folks who come see her for that reason do too. I never understood it. Closed-minded, she said. Practical, realistic, I said. It was one of many breaks in our relationship. Which made what I was about to say doubly difficult for me.

"I want to talk to you about a dream I had," I finally relinquish.

Susan looked at me as if I have spoken in tongues. Her eyebrows curl around her eyes, her mouth opens once, then twice without speaking, and then she begins to laugh. She laughs hard, until she has to stop because she wasn't able to breathe. She stands up, bends over, catching her breath. "Sorry. Sorry. That's just. I'm speechless. I thought that's what you said in your message, but I assumed I misheard you. You want some coffee? I'm getting some coffee." She heads to the kitchen, and I wait.

"Sure. I'll take some coffee. Do I need to get you an inhaler to continue my story? Or a paper bag to breathe into? I don't want you kicking off right here in front of me from laughing at me," I say in a hurt voice, but I'm not really hurt. I always loved to make her laugh, even if it was at my expense. Maybe especially when it was at my expense.

I can hear her giggling to herself a little in the kitchen. It's amazing how good it can feel to be around her, even after these years, even after all of the heartache. That crap they say about time healing wounds isn't quite true, but maybe it does help them scab over enough to tolerate the bad for the joy of the good.

"I really am sorry, Walt. But you have to admit it's an odd thing for you to come to me about." She hands me my coffee. I don't have the heart to tell her I'm on chai now, but I notice she's sugared and creamed it just right when I take a sip.

"I don't blame you, I don't blame you," I say. I think it's ridiculous myself. But I've never had a dream like this. I don't even know where to start."

"Why don't you start with The Cormorant?" she says, and I barely manage to not drop my coffee.

***

She laughs again, this time with a little bit of love mixed in. "I shouldn't tease you, not about this. It takes some bravery for you to find your way here after so many years, and to share these

50

things with me," yet she chuckles even as she says it. "I simply can't help myself. We're swimming in irony, Walter, swimming in irony."

I sit back on the sofa, take a breath, chuckle a little myself. If I can't laugh at myself, at least sometimes, I'm doomed. Coming here to talk about my dream, even coming here to talk about the dead body walking around Oakland, is itself an admission that I don't know everything, which isn't something I could easily admit when Susan and were together. I wouldn't say that I've changed that much, really--I never believed I knew everything, but I did believe that there were some things I knew for certain, things that maybe I shouldn't have been so sure about. Once I hit seventy years old, some of my certainties began to shift. Taking more than a few steps toward The End of things helps with that. You see it coming, and you either admit you don't have it all figured out, still, even after seven plus decades, or you solidify into somebody who is ok lying to themselves, just to be "certain".

"I feel like I'm drowning in irony, a little bit, Susan. I do appreciate you seeing me. How could you possibly know about my dream, though, about the Cormorant? I haven't told anybody about it."

"I didn't know, not really. But I suspected. The Cormorants have been returning to the lake in numbers we haven't seen in decades. And the night herons, the ducks, and marsh insects, fish, of course, and other birds. There are at least two families of pelicans now." She's entered into her professor mode of speaking, and I don't mind in the least. I always loved it when she would get into her marine biologist zone, where she was an expert about things that sort of made sense to me. And then she takes a quick left turn, as always, and I'm lost again: "I've been dreaming about a large, black Cormorant, and she's been trying to communicate with me. Intense dreams, spiritual dreams. That, combined with a surprise text and then phone call from you," she pauses dramatically, takes a sip of coffee, "the idea that you were also dreaming of the Cormorant made sense to me. See? Elementary, my dear Watson."

"I thought I was Sherlock in this scenario."

"Yes, you always did." Another chuckle.

"So that's a sort of deduction you've made, an instinct thing, I think. Cormorants at the lake, you know I live right there, I might dream about them."

"If you say so. You always chalked your gut instincts up to intuition. I think intuition comes from somewhere else, sometimes. And you were always connected to that lake, just as Oakland itself is connected to it. It's the center of community, where all of the peoples of The Town can come together and, if not interact exactly, at least be around each other, see each other, acknowledge each other's existence. It's a spiritual place, Walter, and you're part of that spirituality, even if you don't think you are."

It is as if no time has passed between us. We're already deep into the same disagreement in world view that had split us apart. And we both know it. I have to admit to myself that I like what she says about community, but the "spiritual" isn't comfortable for me. We sit and drink our coffee in silence for a minute.

I know I need her help, and I'm in uncharted territory here for a murder investigation, if that's what I'm even investigating anymore. And I have to admit, my dream freaked me out a little. I'm ok with calling it intuition-plus-something-I-don't-know-about for now. I tell her about my dream, and ask: "What do you think she's trying to tell me?"

"Your dream and my dreams aren't so different--I think she's trying to warn us. There is a danger to the lake. But for the life of me I cannot figure out what it could be. The lake is in better health than it's been almost since we've been alive. Some people have concerns about its spiritual health with the gentrification around the lake. That danger has increased, but it's nothing new. This feels, not new, but more final, somehow. As if she's warning us the lake, the town, and everybody here is in danger. I don't think she'd show herself to folks like yourself unless it was the case."

I want to tell her everything I know all at once, about the cult, the interview Darya and I did with one of its members, all of it, but I don't want to distract her with that just yet. I try again to invoke the scientist in her: "If the lake is in better shape than ever, maybe it has more to lose now, if something were to change there?"

"That's a good point. I thought of that. I've been putting out feelers in city hall and community folks that I know. There don't seem to be big plans for changing the lake in the works. People want to develop more around it, but, again, that's nothing new."

"Huh. Well, the other reason I came to talk to you has nothing to do with my dream," I start. She glares at me. "...as far as I know, as far as I know. I'm sure you'll find a connection." Laughter from both of us again. It is very nice to hear her laugh, to laugh with her. I've missed it more than I could have imagined. Could we be friends? Getting ahead of myself, as usual. "This stays between us, please. I'm not even supposed to know, technically."

"You always did like some forbidden knowledge."

"You heard several weeks ago, a body was found in the lake?"

"Yes. A murder, they think?"

"Yep. Unsolved. And then two nights ago, another body, probably another murder, but with some...oddities."

"You know, I love oddities as much as you love forbidden knowledge," she smiles at me, almost flirtatiously. "And when I say 'oddities' I don't just mean my choice of lovers." She's teasing me again, and it sure does feel nice.

I move on, hoping I'm not blushing. I tell her about the body, how it was found, the mussels, the disappearance, and finally, about its seeming resurrection. She asks me some specifics about the mussels, where the body was found, what the shells looked like.

"That's more than an oddity, my dear friend. That's some career-making marine biology weirdness going on there. First of all, mussels don't attach to soft flesh, generally. They need something hard to cling to. And while they grow in colonies, they wouldn't grow in those numbers on something that is moving around. They can be found on some hard-shelled creatures, but not in those numbers. There's just not enough hard shell to go around on, say, a crab. And, as I say, they have to have something to latch on to."

"I love that the facts about the marine life bothers you more than a dead man walking around," I tell her.

"I don't know, I don't know. Seems like he's not dead, right?"

"He was underwater for hours and hours. He was dead."

"And yet, he's walking, seeing. There's a hole in the logic somehow. Maybe he wasn't in the water that long?"

"Maybe. But it's unlikely."

"Can I see one of the mussels themselves?"

"Huh, I don't know. I suppose Cindy at the morgue might still have a few from when she removed them, yes. I'll check into it. And I sent you a link to the videos for you to look at if you want. But you won't get much detail on them for doing biology. They're not very good resolution."

"I'd still like to take a look. Thank you."

A thought strikes me. "Do Cormorants eat mussels?"

"Not usually, no. Fish, insects, that sort of thing. But I doubt it's the mussels she's warning us about. Think like a scientist--it's all interconnected. In a healthy ecosystem, the mussels help clean the water, but if there are too many of them it's not healthy. Some birds eat them, but not too many, so the water stays cleaner."

"But mussels on a dead body, which you've already told me is sort of unnatural for them, the soft flesh thing," I was talking slowly, brainstorming, bouncing ideas off of her just like old times, "maybe she's warning us that these mussels aren't healthy for the lake, or that..." I trail off, unsure of where I'm going.

"Maybe something is perverting it all. Some toxin, or some spirit," she adds that last part dramatically, knowing it will cause an itch in me.

"Or some cult?" I say.

Now it's her turn to be surprised. "You know about the cult?"

9

Before I can follow up with Susan about the cult, I get a call from Darya. "I'm sorry, Susan, I have to take this. Darya only calls when it's an emergency, otherwise it's texts, texts, texts."

"That's fine," she says, pulling out her phone, tapping quickly. I can feel that there's something she wants to show me.

"What's up, Darya," I say, "Everything ok?"

"Sorry to interrupt. Harks and a team are about to go down to the auditorium. She really wants you and I there to see what goes down. One hour."

I thank Darya, tell her I'll be back to the office soon. I tap away for a rideshare. "Susan, I'm sorry, but I have to rush off."

"I understand. You never did stay long," she means it, but she winks at me. I think maybe we could be friends now. I look forward to it, maybe a little too much. "Before you go though: Have you run across this person in your dealings with the cult?" I look at the picture on her phone. It's a grainy still, a black and white picture, perhaps a picture of a picture. I see a white man in his forties, dark eyes and gray-white hair. He's standing in front of the Oakland auditorium, wearing a white robe, holding a...holding a white hood in his hand. He is smiling for the camera. It's a grim smile, a smile that an android who had only seen a few human smiles might make. A facsimile of a human smile.

"Is that a Klansman?"

"It is. It's from 1924. He was involved in some particularly shady things with the Klan in Oakland"

I finish my coffee and stand up. "Not just in the Klan, but shady as well?"

"You're not as funny as you think you are, Walter."

"Will you send that to me? I'll keep an eye out, but that man would be long dead by now."

"You would think. Keep an eye out for him anyway. We believe he's got something to do with those cultists."

"I will." I'm torn--I really want to hear more about what she knows, but I'll have to get back to her. I'm also bothered. Not by the fact that she would ask me to look out for a long-dead Klansman. I'm bothered by the fact that he does look familiar to me. I'm certain I've seen him somewhere before. Maybe Darya showed him to me during her research on the auditorium? "Again, thank you. Thank you." She walks me to the door and I stop for a moment, look at her, really look. "You're the best, Susan." I give her a chaste hug, hoping I'm not pushing my luck.

"You be sure to tell me if you have any more dreams, Walt." She's teasing me again, but she means it.

"I will. Of course I will." I head outside and my ride is already there. I climb in the back. Susan is already back inside when I look up as we pull away.

***

Darya is waiting for me when I get out of the car at the office. "I brought a taser," she tells me. "Don't lecture me about it, I don't want to be without it if those robed asshats give us any trouble."

We start walking over, more briskly than I'm used to, but we both want to be there before Harks gets there. "No lecture. They won't be giving us any trouble, because we'll be watching, and from a distance."

"That's fine with me. But if they close that distance, I have a taser."

We find a spot on the lake path with a bench near the auditorium. The bench faces the lake, away from where we want to watch, so Darya takes out her phone, makes like she's taking selfies, when she's really just watching over her shoulder. We wait. And we wait a little longer, but it's starting to look like Harks and her team isn't going to show up.

"I'm texting her," Darya lowers her phone to her lap, and I turn to look toward the auditorium. There's nothing going on there, nothing at all. I see passers-by at the lake, but no cars in the auditorium parking lot, no robed people, and no police.

"She says it's off," Darya is irritated, and confused.

"Huh. She say why?"

"I'm finding out." I wait. "She's going to call you."

Harks calls me a few seconds later. Turns out she was told that the auditorium is off-limits. "It comes from all the way up. Past the police commissioner. City council or mayor or some bullshit." I've never heard Harks talk that way about the people above her in the chain of command, even the mayor, who isn't the most popular mayor we've ever had. Harks has always been more than professional in that way, even if she does do things like sneak videos out of the morgue for me.

"That is...interesting," I say calmly. "There must be a reason." I'm pondering, but Harks is still fuming.

"It's interesting, all right. Fucking Oakland politics. I don't know if I can handle it much longer."

"You sound like your father, and he worked there for most of his whole life," I respond, trying to calm her again.

"Yeah, yeah, always bring my dad into it, Walt. I know you're right, but right now, I could quit and never look back."

"I wouldn't blame you. But Oakland would miss you. Needs you."

"Save the pep talk for later, Mr. Denin. I have to go. I'll try to find another way. Just maybe stay away from that place, Walt. If they have folks up this high batting for them, they might be dangerous. More dangerous than we thought."

"Well, I think they're maybe killing people and throwing them in the lake, so more dangerous than that?"

"You're joking, but yeah. Maybe."

She clicks off and I fill Darya in. She's just as angry as Harks: "So. They killed somebody, maybe two people, and they just get to hang out by the lake? That's fucking ridiculous!"

"Don't they say anything about cursing in that religion of yours?"

"It's called Bahá'í, for the billionth time. And yeah, they don't like the swearing. They also say I can't marry my girlfriend, so it's complex. *Fucking* complex. Doesn't this," she points at the auditorium, "make you want to swear? Sorry, 'curse'?"

"It does indeed." I take out my cigar and chomp a bit. "But there's nothing we can do about it. Let's do what we can and find out some more about these folks. Quietly. I'll tell you what I learned from Susan, too. Hey, what would you say if I told you Susan said that maybe these cultists have some ties to the Klan."

Darya looks surprised for about half a second. "Well, that at least makes more sense than anything else we've learned about this case. The Klan ran Oakland back in the 1920s. You know that?"

"Why, because you think I lived through that? I'm not that old. But yes, I did know that. They ran Oakland for about two seconds."

"Too long."

"Agreed."

***

We head back to the office, dispirited, yet still angry, which in my experience is a dangerous place to be. "Hey," I say, "why don't you take the afternoon off. Go take your girlfriend to lunch or something. Work on your paper. Your whatchacallit, thesis."

She looks up at me, first frustrated, then looking like the cat who caught the canary. "You trying to get rid of me?"

"Yep. Get out of my hair for a while."

"What's left of it."

"Don't push it. I'll see you in the morning."

"I'll take you up on that, boss. But no lunch or paper writing for me. I'm going home and going to bed. That all-nighter took more out of me than I thought."

"Don't tell me you're getting too old for this?"

"Maybe. I mean, look at what the job did to you."

She grabs her things from the office and says goodbye. I can see that now that I've given her space to go home, she's exhausted. I guess I am a little too. Honestly, I don't want to dream again just yet, too many slimy tentacles in my dreams lately. I sit down at my desk and research a bit more about the Klan and the auditorium, thinking maybe I'll see that picture Susan showed me again.

I'm so focused on what I'm doing that I don't hear them come in at first, don't hear the door open and shut. But when I hear the deadbolt lock, I look up. Little Red is standing in front of me, in street clothes, sans robes. She's flanked by what can only be described as two men pretending to be intimidating. Fine time for Darya to not lock the office door. I turn my chair toward them, speaking casually. "I'm sorry, we're not taking new cases right now." I decide to take a chance, provoke her a bit, "see I'm already investigating this murder cult by the lake, so I have my hands full." They don't make a move. She smiles a creepy little smile, looking around at the office.

Finally, she speaks: "Well, I thought I could help you with that. You see, I found this over by the lake. I thought it might be a clue." She reaches into her coat pocket and takes out a small black totem, a statue of a monster that I have seen only once before, and only in a dream.

***

I'm a little bit ashamed to say that I didn't completely keep a straight face. I reacted, and she saw that I reacted. How many years do I have to practice a poker face before I get it right? I smile, trying to hide my shock at least a little. "It's cute. Did you pick that up at Oaklandish or something?" For a split-second, she loses her composure as well. Apparently she doesn't like being made fun of. It occurs to me that maybe she is in the Klan. Those folks have no sense of humor. She recovers quickly, however, and now her tone is more serious. She holds the totem in the palm of her hand. It is beautiful. It has a dull gleam that shows on the surface but feels like it's coming from deep within it, rather than as a reflection. My eyes are drawn to it, despite the fact that three strangers are in my office who probably harbor some ill will against me.

When she speaks again, I can tell she is trying to keep her voice calm. I actually did make her angry, I think. She speaks slowly, calmly, almost rhythmically. "Walter Denin. Are you certain that this doesn't help you at all? Take a closer look." She doesn't step closer, but I do get a closer look--my gaze is drawn into it. I see the tentacular arms of the creature, the creature from my dream now right in front of me in the form of a little statue. The arms are flowing from its body onto the base of the totem. They're made of stone, and not moving like in my dream, but they still seem to flow, to writhe though they are solid stone. It is a beautiful carving. The many eyes of the creature are stylized in the totem, hinting at eyes rather than trying to imitate real eyes. They are everywhere on the creature's head, everywhere except its mouth, which looks both open wide and closed, due to the genius of the sculptor. It's exquisite. I find myself looking even closer now, though I am not moving toward it at all. My view telescopes in on it, and it feels wonderful, looking more closely. I see the room reflected in the black polished stone, the reflection of Little Red's hand, and now even my own impossible reflection. Impossible because I know I am across the room from it, and yet I see myself clearly. I see every wrinkle, every scar, every imperfection of my face and body reflected in its stone eyes. In the background I can hear her saying my name again, talking to me, but it is a low, methodic drone to me. I'm far more interested in getting an even closer look at the totem.

I have a deep wish to go back into my dream, where the totem, the one I saw there, was accessible to me. If I could get back there, to the dream, I could see even more, see into myself. I know this truth better than I have ever known anything in my life. Certainty wells up inside me. The room dissolves around me, and I see the totem begin to move, to undulate in her hand. It's eyes begin to open, real eyes, dark and red and looking around, but also looking into me. I feel myself going back to the dream, going into one of those eyes, falling into the gaping maw that is somehow enveloping me, though the totem is still in her hand. Impossible. But I will go back to the dream. I want it more than I've wanted anything, more than I've wanted love, or sex, or death. Still in my chair, yet I'm moving into its center now, my being enveloped in the cold, wet flesh it has become. My dream. My dream. The totem, and then...and then the Cormorant.

I hear a slam, and it seems to come from far away, like a cannon set off in another part of town. Then another slam, and another, and they follow each other like the end of a fireworks show. I am fully back in my chair suddenly, snapped back, and feel a hangover-like headache quickly grow and penetrate every part of my skull. I'm not sure where I am for a moment. And then I remember, I realize, I'm in my office. I see Little Red pocket the totem, and turn toward the banging. Somebody is knocking on the glass of my door, on the windows facing the lake, repeatedly, in weird inhuman rhythms, and I see shadows around the room. The glazed glass doesn't let me see directly out onto the lake, but I see the shadows, and finally recognize what they are: gulls. There are gulls throwing themselves against my door, against those windows, repeatedly. I hear Little Red swear under her breath as I see the two would-be goons backing away from the door, their backs toward me. I edge toward my safe, which is just a few feet away, aiming to get a taser I keep there.

The birds are coming in greater numbers now, their shadows darkening the room. They're trying to get in? And finally a window breaks, and they are in. They almost flow in, tens of them, maybe even more than a hundred, more gulls than I've ever seen on the lake. They are focused on Little Red alone, but the room is still chaos with them flying around, then swooping onto her. She yells in a language I don't understand, a booming yell, and they fly back for a moment, all one mind, but then they're on her again. The goons are already opening the door, running, and she pays them no mind. She's got her hands full. I reach for the safe's keypad, but then stop. It doesn't look like I'm going to need it now. She's leaving, gulls squawking and practically pushing her out the door. She's trying to bat them away, trying to shout at them, but they don't let her do even that, flying at her face, even shoving beaks and wings into her mouth. She strides out of my office, out the door her henchmen had left open, and then runs.

I sit stunned as the mass of gulls follows her out. She is running at a fast pace now, toward the auditorium, and the gulls are following. I watch her start to round the bend, and think about following, but then think twice of it. My head is pounding. My heart is beating fast. She did something to me, and I'm not following her, not wanting another dose of...whatever that was. The birds are gone now, except for some feathers in my doorway and around the broken window. I'm glad the window is broken. Without it, I wouldn't believe what had just happened. I stare at the lake, and it all looks normal. People milling about. There is no preponderance of gulls, no stone totems coming to life before my eyes. But there is a broken window, and my fast-beating heart. I hear a scuffling, and see a neighbor of mine pull up on his bicycle, taking off his helmet. He looks toward where the Little Red ran away to.

"Walt, you ok?" he asks.

"I think so, yeah." I find myself patting my own body, as if I'm making sure I have my wallet and keys.

"What the hell was that?"

"I'll have to get back to you on that one, Josh."

***

Josh helps me clean up the glass and feathers. He's a good kid. A kid in his thirties, but still. It's nice to have good neighbors. I assure him I'm fine, that the birds just went a little crazy and broke a window. They have flown into our windows before, something about the way the light reflects off the lake and then the window, something about their reflections maybe. But there has never been anything like this. I didn't think there were that many gulls on the whole lake. I'll have to ask Susan about that, maybe. I'm more concerned about how that asshole came into my office and somehow almost, what? Hypnotized me? Like in that movie where the evil white lady hypnotizes the Black kid with a teacup and a spoon. Somehow her voice, and the totem...

The totem, the one that I had a freaking dream about before I saw it. That isn't intuition. That isn't my subconscious. This is new territory for me, and I don't like it, not one bit. I've got tasers for tough guys, and my gun locked up if I really need it, but what the hell do I do against people

58

who have, what, some sort of magic? I can't even entertain the idea. It doesn't fit with what I know about the world. I've almost convinced myself that maybe I did see the totem somewhere before my dream, and maybe hypnotism, yeah, that is a thing that works just like she did it. Almost. And then I see my broken window, a bloody feather still stuck to a shard of glass. There's something else going on here, and I need to find out what.

10

One nice thing with renting an office in a larger building like this is that I don't always have to fix everything. I call Stacey, the super for the building, and she sends some people out to fix my window. Darya was going to be pissed that she wasn't the first to know what happened, but I swore I was going to let her have the evening to herself. She'd more than earned it with her little morning escapade and I selfishly needed her fresh for what I felt was to come. Also, I am not quite sure myself what happened. So I call Susan. She listens to my story without interruption. After I finish, she asks a few questions about the totem that Little Red had somehow used on me. She is all business, which I appreciate. The whole thing with the totem, my being almost hypnotized or whatever that was, and the birds, had rattled me. Especially the birds. I don't get rattled easily, but I'm good with admitting to myself when it does happen. I don't like the idea that this person could come into my office and somehow begin to control me. Or that she only failed by some freak bird show. I ask Susan how I could protect myself if Little Red came around again brandishing her mind-control troll doll.

"Well, Walt, first things first, don't look at the damn totem."

I laugh. "Ok. Noted. Anything else?"

"If she's holding that thing, and speaking to you, you're in danger. Knock it away, make noise so you can't hear her, turn off your hearing aids, whatever you have to do to disrupt that. Now that you know you were affected, it should be more difficult for her to do that to you again."

"Alright. Makes sense. How do you know all of this? Ohlone Shaman stuff?"

"Careful, little white man. It's some experience with shamanism, maybe, but mostly common sense, which you sometimes lacked. It's like science, or deduction, Watson--statue in her hand plus her talking equals Walt talking a nap, so remove part of the equation. Also, I do know a bit about that particular totem. I was going to tell you more of that when you rushed off."

I thank her, and tell her about why I had rushed off, and how the police raid on the auditorium had been a dead-end because of the higher ups at OPD and City Hall.

"You want to know more about what's going on, Walter, I could tell you some. But really I think I need to bring in Eddi on this one. They know more about what's going on, and they can tell you about the history of that statue better than I can."

"You've been holding out on me, Susan," my curiosity more than piqued.

"That stuff is need-to-know, my friend, and up until recently, you didn't need to know. I'll give them a call, tell them you need to talk. You know who I'm talking about, don't you?"

"Yes, I know of Eddi. I haven't really met them, except in passing. They still live by the lake? In that condo building that Huey Newton lived in?"

"They do. Same place. It's not common knowledge though, Walt, so keep it to yourself. Eddi is something of a private person, really, despite being the center of a lot of circles." Susan's voice of caution was familiar to me. She was telling me some truths that I needed to keep close. This case was getting odder and odder.

"I appreciate you connecting us. What do you think I can learn from Eddi though?"

"Well, I know some things that...let's just say they're not things I'm at liberty to discuss. Eddi can discuss them if they want to."

Genuinely surprised, I ask, "You work for Eddi somehow?"

Susan laughed, "No, no. But we do work together from time to time, and I respect their deep knowledge, their connection to history. They've helped out with some of my work around saving shellmounds, and I've helped them with some work on...other things."

"Mysterious talk again. Some scientist you are."

"Science sometimes intersects with the greatest mysteries, Walt. That's something you may learn yet."

We hang up, and I shake my head to myself. I'm frustrated and a little afraid at this case, but I'm glad we're talking again. It's a good feeling, having Susan in my world again.

I do a little more research on the current owners of the auditorium, or try to. Darya is going to have to tackle that one for me. My google-fu is not strong enough for this one. A few hours later, the sun is going down and I get a text from a number I don't know. It's Eddi, asking if I can come meet them to talk. I say yes, and thank them, ask them when. They want to meet now, and I wonder if I should bring Darya in on my conversation with Eddi, as a buffer of sorts. Then I hear Darya's voice in my head: "What, you think all people of color know each other, Walt? You think I can do the secret handshake to make you feel more comfortable?" Ok, I tell the voice. I'll go alone, old white guy going up to the penthouse condo that Huey Newton used to live in, sure, why not. It's not as if I'm not being invited. I sigh, not sure exactly why I'm hesitating. It feels invasive, somehow, but Susan thinks I need this person's help, so I go.

***

I decide to take a rideshare, even though it's close enough that I can see the building from my office window, across part of the lake. I don't want to have to get in a footrace with the cultists, and I'd have to walk by the auditorium to get to Eddi's place. Lots of folks don't know that one of the most famous activists in American history used to live right by the lake. Huey Percy Newton, co-founder of the Black Panther Party for Self Defense, back in '66. It's said he hated living in that building, but was asked, persuaded or forced by the Party to live there. It was symbolic--lots of powerful, rich white folks lived in that building back then. It was pretty fancy for its time, with a doorman and everything. These days there is no doorman, just a keypad to call up and get buzzed in. Back then, the symbolism bothered a lot of powerful white folks, and that was part of the point. I knew some of those people who were bothered. I liked that they were bothered, though I'm sure it wasn't a fun place for Newton to live, really. People who lived in Oakland during that time know it as a wonderful, magical time, though of course it was also a dangerous and volatile time for being a Black person. But what time hasn't been, in the United States of America? Still is.

And here I am.

I am a little surprised to feel like the Panthers are still being invoked here, by the lake, in the form of Eddi. The spirit of the Black Panthers are everywhere in Oakland, of course, and across the country, but it's still amazing to me the ways in which that spirit flourishes. Eddi is interesting to me, a younger person in their late-twenties I would say. Most folks around the lake know Eddi, being a regular presence and also easy to remember in various ways. At once shy and reserved, but also loud and full of laughter. They spend a lot of time just walking the lake, like I do, which is how I know of them. It's unclear what they do for a living. Maybe they did figure out a way to make money just walking the lake? I should ask for a job application. Eddi is what the

61

kids these days call "nonbinary". It's tough to get my mind around the pronouns, but not around the concept. Pretty sure there have always been nonbinary folks in the world, even if folks didn't call it that. People said "two-spirit", sometimes, if they were from some Native traditions. They said "faggots" sometimes, if they were down at the White Horse in the late 80s, reclaiming the word even though maybe it didn't quite fit just right. I know a few people who used "dyke" in the same way, and who now use "queer" or "nonbinary". I like that I live in a world where being nonbinary is the least interesting thing about somebody.

I call Eddi from the front of the building and they buzz me up.

I've never been up to the famous penthouse before, and I find myself getting a little nervous in the elevator ride up. I dig out my cigar, chew it a bit, decide maybe that's a little too informal for a conversation with a stranger. I can't help but chuckle at myself. Over seventy years on this earth and I'm nervous about meeting a 20-something Oaklander. It's silly. Yet I feel the history here. It's not even a nice building, really, even with the term "penthouse" trying to glam the place up. One of the few buildings right on the lake that is more than a six stories tall, built just before the city started regulating heights of buildings closely, built quickly. The carpet in the elevator isn't dirty, but it isn't new, either. It's not even known as a much of a piece of Black Panther history, really, in part because Newton didn't even want to live here, in part because more important places--places where Panthers fed kids, places where they met to plan a local and nationwide movement, and yes, places where they died, places where they lived, really lived, seem more important to most folks.

But I like the idea that Newton lived here, looking over the lake, looking over what I consider to be the heart of Oakland in various ways. I'm romanticizing it, almost certainly, but that's part of what it means to be the heart of a town, isn't it? Part myth, part reality, symbolic of hope and togetherness in this case. For me at least

The penthouse is really a rooftop dwelling, taking up the entire top floor of the 24-story building. Lots of glass walls, space to walk around on the roof. I've heard there's even a little Zen garden up there. When the elevator door opens, I've regained a little bit of my composure. I walk down the short hall to the entrance, seeing a young woman sitting near it in a chair that was built for sitting in and reading, right next to the end of the hall, where a window allows the dimming sunset to glow. She is indeed reading when I walk out. She's not anybody familiar to me, and she's white, which surprises me for some reason. I was thinking about the sixties and the Panthers so much that somehow I thought I had stepped into the past and was infiltrating a Black Panther meeting.

"Hello," she says. "You must be Walt. I'm Jela," she reaches out her hand to shake mine.

"Nice to meet you Jela, yes, that's me. Eddi buzzed me in." I glance down and see that she is reading a thick book, paperback that looks familiar. I place it finally when I get a closer look. "I see you like science fiction," I say, pointing to the book.

"Sometimes. This one is an odd one. I was told to read it by so many people, I couldn't resist. It's taken me a few tries to get this far though," she holds it up, her finger maybe a third of the way in to the 800-plus page tome. "You've read this?"

"Once," I say. "A long time ago."

"Is it worth finishing?"

"I'd say yes. At least once. I met him one time, y'know?" I'm clearly trying to impress her now, and she raises her eyebrows in an acknowledgement of that fact.

"Oh yeah? What's he like?"

"Charismatic. He's got a kind face and a firm handshake. They say you can start that book from any page and then read it through and back around and it still makes sense."

"I'm not convinced it makes sense yet, and I started from the beginning."

"Well, let me know what you think when you're done."

"You can go on in, Walt. It's open. They just wanted some privacy," Jela says, sitting back down, settling back into her book. Eddi has a surprise guest for you. I think you might know them."

After my interaction with Little Red and her friends, I'm not sure I want any more surprises today, but Susan vouched for Eddi, so I think I'm in good hands. I try the door, and sure enough, it's not locked. It opens directly in to a large room, and I can already see the cityscape beneath us. Two people are sitting on a leather sofa in the center of the sunken living room. One of them is Eddi, who gives me a little wave and stays seated. Getting up from the sofa is a man with a familiar face, but one that I hadn't expected to see here. It takes me a few moments for my brain to catch up with my eyes.

"You ok, old man?" Stoney says walking toward me. "Come on in, I'm about to earn that twenty bucks."

I shake Stoney's hand, then give him a hug. I'm not usually a hugger, but it feels right. Part of why I didn't recognize him right away is that he's clearly had a shower, is mostly cleaned up and wearing some clean clothes. He still smells of beer, but that may be my imagination.

"Nice digs," I say to Stoney. "You're moving up in the world."

"Literally," Stoney says, indicating the skyline, cracking himself up, laughing and squinting as we head into the living room.

"Hi Walt," Eddi says from the couch. "Have a seat. Would you like anything to drink? Tea? A beer?" His manner is so calm and collected that I could imagine we were just here as friends, for a chat about sports, or the weather.

"No, no, thank you. I'm ok." I sit in a chair opposite the couch. The room is relatively sparsely decorated, and it's huge. Windows on two sides show a view of the lake (and then the bay, and then San Francisco) and another of the Oakland hills, homes there already turning on lights, creating a field of dimly glowing stars. I look back and forth between Stoney and Eddi, waiting for somebody to say something.

"You're wondering what I'm doing here, eh, Walt?" Stoney says, enjoying my confusion.

Eddi chimes in, "Stoney and I go way back."

"Not that far back, son," Stoney says, "You don't go that far back yourself."

"Pronouns, Stoney, pronouns! You know I'm not a son, Stoney, any more than you're a daughter," Eddi gently corrects him.

"I don't understand all of that gender stuff, Eddi. You're Eddi, so you're a man. But you're like 12 years old, so you're a son." Stoney is still smiling, but it's clear this is a conversation they've had before.

"You talk a lot of shit for a guy who needed a place to stay last night," Eddi replies, sipping on a soda. They're smiling too.

"Yeah, yeah. You needed information, and that was the price last night," Stoney says, waving his hand sideways at Eddi.

"You came to my door!" Eddi is laughing now.

"It was information I knew you'd want."

"Yeah, and you knew I have the best shower in Oakland."

"Well, that's true. But I don't know why you care so much about pronouns anyway."

"Sure, Stoney, Sure," Eddi says. Then, indicating Stoney, "Do you want HER to tell you what SHE saw last night?"

"Alright, alright, point made. Lordy. Kids and their high ideas these days," Stoney is actually a little frustrated now.

I interrupt their banter: "So I take it my twenty bucks wasn't better than a good shower."

"Also true," Stoney smiles.

Eddi's tone changes a little when he next speaks, and I feel it in the room. Stoney and I both react to it, sitting straighter, listening intently. I think for a moment that maybe Newton is still hanging around here, in some way. "We were just talking about a mutual friend," they say.

"Susan?" I ask, thinking I know the answer. "I didn't know you knew Susan, Stoney."

"I know a Susan, but that's not who we were talking about," Stoney responds, folding his hands in front of him and looking at the floor. Whether he has been drinking or not today, I can tell he wishes he had a beer in his hand right now. I sort of feel the same way.

"I'm confused," I admit, "who do we all know?"

"Stoney came to my door last night pretty late, after midnight. He was pretty shaken up. You want to tell him, or do you want me to?" they offered.

"No, I'll tell it, I'll tell it. It was that guy, Walt. The guy from the lake. With the shells all over him. I watched him walk straight into the lake."

11

Stoney stands up as he tells the story. He's visibly agitated in a way that I've never seen in him before. Or maybe I've never seen him this sober? He paces around the room, behind the sofa, behind me, then over toward the entryway. He does this so many times that each time he heads toward the entryway I wonder if he's thinking of making a run for it. He wants to tell the story, but he doesn't want to be the one telling it. Yet he wants to be free of it. I can identify. I find out that he's asked to stay with Eddi just for a few days, and then Stoney's cousin from the central valley is going to come pick him up and let him stay there with him for a while.

"I'm getting out, Walt. It's a heartbreaker, but I can't tell what's real and what's not in Oakland anymore. I have to get clean, get some distance."

It's understandable. Maybe Stoney has finally hit rock bottom, seeing what he saw last night on the lake. And what he saw is enough to drive anybody to sobriety.

"I was getting settled in, right where you usually see me," Stoney indicates both Eddi and me. "I was tired, really tired. And I had a good day yesterday, so I maybe had had a bit more to drink than usual, sure. I was looking out at the lake, sitting in my tent with the flap open, getting ready to turn in. I usually put up a few things around my tent, just in case somebody I don't know comes calling, y'know. Empty cans, stacked stones, anything, really, that somebody who means to do me harm might not see if they approach the tent. Didn't have to do that when we were all living near the auditorium, but..." He trails off for a moment, then goes on: "But I hadn't even gone to sleep yet, the tent flap was still open." He pauses, checking to make sure we're still paying attention.

"I didn't hear him coming, but he kicked over one of my cans. Kicked it pretty hard, and it rolled onto the path and almost into the lake. I jumped up, almost fell over. I was more drunk than I had thought." Another pause. "But I saw what I saw. I wasn't that drunk. Nobody is that drunk," he was reassuring us. I believed him. At this point he was my most reliable witness of the craziness that was happening around the lake, not counting Harks and the medical examiner. Eddi raised their eyebrows, not quite convinced, but not wholly skeptical. Eddi is hard to read. He had heard the story already, of course, and had some time to think about it.

Stoney tell us that he stood there, straight up, not believing what he was seeing. He was seeing a man covered in mussel shells, the man he had seen dead by the lakeside just a few nights prior. The man was standing, shuffling toward the lake with small steps. His head slowly turned to look at Stoney, and Stoney saw one eye uncovered, staring out at him.

"He never stopped walking toward the lake, though. His head turned to look at me, and I saw that eye, and it blinked, I swear, a bunch of times at me, but the rest of him just kept moving forward, not looking where he was going, like there was a rope around him, pulling him to the lake." Suddenly Stoney looked at Eddi, referring perhaps to an echo of their previous conversation, "That was it, Eddi, that was it. It was like a rope was around him, pulling him in. He was resisting, or something, even turning his head was hard on him, maybe." Stoney stops, sits down, finally, and stares into space, lost in his memory. "He looked at me the whole time he could, shuffling to the water, until his head didn't turn that far, you know? He was glistening, like he had just come out of the water, even though he was heading to it. That's it, Eddi, that's it, he was being pulled in."

65

He explained the man shuffled straight into the lake, slowly, methodically, arms at his sides the whole time, walking as if he was just going to go across the lake to the other side, maybe. The lake doesn't get very deep until you get to the center of it, and Stoney could see in the moonlight that the man just kept walking, until he got to a place where his entire body was underneath the surface. And then the water was still. Stoney stopped the story now, leaning back in the sofa. He closed his eyes. "I think I have to go lay down, fellas. I'm sorry."

Eddi helped him up, and we both told him to be quiet with the apologies. We'd talk to him later. He should go rest. He went down the hall alone, shuffling too, tired. Seeing impossible things is tiring, I suppose. Those shocks to your worldview tire you out.

"Stoney couldn't figure out what was going on last night, so he came to me," Eddi tells me. I don't ask why Stoney didn't go to the cops--he's Black and homeless, and even though most of the police around here know him, what they remember is that he's often drunk. They'd guess he was seeing things, nothing more, and I couldn't really blame them. Up until a few days ago, I might have guessed the same thing.

"Sounds like he did the right thing. I'm glad he has friends around here," I tell Eddi. "I won't pretend it doesn't sting a little bit that he didn't come to me."

"He and I go back quite a bit. I know his cousin. He's not family, but he's like family."

"I see. Makes sense. I wish I could help him more right now."

"Be careful what you wish for, isn't that something they say?" Eddi smiles, sipping their soda.

That gets a little chuckle from me. "They do, they do say that. Sounds like maybe you know something I don't, Eddi."

"I'm sure the reverse is true as well, Mr. Denin. Walt. But yes, I know a bit about what Stoney was talking about. I'm not sure how much Susan told you." I'm struck by how adult this young person sounds. And they're so...relaxed. We've just been hearing about dead bodies walking into the lake, and they seem like they just got back from a leisurely stroll. I mean, they are an adult, but anybody under forty just seems young to me now, and all the things that come with that judgment come up.

"Not much. She usually just points out my ignorance and I go from there," I say. Now I'm the one feeling restless. I get up and go look out to the windows that overlook the lake. After a few moments, Eddi follows me, and we look out at the lake. From here it's easy to see why it's called the "jewel of the Town". Small white lights circle it's edges, and there are a few joggers jogging and couples strolling around it. The water level is pretty high tonight--its fullness varies with the tides and with some man-made help, connected as it is to the bay.

"You haven't asked how a young person like myself can afford to live up here. It's usually the first thing strangers ask, if sometimes obliquely."

"Your business, I suppose. Though of course I'm curious, and Susan hinted at some things. Huey Newton lived here a long time ago, before you were born. I'd guess you know that though. You live here now. Hard not to invent a connection, even if it isn't real."

"A connection. Hmmm. Yes. There is a connection. We can talk more about that, but first, you said you wanted to help Stoney more. Want to help us all?"

"Could you put that more mysteriously?"

That gets a belly laugh from them. "Probably not, probably not," they reach out and pat my shoulder. "OK, I hear you Walt. Some answers. I want them too." They move back to the sofa, falling into it, showing for the first time that they, too, are tired. "Susan wanted to tell you more, I'm sure, but she's good at secrets. Which I'm grateful for. So I'll start with the question you didn't ask, and go from there: Friends of the Black Panthers own this place. Bought it outright from the last owner. The 'Friends' were never Panthers themselves, but they were wealthy folks, Black folks and others, who thought that the Panthers still needed a presence around the lake."

I'm confused now, and I tell them. "With respect, Eddi, the Black Panthers are no more. Not in that way."

"No, not in that way, but in myriad other ways. We took a page from our oppressors. White people love their secret societies. So much for not being able to dismantle the oppressors house with his tools, I suppose. And yet, it's working, after a fashion."

"You're part of a secret society of Black Panthers? That sounds...well, like a superhero movie or something."

"How do you think that movie got made in the first place?" They look serious for a few beats, then laugh. "You'll never know. It's need-to-know."

"That's what Susan said."

Serious again: "Well, back to Stoney and his man-monster. I'm here in this apartment because one of the Panthers' goals is to protecting the lake. Including protecting it from things like what Stoney saw. We hope."

"How does that work?"

They sigh a small sigh. Feels like they want to tell me more, but they are hesitating. "More on that later, but first, you should know that I can help solve your 'murder' from the other night."

"Not sure it's even a murder, if the dead man walks around as he pleases."

"Point. What if he's not dead, maybe, not in the traditional sense?"

"There's another sense?"

"I think so. Susan thinks so too, and some of those with her. Do you believe Stoney saw what he saw?"

"I do. I really do. But I'm still not sure what he saw was a dead man."

"I'm sure that it was. And that it wasn't." They take a drink of their soda, and then: " I knew him."

"You knew him?"

"He was one of ours."

* * *

Eddi explains that the man in question, the dead man who may or may not be dead, is named Frank Marshall, and he was working for Eddi and their group, which I still sort of refuse to believe is somehow affiliated with the Black Panthers of old. Marshall was a volunteer. He had been a tech guy, new to the area, and decided his work culture wasn't really for him. He ended up doing some tech stuff for Eddi for a few months.

Then about six months ago, Eddi's group noticed that something odd was going on out at the Oakland auditorium. Turns out Stoney was as good a lookout for Eddi as he had been for me, though Eddi paid better--when the homeless tent encampments had been cleared out by the cultists, Stoney had reported that back to Eddi. Seemed fishy, so they looked into it.

"There's some east coast consortium who bought the place, and we're having a hard time really teasing that all out, honestly, especially now that we've lost Frank," he tells me.

"Have you run into Victor Immack's name, in this investigation?" I ask. I figure there's nothing gained by not sharing this information.

"We have not. You have?"

"He's connected somehow, but we're not sure exactly how yet. My associate Darya is still digging."

Eddi takes their phone from the coffee table and either texts somebody or makes a note. "Thanks. We'll check on that. What we did find out is that there's a lot of money involved. Some of the same people in the consortium have been looking into buying property around the lake, but not actually buying any yet. Lots of inquiries *from* them, no sales *to* them. Usually that indicates individuals, or individual companies who are looking to work together to buy a huge chunk of property all together, leverage their grouped resources. That could be what's happening, but we don't think so."

"I'm a little out of my depth here, Eddi. I'm not generally investigating real estate cases."

"Sure, sure. Just giving you some background. These...cultists, I like that, because that's just what they are, aren't they? These cultists are related to the consortium somehow. So individuals join the cult, pay to join it, and they get...something. We didn't know what, so that's why we sent Frank in."

"You paid to get him in?"

"We did."

"Who are these people funding you, Eddi?"

"Need to know!" he laughs.

"I need to know if they need to adopt an old man with some private investigator skills, is what I need to know."

"Well, the plan included getting our money back down the road."

"But it didn't include Frank dying."

"It did not."

Eddi tells me that Frank got in ok. He tells me that Frank, while generally "passing" for white, was Black. Frank went to some meetings, paid his money. I tell Eddi about my conversation with John Trier, the escaped cultist Darya and I talked with. He makes another note in his phone. Frank had been reporting back, had been to the auditorium twice, even dressed up in the red robes once. And then, a few nights ago, for his third meeting there, he was to do some sort of all-nighter. But he didn't come back the next morning.

"I think they somehow found him out," Eddi says, shaking his head. "I'm not sure how. We're very careful, and we know how to do these things. F.B.I. infiltrated the Panthers for enough years, we learned from that. But they must have 'made' him. Because he's the one that walked out of the morgue, and he's the one who walked into the lake last night."

We talk for a while. Eddi tells me almost nothing about the New Black Panthers or whatever they're called now, but I glean a bit. They are doing work in Oakland and around the Bay Area, and are also doing some work nationwide. Mostly they operate quietly, secretly. I wonder if the original Panthers would approve--their whole thing was doing everything publically. But what do I know. Just an old white guy from Oakland. They tell me about the lake being a "spiritual center" for Oakland, which sort of makes sense to me. They keep emphasizing it, and I ask a few questions. I find myself wishing I had brought along Darya. She's better at this spiritual stuff than I am. I don't mention my dreams to Eddi, but I get the sense that they would understand something about the dreams if I did.

"Have you gone to the police about Frank?" I have to ask.

"Not officially. We have some folks there, in the department, and they're keeping an eye on things. I'm not sure if getting more police involved will help us. And it just makes the higher-ups nervous."

"Who are your higher-ups?" I prod them one more time.

"Not mine, Walt. The city's. Word is the mayor herself had a word in keeping the cops from going into the auditorium. Given that, I don't think she's going to care much in a positive way about Frank, unless we could convince her he'd help her get re-elected."

"I don't disagree."

"What do you think we should do, Walter Denin?" Eddi sits back, arm over the back of the couch. They have a quiet smile on their face.

"I don't think you agreed to meet me to tell you a plan. You seem like a person who already has a plan."

Eddi's smile broadens. "I do. I do indeed. You want in?"

"Depends. What is the plan?"

"We're going to go in there, illegally I might add, and take a look around, and if we have to, maybe bust some heads."

"That's your plan?"

"It's part of the plan."

"I'm not really the head-busting type. Eddi. Especially these days."

"Yes. I know. Still, I'd like you to be there. I'd like your eyes-on. We'll keep you safe."

"I'm flattered that you think I could go with you to the head-bashing, I really am. You're friends with Susan, so maybe you think all people our age are as spry as she is. I'm not."

"We'd really like you to be there, Walt. You have a special perspective," Eddi says. I can't help but think perhaps he already knows about my dreams, from Susan.

"I'll do you one better."

"How so?"

"I have an associate who would absolutely love to go with you. And she's got better eyes than I do anyhow." Darya will be happy to hear it.

"She'll be ok with it? Again, illegal break-in, potential violence?"

"You might have to hold her back."

"You'll have to hold me back, too," Eddi says. "We traced one of the leaders way back. They have some family history in Oakland. They're probably really proud of their family tree. It has roots in the Klu Klux Klan."

I call Darya.

69

Interlude
Oakland 1924

Moonlight streamed down onto the calm surface of the lake as he approached its edge. He pushed aside the lakeside plants and stepped to the edge of the marshy shore, his shiny black shoes toeing the mud and brackish water. The stone in his hand thumped with his heartbeat now, as he began a chant low in his throat. The words were known to only a handful of beings, but he kept them deep in his lungs at first, holding on to his secrets until his dark dreams broke the surface of the lake. Lake Miskatonic, it would be called, from now, for all of eternity, a place of chaos unlike any before on earth. The birthplace, the place of re-birth, of Madness itself.

He could still hear the distant chanting of the Klan members in the building behind him, ignorant fools doing his bidding while they thought they were doing their own. Their hatred was bounded, by race hatred, by fear, by smallness, while his was unbound, the source of all other hatreds, the source of every joy devolved into tears. His chaos was superior to theirs, yes, but it didn't matter, wouldn't matter in a few minutes. When the creature he now summoned reached our plane of existence, none of that would matter any longer. Races didn't matter, people didn't matter, only the dark maw of the universe falling inward onto itself. He felt the stone heating up now, and knew with no doubt that he, alone, would retain his memory of this moment, that he would be the First among the humans to greet their master. Not their maker, for this creature revealed there *was* no maker. It superseded all gods humans could have invented. It came Before. It would consume those behind him, and then Oakland, and then the world.

He raised his arms in praise, continuing his chanting, focusing the energies of his oblivious followers into the stone, which in turn sent the energies to the lake. He felt the lake itself stir. The night was quiet. Even the birds seemed to have left the lake, knowing somehow to avoid it this night. He closed his eyes to focus as the surface began to ripple. Something large in the center of the lake was moving beneath the surface, and he could hear the small waves begin to lap against the reeds, against the muddy shore. He rejoiced and let his chants escape his throat. It was too late to stop it now, he knew, even if the men in the auditorium heard him, or a passerby. It was almost done. He chanted loudly now, eyes closed. He could see the lake with his mind's eye, see the creature beneath its surface. He had done it. The lake, the men behind him, the stone, his will, they had opened a schism in reality, the bottom of the lakebed splitting, and his summoned creature climbed out into our world. He began to walk into the water. He would greet the summoned being face to face.

But his feet wouldn't move.

Opening his eyes, chanting faltering for only a moment, he looked down and saw that his feet, his legs, inexplicably, were buried up to his knees in...something. White and silver shards held him in place. The stone's pulse slowed, and he refocused his energy on it, chanting loudly again, as he tried to move and failed. The...shells...they were empty shells he recognized now, seemed to multiply rapidly, moving up his body, created out of nothingness. Small, meaningless little shells of mussels, oysters. Some were only shards, some whole empty shells. They poured up from the mud beneath his feet. Up to his waist now, he held his arms aloft, holding the stone in both hands above his head. The being he summoned was still coming. He could feel it. Turning as much as he could, held fast by the shells, he saw five men behind him, Klan robes

70

on but hoods off. They danced, and held totems of some sort in their hands, chanting their own chants. Swirling around them were hummingbirds, a hundred of them. How had he not heard? Where did they come from? Who the fuck were they?

They paid him no mind, even though they formed a semi-circle around him, dancing methodically, quiet chanting breaking his own chants, sound against sound. He forced himself to look to the lake again, and something was breaking the surface. The shells were to his chest now, and he had to work hard to breathe with the pressure of them surrounding him. It was almost over. If he could just hold on for a few more seconds! The stone grew hot in his hand, burned him, but he held fast. The creature broke the surface, and the moonlight showed its muddy flesh, shiny black like a dirty mirror, a monstrosity bringing chaos in its wake. He rejoiced. He was going to make it. Holding the stone aloft, feeling it burning his flesh with salty fervor, the shells covered his chin, his mouth, his head. He struggled to chant, to breathe, as the men behind him danced. He felt the creature coming, it was almost all here. A few more moments and he will win.

And then the stone was gone from his hands, yanked away by something. He screamed, the relief from burning pain fueling his disgust and horror. No! The mound of shells constraining him fell away instantly, freeing him to see the surface of the lake settling again, small waves getting smaller, as his hopes of chaos faded from sight. The stone! If he could get the stone again! He turned, and the five men had stopped dancing. Still they didn't look at him. They had taken a knee in front of a large black Cormorant, which stretched out its knack, setting before them an object: his stone--and yet not his stone. He screamed again at the men, who didn't hear him or didn't care. The Cormorant set down the fist-sized totem of a chaos creature, and then flew at him, directly at him, knocking him into the lake.

12

The Klan back in the 1920's really had little to do with the Klan that came out of the ooze after the American Civil War. The Klan in the 1920's was part of a political machine, and focused more on "rooting out" the Catholics and Jewish folks from government than it did on worrying about African-Americans. In Oakland, the Klan ran on a ticket to "clean up" the government in Oakland, to get rid of corruption in government. Racists often win running like that, since it gives angry whites who might be losing power to some degree somewhere to put their anger. And they did win in Oakland, briefly. Of course when they turned out to be as corrupt as those they were replacing (and more racist, to boot!), they were quickly voted out, but their roots are deep in Oakland, something we're not proud of, and something that has been swept under the rug to a great degree. Most folks living here don't know that history. It hasn't just been forgotten. It's been covered up, swept under the rug.

By the time the Civil Rights movement had some to Oakland, by the time the Black Panthers were feeding school children breakfasts, the Klan had gone fairly deep underground, enough for them to be thought of as just a memory. But of course they were still around. I'd see them pop up their ugly heads from time to time. They were quickly beaten back down, as far as I could tell. I definitely took my eye off of that ball, though. To hear that they might have something to do with what's going on now at the lake felt personal.

Darya meets me at the office. She had slept, and spent some time with her lady, and it shows. She's bright-eyed, and focused. She's already brought up some schematics of the Oakland auditorium and is looking at them by the time I get back there in my rideshare. She starts in without a greeting, as she often does when she's focused in this way.

"Here's where I think we should find our way in, around the far side. There are two service entrances. They're probably locked, but I suspect Eddi and their team has a way around that."

"Wait. Let's talk about this first, Indiana Jones. I'm not even certain we...you, should be doing this."

"Too late. I'm doing it. C'mon, Walt, this is what we do. You're always talking about "the gray area" that P.I.'s live and work in. This is it. The gray."

"Maybe. But I feel like we don't know enough. And it feels dangerous in a way that I'm not certain you're willing to admit."

She stops looking at the schematic and looks at me, stands up straight. "I hear you. I do. I'm not taking this lightly. You might not understand something, employer of mine: I understand the danger far more than you do." I try to interrupt her, and she holds up her hand, "Wait. Listen. Please just listen. I know you're old and wise and all of that. I do. And you are. But I've been dealing with this stuff in ways in my short life that you have never and will never have to." She pauses, waits for me to speak. I look down, and sink into the office chair, and indicate for her to continue. "I have faced violent racists all of my life, Walt. Not in groups like this, not with the weird stuff going on, sure, but at the very least, please admit I understand the danger."

"You're right."

"What?"

"I'm not going to say it again," I laugh. I know how much she likes hearing me say it, and I'm amused just a little that I've confused her.

"Ok, great. We're on the same page."

"I want you to take the taser, and take all precautions," I say. "And I want to go as well. I won't go in, but I want to be nearby, watching the door. Somebody has to be backup."

Now it's her turn to be the concerned parent. She convinces me it's a bad idea, and I know she's right again. I hate to admit it, but I really am too old for this stuff. My brain is good, but my body isn't going to do well in a fight.

"I'll stay in contact the whole time, Walt. Call you before we go in, keep the channel open. How does that sound?"

"Sounds like a good start, but Darya I just don't know. I knew you'd be interested, but the more I think about it, the more dangerous it feels. Eddi and those folks seem to be ready for something like this. I can't ask it of you."

"You're not asking. I'm telling."

"This is above your pay grade."

"Yeah, but they tried to rough me up. They're messing with the lake. Our lake. And they're Klan. It's not just our job. It's what's right."

"You've see too many action movies."

"Maybe you haven't seen enough."

I look at the floor again. She can handle this. She'll have backup. Eddi knows more about what's going on than we do anyway.

"I had an idea," she said, grabbing her backpack. "I took this from Jen's house. She uses it out in the backyard to get pictures of the deer that come down to eat her garden." She holds it up. It's a fist-sized outdoor webcam. "It's not something we could easily hide, but it will broadcast to the office here, and it's got a motion sensor. I can put it out when we go in, and it will go off again when we come out, so you'll have another way to check on me if my phone doesn't work inside the auditorium. And I'll just grab it on the way out."

"Does your girlfriend know you took that?"

"No, and if everything goes right, she never will," she says, sitting down at her computer. "Let me get it set up. I'm supposed to meet Eddi in fifteen." I let her work. I check the tasers to make sure they're both charged and set one next to her. She doesn't need to be reminded, but it will make me feel better if I'm certain she hasn't forgotten it.

So much control I have to give up. Illusions of control, really. Aging shows me that, for sure, that most of the things I thought I had a handle on, I really never did.

Darya texts some pictures of the schematic to Eddi, grabs her backpack, the taser, the camera. "Ok, I'm off."

"Don't kill anybody," I say.

"No promises," but she smiles.

I feel paternal suddenly, and want to give her a hug, a fist-bump, an inspirational few sentences, but I do none of those things. Instead, I say "I'll see you in a little bit."

I settle in, in front of the screen that will show me what the camera sees, at least when there is movement. I'm antsy. Something feels off about all of this. If I didn't trust Susan so much, and if I hadn't gotten a good feeling about Eddi, I might have discouraged Darya from doing this. Maybe I'm more worried than I should be. Maybe I really am losing my nerve, too old for this job.

Ten minutes go by. She should be there by now, and sure enough, I see a picture of her waving at the cam, testing it. It's sending a picture every few seconds, not video. She calls me to verify: "Look good?" she asks through the phone. "Good," I respond. "Good luck." In the picture I see six people dressed in black, wearing backpacks. I suddenly wonder if the cultists have cams set up themselves, and can see Eddi's group coming.

"I'm turning the volume all the way down on my end, Walt, so I won't be able to hear you. Don't want you to give me away. Talk to you in a bit." Great. This is the worst situation for me, sitting on my hands not able to help at all, really, just waiting. It's times like this that make me wish I still smoked my cigars. I take one out and chew on it though, which helps a little. I see snapshots of them going up to the service entrance with what I think must be some sort of lock-breaking mechanism held up to the door. And then they are in. The phone rubs against the material of Darya's backpack, where she must have stowed it. I hear whispers from her compatriots and then see a few more shots of them going in. The door shuts, and I don't get another shot for a minute. Another minute. I keep track on my phone as the minutes go by. Five minutes. Ten. I don't hear anything from her phone any longer; as soon as she went in she must have lost service. Then, a minute later, I see snapshots of action--the door opens, people run out, Eddi's black-clad team, running, not moving quickly but running as if their lives depend on it. I curse the fact that I don't have video, because what I see is a horror slideshow. I stand up reflexively, even though I am not there and cannot help. Three people run out, I think, and then a fourth a few moments later. Then a fifth and sixth, but there is something behind them. Something darker than the night around it. A tendril, an arm, what the hell is it? Reaching out from beyond the doorway. One person gets away, and I think maybe it's Eddi, just from the build--the camera isn't good enough to show me their face very clearly. But the last person has a tendril around an ankle. Each 'snap' of the camera shows me another thing I don't want to see.

Snap! The person's on the ground, clawing toward the camera.

Snap! They're halfway back into the doorway.

Snap! The door has closed, black tendrils surrounding its edges still.

Snap! The door is shut and nobody is in sight.

And Darya did not come out.

***

I stand and watch the screen for a few more minutes, trying to call Eddi and then Darya repeatedly. Voicemail for both of them. I grab my jacket, put the other taser in the pocket. It's stupid, and I know it's stupid, but I have to go get Darya. I'm halfway out the door when I decide I need backup. I write a text to Detective Harks telling her what I'm doing, what's going on. I set it to send in an hour. I don't want the cops showing up there right now, getting Darya hurt, if she's not hurt already, but I do want them to show up if I go missing as well.

I take a deep breath. If I can't get Darya out, hopefully Harks will get the text and send in the cavalry. I also send a text to Eddi telling them what I'm doing. I really should wait for some help, but I'm not going to. I know better, but I don't care. I head out, jogging an old-man jog as fast as I think I can handle. It's darker than dark tonight, the moon is hiding. The little lights that circle the lake aren't enough tonight, so I've got my phone out shining its flashlight. A thought goes through my mind that it would be funny if I got mugged on my way to save Darya.

When I get near the auditorium, I'm winded, and I lean against a tree for a few moments to catch my breath. I can barely still see the camera Darya set down on the ground near the door.

74

It's still there, an unblinking eye, and for some reason that gives me hope. Probably because I'm grasping at straws. There is no sign of anything here, none of Eddi's pals have hung around, and there is no evidence of any supernatural bullshit tendrils around the door. Pulling the taser out of my coat pocket, I walk up to the door as quietly as I can, and put my ear up against it. I hear nothing but my own raging heartbeat, and that, too, gives me hope. I can't believe I let her do this, I think to myself, knowing I could have done nothing to stop her. I try to put my anger at myself on the back-burner. I have a job to do.

The lock for the door is just gone, a small hole where it used to be. I make a mental note to ask Eddi how I could guard against their little box of tricks. I quietly open the door an inch, then two, and take a look in. I can't see much in the darkness, but it looks like a hallway leading off to the left, empty. I slip in and let the door close silently behind me, holding it until it shuts. I can't see a fucking thing, really, so I listen, and I can hear rumbly noises down the hall. People talking? It's hard to tell. I risk taking my phone out, and let the light from the home screen shine. Yep, just a utility hallway. At the end of the hallway, 10 feet or so, there is an open doorway, and I now can see some sort of curtain hanging there, with a reddish light showing dimly under the bottom of it, near the floor. Putting my phone away, I move forward, taser at the ready, and peek through the side of the curtain.

Past the curtain I see a concrete walkway bordered by the auditorium seating, which goes up at a steep angle. The red light is coming from down that walkway, toward the center of the auditorium floor, where it looks like some light sources have been set up, maybe seven or so. Are those braziers? With coals? Something like that is creating the light. Well, hell, at least they aren't lighting the place with burning crosses but what the hell is going on here. What is it with cultists and open flame? There is a feeling of utter madness coursing through me, and I chalk it up to my worry about Darya. Once we get out of here, we're dropping this case. Fuck this.

If I could get higher up, that would help, but it looks like I have to go forward first in order to go up into the seats. I hug one wall, inching forward. I can see a bit more now. There is an altar of some sort in the center of the auditorium floor, stone, maybe, encrusted with the shells of thousands of mussels. Around it stand just ten or so people in the red robes, milling about, talking to each other in hushed voices. From time to time they peer over the edge of the altar-- which now looks more and more like some sort of container, like a rectangular bathtub, or...or a coffin. I move more quickly--they clearly aren't paying attention to the hallway, or expecting me, which I will use to my advantage. I sneak around the front of the auditorium seating and begin heading up for a better view, when I see that Little Red is a few steps above me, looking straight at me. And then, from behind me, five more robed cultists approach. She looks at me almost pityingly.

"Now where were you hiding?" she asks me, or maybe herself. "I was surprised when I couldn't find you among the intruders, but you must have been just sneaking around, eh, Mr. Denin?" She clicks her tongue at me and I want to punch her in the gut. I finger the taser thinking about that, too, when the people behind me rush me, grabbing my arms, taking my weapon. It's not a fight. I give in easily, and look around. It's as if they were expecting me, like she said. "Don't you worry, Walter, we'll find all of you, and we'll make sure this sort of intrusion doesn't happen again." She gives a gesture with her hand and I'm escorted by two robed women over toward the altar, where the other cultists are now circling up.

"Do you like what we've done with the place? Spruced it up a bit since the last time we were here, wouldn't you say?" As long as she's still talking, that hopefully means that Darya is alive that much longer. Where the hell is Darya? I think that maybe I've messed up, maybe she got out before and I somehow didn't see it. And, of course, I've now walked into a trap. This wouldn't have happened twenty years ago, when my mind was a bit sharper. Would've thought I'd grown wiser, but back then I worked alone so there would have been nobody to rescue.

"You were so chatty before, Mr. Denin. Now you seem quiet. Overwhelmed?"

They bring me forward and I get a look at the stone coffin. It's encrusted with shells, and inside is a dark pool of water, with little waves moving about. Maybe the water flows into it from below? I see the braziers better now, and that is what they are. Columns of stone with bowls at the top for oil or some substance which is burning a reddish light. I can't help myself: "You know, LEDs are better for the environment." My hands are free now though I'm surrounded. I take out my cigar and have a chew on it.

"The environment," she says. "You won't have to worry about that for much longer. We're making some changes to the environment, aren't we?" She looks at her followers and for the first time I see that they aren't mindless cultists, but rather scared young people, somehow under her thrall. They're doing as she says, but the looks on their faces tell me her hold on them is tenuous. That could work in my favor. Well, as long as they're all focused on me, hopefully that means Darya can get even further away.

"Sure, sure, but all those dark, smoky tendrils, they can't be good for anybody's health, can they?" I prod her.

She looks down, regaining composure, then up at me again. "They certainly aren't good for people who break into our sanctum, and disturb our work. But thank you for providing...fodder for that work." She indicates the stone coffin, and I don't quite understand. Then it dawns on me that Eddi's compatriot was dragged right in there, and that maybe that pool goes down further than I thought. And, of course, that I am next. "Oh, you get it now," she says. "I can see it on your face. You are fuel for the chaos fire, Walter Denin, and that is all that you are. But you, you are a bright, bright source of fuel. You don't even know it. I don't think a hundred of those lackeys could have provided the energy that you will be providing me now."

"I'm not going to do anything for you, you crazy fucker." I say.

"That's it, keep the anger going. Its fuel burns even brighter," she says, as she pulls the totem from her pocket and the cultists begin an almost familiar chant.

13

I think of what Susan told me after my first altercation with Little Red, and try to cover my ears, but the cultists hold my arms. Maybe I should have kept in better shape. Time was, two people holding my arms would have been asking for those arms to be broken. I close my eyes, but the sound of her voice, hypnotic in a way a deep space pulsar is hypnotic, is irresistible this time, coming into my being not through my ears, but through my bones. It is a filthy, musty rhythm, and I feel it coming from somewhere...else, not from the chanters or from Little Red. I want to fight it, but I have no way to do so. I should have spent some more time with Susan, talking to her about it, giving in to her spirituality-talk. As I begin to fade, they move me toward the sarcophagus, which is of course what it really is, and also some portal to the energy they are wielding at me. I should have spent more time with Susan period. I find myself wishing for things, remembering how it felt to want things deeply. They pick me up, readying me to lay down in the saltwater coffin. I can hear and feel the water there pulsing with the chant, with energies from deep below. I want to see Susan again, to save Darya, to walk the lake one last time. But I'm fading. I won't do any of those things again. I can't hold on. Maybe I'll see The Cormorant before I go, I think, one last beautiful bird on the lake.

And then there is screaming. And it's a relief, the screaming--it's not mine, and the chanting has stopped, leaving a wake of silence pierced only by a shouting scream. The cultists around me almost drop me, letting go quickly, but I stand on my own, just outside the stone coffin. I am free, in more ways than one, my brain and body once again my own. It is Little Red who is screaming, I see now, and the cultists are running toward her. They want to help her, but it's unclear how they can. She is on fire. One of the braziers has fallen, and she has been immolated in fiery oil. The auditorium brightens with the light of her and now I see one of the cultists, hood up blocking their face, approach her. Little Red still stands, which seems impossible, and the totem is still in her open palm. She is screaming, but trying to not move. I do not understand. Then the cultist nearest her reaches out to help her, right through the oily flames. I'm stunned, as are the rest of the cultists, all of us for a few seconds just watching it all happen.

But the helpful cultist is not helping. They grab the totem from her hand, and run toward the altar. Something breaks in the Little Red when the totem is taken from her. She collapses now, flames beginning to consume her, and her screaming changes tone. Is she dying? I see the cultist running toward the altar, then running at me, as the rest of the cultists begin, finally, to approach and surround Little Red. They are confused, as if some sort of spell has been broken, but they still have the basic humanity of wanting to help the burning woman. All except the one with the totem, who comes right up to me, hands me the totem, and says, "Let's get the fuck out of here" in a familiar voice. Darya leaves the hood on, grabs my hand and we run toward the doorway we had each come in through, the path to it blissfully unguarded. I can't help but laugh out loud.

I stutter out: "I came to save you."

"Nice going! Almost got yourself killed!"

Behind us the cultists are beating out the flames with a discarded robe, and the screaming continues. I risk a glance behind me, and what I see stops me in my tracks. "C'mon! We have to go!" Darya is urging me on, a few paces ahead of me, but now she sees it too. We see tendrils coming out from the sarcophagus now, black and smoky, moving slowly toward Little Red, who is beginning to stand. The tendrils encircle her and grow, and the cultists are backing away, realizing perhaps that this wasn't all a dream after all. I feel for them. This shit is real. There is a thumping now, though nobody is chanting, and I feel the totem pulse in my hand. I shove it into my coat pocket, and we are still watching, because the spectacle is beyond anything we've seen before, yes, but also because it's difficult to look away from what is happening, like a car crash happening right in front of you.

The tendrils encircle Little Red, the flames out now, and with the pulsing beat from the sarcophagus, constrict around her, darkening until we can't see through them at all. They pulse with the rhythm, the strange beat growing louder. The screaming has finally stopped, and then we hear a low rumble coming from her, and then another scream. It starts low and quiet and builds as the tendrils quickly retreat, exposing her body. Except it isn't her any longer, not really. A tall, thin man stands in her place. He could be a brother to her, except I know instinctively that this has been who she was all along. This is a revelation, not a newness. He is not burned at all, and his *white* robes are clean as if they had just come back from the cleaners.

Darya whispers to herself, "You have got to be kidding me" and now it's my turn to grab her hand.

"Let's go," I say. She nods, and stands in place. I give the man one last look, and he is looking directly at me. He raises one arm and points. I know he's pointing at us, but I feel a tug from my pocket. He wants us, but it's the totem he really wants.

In a deep voice, one that hums with the darkness of the creature which revealed him, he commands the remaining cultists: "Bring. Them. To. Me."

We run.

***

I feel invigorated by the release of her...of *his* hold on me, and I can almost keep up with Darya, who is waiting for me. We have twenty yards to the doorway, and we cover it quickly, not looking behind us now. The light is low, and Darya takes her phone out, lighting the way, but I see already that there is something wrong with the doorway we're heading for. Two cultists stand in front of the curtain, or Klan members outright, as their robes are white, not red. They don't appear to have weapons, but they are big bastards, both at least six-five, broad-shouldered. They stand directly in our way, right in front of the curtain. I steal a glance behind us, and the cultists back by the altar seem to be still confused, standing around. I hope they are trying to fight his control maybe, though The Leader is striding calmly toward us.

"He looks pretty good for having been on fire," Darya says to me as we stop moving toward the doorway, gauging our options.

"Nice move with the brazier, by the way. Very Game of Thrones."

"Oh yeah? I don't watch that stuff. You don't pay me enough to afford premium streaming."

"Tell you what," I say, looking up toward the stands, then back to the door, and back again to The Leader, "we get home alive, I'll look into giving you a raise."

"It's cute you think I'm still going to work for you after this," Darya tells me, brandishing her taser. "Maybe we should think again about getting some guns."

The red-robed cultists are falling into line now, moving toward us, and we're being pinned between them and the giant Klan men by the doorway. The Leader is frowning still at us. I get my first good look at him, and I could swear I know him from somewhere. Angular features, white hair, dark eyes. I pull out my taser now, readying myself for a last stand that doesn't look good for us.

"We've gotten out of worse scrapes before," I try to sound confident.

"We really haven't."

"Ok, right, we haven't. What say we try to go through the goons at the curtain before the others get to us."

Darya starts moving before I've even finished my sentence, and I follow her. As she approaches the men they stay put, blocking the doorway, hands in fists ready for a fight. We can't see their faces with their hoods, and I have a strange idea that there's nothing at all inside those robes. Darya walks right up to one and tries to tase him, and he knocks her on her back with a casual swat of his hand. Darya is caught off-guard. "I don't think we're getting out that way," she says as she gets up, the Klan men not moving toward her at all. We are now almost surrounded, two ridiculously large men in front of us, five red-robed cultists and The Leader right behind them. I decide to switch tactics.

"What do you want, Mr. Wonderful," I say to him. "This?" I pull the totem out of my hand and hold it up. His eyes widen in something I can only call lust.

"Give it to me."

It's an odd kind of stone, almost like a shiny kind of shale. It feels like it should be fragile, but it's clearly not. I don't have any moves left, except this one, so I make it, no matter how ridiculous it might feel: I put it back in my pocket leaving my hand there. "No. Finder's keepers, Mr. Magic." He starts toward me again, and I quickly pull out my hand and throw with all of my might up into the stands to the side of us, saying, "You want it, go get it!" It lands in the seats with some clunky bounces, and he shrieks, heading toward the stairs to the seats.

Almost as an afterthought, he says to his followers: "Kill them."

***

I look at Darya. "It was worth a shot," I say, shrugging my shoulders, as the red-robes close in, and the white-robes continue to block the doorway. The cultists in the red robes are moving slowly toward us, their faces oddly empty of expression, their eyes glassy. There is still a "thooom-thooom" base coming from the sarcophagus, and I hear The Leader scraping around in the seats for the totem, distracted. For a moment I almost think we can take them in their distracted, not-fully-conscious state. And then I hear a slam behind the Klansmen, and I turn just in time to see the a person slam into them from behind, knocking them stumbling forward. It's Eddi, and they are quickly followed by Harks, who looks around, summing up the situation. "Police. Back up, now," she says loudly, but calmly, bringing her gun up to chest level, pointing it at the two Klansmen who are getting their bearings and turning toward her. They hold up their fists again, and move toward her. I notice the red-robes have stopped moving toward us, their eyes wide. Without a second warning, she lowers the gun slightly, and pulls off two shots in quick succession, aiming at the leg of first one Klansman, and then the other. And then the fiftieth crazy thing today happens.

Instead of yelling in pain, or falling to the ground, or even just recoiling from the sound of the gunfire in this enclosed space, they move toward her and Eddi. On instinct I look up and see

79

The Leader looking over the edge of the seating toward us, eyes heavy-lidded, mouth moving. Harks shoots again, to no avail, as one of the Klansmen knocks Eddi down with one hard punch to the chest. "Harks!" I shout. "Forget them! Aim for that guy in the stands!" I point to The Leader, and Harks doesn't hesitate as the Klansman gets closer to her. She briefly aims up toward the stands, and shoots. I'm already fairly certain she didn't aim to hit him--she's a fair shot--but she does hit the cement railing he's leaning against, and he is indeed startled out of whatever trance he'd put himself in, his hands coming off the cement, his eyes opening, and his mouth open in shock. At the same moment, the white-robed Klansmen drop to the ground like sandbags, and then there is only their robes, lying where they had fallen. To her credit, Harks ignores that impossible event, and keeps her gun trained on The Leader.

"You!" She yells. "Get your hands up." His hands are already halfway there in shock, and then he drops below her line of sight before she can get a shot off. His voice resonates still, as he tells the remaining cultists to stop us at any cost.

But we're already moving to the doorway, Darya helping Eddi up from the knockdown they took, and we are moving behind Harks through the curtain. I hear two more shots behind us, and then we're down the hallway and out the door, Harks behind us, and the cultists on our heels, into the night air.

***

I notice immediately that we're moving like a unit, as if this is our normal Thursday evening thing, running from a white-supremacist sorcerer and his followers. Darya takes the lead while Eddi and I sort of support each other as we go, since I'm old and Eddi has just had the wind knocked out of them. Harks is bringing up the rear, checking our backs for pursuit, gun still out, but pointed at the ground. As we move onto the lake path, Darya stops and we all catch up. She looks at me. "Where to?" I look to Harks, then Eddi, the two people who really should be making this decision. Harks is a good cop and Eddi leads some sort of secret Black Panther society, what the hell are they asking me for? But I do know where we should go.

"You have a car?" I look at Eddi and Harks.

Harks responds. "I'm right there," and points a little ways down the path, where street parking meets the lake area.

"A Subaru?" Darya says just under her breath. "Maybe I have a chance."

"What?" Harks asks, confused. I start to move toward Harks' car. I don't see any cultists behind us just yet. I hop in front, Eddi and Darya in back, and as Harks starts the car, the rest of us do see something behind us. Red-robed cultists opening the door of the auditorium, and darkness pouring out in thick, smoky tendrils. Eddi cries out, "Go! Go! Go!" as the tendrils move quickly toward us, thickening as they go. Harks pulls away quickly, and we're heading down Lakeshore drive in the middle of the night. I give a fleeting thought to anybody else who might be down by the lake, and am grateful I know Stoney's not down there any longer.

"Wait. Where to?" Harks asks.

"Head toward west Oakland. We're going to Susan's." I say. "We can't go to my office--those assholes know it. And Eddi's is probably known to them too. I don't want to put Susan in danger, but I'm hoping they don't know about her."

"We'd be safe at my place, but my people are shaken. I'm with you folks for now," says Eddi, their voice betraying some uncertainty, first I've heard from them.

80

Darya, from behind me, says, "That's a good call. Oh, and hey old man, I forgot to thank you for the rescue."

"I hear you. Next time I'll stay home and let you do your thing. What exactly is your thing again?"

"Pulling your ass out of the fire, apparently."

"More like setting people on fire," I say, which gets a 'what-the?' sound from Harks.

Darya directs Harks toward Susan's while I text Susan, not knowing if she'll get it in the middle of the night, but wanting to give her a heads-up. Then I turn to Eddi: "Hey Eddi, is there any chance you could get a few people over to Susan's? After all of that crazy there is a slight chance they may actually trace us to her place."

"Sure, sure," they say, pulling out their phone.

"How could they trace us, though?" Harks asks, keeping her eye on the rearview.

"Well, we do still have this," I say, as I pull out the totem from my pocket. "Though now I do have to buy another new webcam. I gave my last one a pretty good toss."

14

Darya reaches up and grabs the totem out of my hand. "You little madman! That's pretty risky, all for this little thing. She begins to roll down her window. "I'm getting rid of this thing now."

I panic. "Darya, no!" I say, trying to reach back and block the window from where I'm sitting in the front seat. She quickly rolls the window up, laughing.

"Just playing with you, Walt. You're as gullible as the Klan leader back there," she says, laughing.

Eddi reaches over and takes it from her, holding it in his lap solemnly, carefully. "Let's not play with that, please," they say, closing their eyes and leaning their head back. They are once again amazingly calm.

"Eddi, are your people all ok?" Darya asks.

"Hang on, hang on!" Harks cuts in harshly, shutting down all of our talk. "Do I look like your driver?" We pull up to the curb in front of Susan's house. "We'll go in, and all of you can tell me what the hell is going on? Sound good? Good." I feel as if my mother has told us to quiet down or she'll turn this car around. We're all quiet now, and as we approach Susan's porch, she opens her front door. The neighborhood is quiet, and I realize that I feel exposed on the way into her house. We're the only ones around, two in the morning, a motley bunch invading an old woman's home. She says a quiet hello to each of us, and I realize that it's her, rather than me, that is the connecting thread here. She knows us all, even Harks a little bit, from her activist work--though at times the two of them have been on opposite sides of a police line. As we crowd into her living room, we sit. A younger woman who is already there stands up as we enter.

Susan introduces her, "Everyone, this is Sii, she's a scholar friend of mine who may be able to help us." Sii is probably in her late twenties, and it looks as though Susan got her out of bed sometime recently--she's even wearing pajama bottoms, and a baseball cap holds her long hair away from her face. "I'm here to listen, for now," she says, her deep voice that of a confident academic. She reminds me a little of the Susan I had met all those years ago. She continues briefly: "Susan asked me here to help. I am also here to make certain that Ohlone interests are kept in mind through all of this."

"And just what *is* all of this?" Harks asks. We all look at her, not knowing where to start, and that elicits some knowing laughs from all of us, rounding the room out, until Harks herself is also laughing. We sit.

Susan takes charge, looks at me, her gaze as calming as ever, and says, "You ok?" Then, looking around: "Are you all ok?" We respond with a quiet chorus of nods and murmurs, each of us unsure of the real answer to that question. Susan continues, "Well, then, Walt, why don't you and Darya begin. But before that, do you have it?"

"Have what?" I respond, unsure, a bit confused now.

Eddi saves me: "I believe she means this." They hold up the totem, handing it to Susan. Susan holds it delicately in both hands, like one might hold a butterfly. She hands it to Sii, who takes it confidently, looks at it for a few moments, nods at Susan, and then walks out of the room with it.

Darya half stands up, then sits back down, her hand out toward Sii as Sii walks out, "I don't want to be 'that guy', but I worked pretty hard to get that thing," and then, after a moment, "And Walt pulled a fast one to hold on to it."

"And we thank you, dear, we thank you," Susan says, reaching out to touch Darya's shoulder.

Returning, Sii says, "Yes, we thank you. Both of you." She pauses on her way back to her seat to also touch Darya on the shoulder. Darya settles back into her seat. I smile to myself--leave it to Susan to bring a beautiful woman in on things to trip Darya up.

I start again, "Maybe you can at least tell us what that thing is, exactly?"

"We will," says Susan. "Please tell us how you managed to get it, all of you. And perhaps we need to fill in the detective a bit more," she said, indicating Harks.

For her part, Harks has already settled back into her chair, hands on her legs. "Sure, yeah. That'd be great," she says, verging on sarcasm, "I shot two ghost-Klansmen today, so if somebody could explain that to me, that would be great. Her hand rubs her face. She's tired, like we all are.

I start from what I think Harks already knows, and go from there, and end with her saving Darya and me from...whatever The Leader had in store for us. The group listens intently, and then Eddi tells their side of things. They don't seem hesitant to tell the story of breaking-and-entering in front of police, which seems a testament to their trust in Susan, really, but also probably has something to do with Harks' reputation. I guess that reputation includes her shooting two "ghost-Klansmen". We all have a bit of a bond now, from our brief time in the auditorium.

Eddi takes a breath, and continues: "We got the door open with no problem, and were able to get in undetected as far as we knew. The cultists were performing some sort of ritual at the center of the auditorium, about twenty of them, which is more than we had known were even in the cult. They were encircling the sarcophagus, with The Leader leading them from outside their circle. She...at that time she presented as a 'she', at least, she had the totem out, and the fires were lit, and there was some strange, musical beat, like Darya said. We watched for a few minutes, and then decided to try to take a look around. The auditorium has a "backstage" area, and we moved through the seating quietly, heading toward that. I really wanted to find either evidence of my missing man, Frank, or something linking these folks to some other criminal activity. I figured we find evidence, we anonymously give it to the cops, and then they'd be hard-pressed to ignore these folks, even in the face of the corrupt mayor," Eddi nods at Harks, who raises her eyebrows, and nods.

"Thing is," Darya cut Eddi off, "The Leader heard us, or saw us, or something, because suddenly they all turned together to look right at us."

Eddi adds, "Even that creepy little totem seemed to be looking at us. I felt it. I instructed my people to back up toward where we had come in, but we weren't leaving. We had seven people, eight including Darya here, and even though there were twenty of them, they were all a little out of it. They seemed drugged, or hypnotized. Their movements were slowed, their faces, their hoods down, were all just blank. No emotion, no...life there."

"Creepy," Sii said. "I've seen something like that before. Go on."

Eddi went on:

"The Leader shouted that we were trespassing, and that we should leave. I motioned my people forward. I think that's when Darya went rogue, but I'm not sure," they said, smiling at her. She nods in affirmation, but lets him continue: "She tells her minions to escort us out, but we keep approaching. I say, 'We're here to find out about Frank. Frank Marshall, you know him. He knew y'all.' The Leader did not like that, not one bit. I think she understood that even though we were outnumbered, we weren't leaving."

"I hate to ask," I interrupted, "But you didn't have guns or anything? I thought that's part of what being a Black Panther is." Eddi looks at me like I asked them if they liked to eat children. I see Darya shaking her head. "I'm ignorant," I continue, "pardon me, but I was fucking there and I knew Panthers who loved guns."

Eddi took a breath and responded, "Walt, I'm not going to walk around Oakland at night with a bunch of other Black people bearing arms. I don't want us all to get killed by police." Another eyebrow-nod from Harks. "That said, we weren't unarmed. We brought out some batons, like police use at protests. The bats seemed to make The Leader's minions think twice as we took them out and extended them. She instructed them to back up and resume their weird chanting, and they did, even as we approached, bats out. I have to tell you, I wasn't sure what to do at that point. I wasn't about to start beating up these folks unprovoked, if they weren't going to defend themselves, so I headed toward The Leader, thinking that maybe they would respond to a threat or two."

"Before I got the chance, though, she held that totem up, and the thump-thump got instantly louder. The chanting, too."

Darya cut in, "I was already up in the high stands by then, watching it all. It was clear to me that that thing she was holding, was somehow a key. I hid."

"Glad you did, too, glad you did," said Eddi. "Because as we got closer to the altar, that's when the 'whump-whump' sounds from the sarcophagus started, and then it happened. Those black, smoky arms started coming out of it. They coursed through the cultists and came right at us. Quickly snaking their way right toward us. I told my people to run, to get out. I'm not prepared to fight tentacles from the deep. That's more your style, Susan," they say, smiling at her.

Susan nods, looks around at us. "Well," she says. "Let's talk about that fight, then."

***

I sit back in my chair, the events of the night finally hitting me. Adrenaline has run out, maybe. I close my eyes, listening. I should have known that Darya would be all right, that going in to 'save' her was a mistake. A rookie mistake, really. Or the mistake of a tired old man. I hear my compatriots talking, planning, and I take some of it in, but really I just want to go home. I was not made for this sort of thing, my thoughts echoing Eddi's earlier words. I don't even believe in the supernatural, my own dreams be damned. There must be some other explanations. I feel myself drifting off, voices of my friends murmuring me to sleep. I'm woken by Susan's words:

"And that's where Walt comes in."

I wake up and everybody is looking at me, then back to Susan. "I'm awake, I'm awake!" I can't quite keep myself from saying. I take out my cigar and chew on it.

84

"I know you're tired," Susan says, "And we'll break this little meeting up in a few moments, but you can't opt out of this, Walt. For some reason, The Cormorant, she wants you involved."

We're surrounded by people, but for a moment it's just Susan and me, again, having the same disagreement we've always had. "I had a few dreams, that's all. Throw in some horrible racists and some, I don't know, mass hypnotism, and that explains all of this." I shake my head, not believing my own words even as they come out of my mouth.

Darya interjects, "And those arms coming out of that coffin? We did not hallucinate that. Dead body walking out of the morgue? Not a hallucination. We have video, pictures. There's something weird going on, Walt, and you know it."

"I don't believe in all of that stuff, you know that," I'm pleading with them all now.

This time it's Harks who speaks, the first time since we've arrived. "I'm with you on all of that, old man. But I also know what I saw, and I didn't see a hallucination. I saw....something coming out of that stone coffin. I saw two men standing in front of me just dissolve when I distracted that guy by shooting at him--a move you told me to make, I'll remind you."

"And not believing is ok, Walt," Darya says, "maybe that's even why The Cormorant picked you or whatever. Did you know that placebos work, that it's scientifically proven that they work? And they work sometimes even if you tell the person that it's a placebo. So just go with us. If you don't believe in 'all this stuff', believe in us. Trust us."

I can't help but crack a smile. I really hope Darya takes over my business when I'm gone. She's smarter than I am, that's for sure. And maybe even better with people than I am.

"There's one more reason The Cormorant may have chosen you, Mr. Denin," Sii breaks the silence. "Out of all of us, you may be closest to death."

Even Susan looks at her askance for that one. I let out an uncomfortable chuckle. "That may be true, probably is true. But why would that matter?" I ask.

Sii continues: "She may not be able to influence any of the rest of us that directly. Her power is weakened by something, most likely by the activities of these cultists, as you call them. But from what Susan has told me, you have lived here a long time, and have lived right by the lake. You have interacted with the lake, the birds, the people around it. You have walked the lake. Unintentionally, you have connected yourself to it spiritually, even if that fact represents the very facts about which you don't believe. You've become a...," Sii pauses, looking for the right word.

"A mascot?" Darya says, laughing.

"A symbol, yes," Sii laughs back. "And as that symbol, The Cormorant has reached out to you. She may not have had any choice."

"She wouldn't be the first to choose me for lack of options," I say. Susan smacks me on the shoulder. "I have to ask though, Sii, if all of this involves protecting the lake, protecting Oakland spiritually, why me? Eddi lives by the lake, they are involved deeply in it, and is a spiritual protector. You and other Ohlone folks are working even now to protect this place, and those around it--you had a shellmound protest just last month! I'm an old white guy on his way out. There has got to be a better choice."

"Maybe The Cormorant is getting old and making poor choices too," Darya jokes.

Sii doesn't laugh when she responds, "She may have chosen you to make a sacrifice. To be a sacrifice." She looks me in the eye, and I feel the weight of her words.

Darya responds more seriously now, "Respectfully, Sii, I'm with Walt on this one. I can't see why you, or the spirits of the lake would sign him up to be some sort of white savior. That doesn't seem right."

"I didn't say 'savior'. I said 'sacrifice'. A kind of self-sacrifice, perhaps."

The room is quiet, with most of the people decidedly looking away from me, and away from Sii.

"I'm not much for sacrificing, I have to say," I pause, look around the room. "But we have all sacrificed to just get here, I suppose. I'm not going to worry too much about what you just said until I get some rest. Will you take me home, Harks?" She nods, and Darya says she's coming with.

"One more thing," Sii says. "Walt, do you have any tattoos?"

I see Susan smiling out of the corner of my eye. "That's pretty personal, but I have a few, sure. Why?"

"Are any of them of a hummingbird?" she asks.

I look directly at Susan now. "Susan told you that, did she?"

"I did not," Susan responds, hands in the air. "She didn't ask me."

"Yes," I say, "I have a hummingbird, over my heart. Do I want to know why you guessed that?"

"For some Ohlone, the hummingbird is a deep part of mythology. Hummingbird is smarter than the other animals, always fighting with The Coyote, who is always trying to kill Hummingbird. Hummingbird always manages to outsmart Coyote."

Darya says, "Well, that's an amazing coincidence but it breaks your theory. I don't think Walt is smarter than any coyote." I laugh, but this is just one more thing that makes me wish I could believe in this stuff. I absentmindedly touch the tattoo over my heart.

"Maybe I got the tattoo to remind myself that I'm not as smart as hummingbirds are," I respond, looking at Susan, who knows why I got the tattoo, as she was there when I got it. It's her favorite animal, and I wanted to be reminded of that.

"Go get some rest, Walter. The rest of us will do some more planning," Susan says. "We think we have a way of stopping this Leader and what he's trying to do. But we will need your help, all of your help. Three nights from now, we'll need to meet by the lake. If we're right, we can stop this once and for all."

Eddi chimes in, "Three nights? That's the day of the monthly vigil. It's going to be a little busy down by the lake."

"We suspect The Leader is counting on that. And we're counting on it as well."

***

When we get back to the office, there is a police car parked out front. Harks explains that she's got somebody she trusts watching me for the night. "He's ok. Officer Treadwell. He's a little green, but he's a good guy. He'll also keep this all quiet. Don't invite him in, old man, he's to stay out there and keep watch." I don't have the energy to protest.

Darya asks Harks, "Hey, do you mind taking me home? Or we don't have to go straight home. I'm restless after all of that." I shake my head.

"Why don't I just take you home. Your girlfriend is probably worried sick about you," Harks says with a nod-and-wink in her voice. They laugh. Well, at least that is out in the open.

I wave to Treadwell, head inside, lock the door behind me, check it twice. I keep the taser with me as I go through the office and into my apartment, and I lock that door as well. My phone vibrates with a message from a new number--it's Sii, sending me a text with a link. "You might find this Ohlone story interesting, Walt."

I'm exhausted, but I can't help but click on it out of a deep curiosity. The link is to an English translation of an Ohlone story:

> When this world was finished, the eagle, the humming-bird, and Coyote were standing on the top of Pico Blanco. When the water rose to their feet, the eagle, carrying the humming-bird and Coyote, flew to the Sierra de Gabilan. There they stood until the water went down. Then the eagle sent Coyote down the mountain to see if the world were dry. Coyote came back and said: "The whole world is dry." The eagle said to him: "Go and look in the river. See what there is there." Coyote came back and said: "There is a beautiful girl." The eagle said: "She will be your wife in order that people may be raised again." He gave Coyote a digging implement of abalone shell and a digging stick. Coyote asked: "How will my children be raised'?" The eagle would not say. He wanted to see if Coyote was wise enough to know. Coyote asked him again how these new people were to be raised from the girl. Then he said: "Well, I will make them right here in the knee." The eagle said: "No, that is not good." Then Coyote said: "Well then, here in the elbow." "No, that is not good" "In the eyebrow." "No, that is not good." "In the back of the neck." "No, that is not good either. None of these will be good." Then the humming-bird cried: "Yes, my brother, they are not good. This place will be good, here in the belly.
>
> Then Coyote was angry. He wanted to kill him. The eagle raised his wings and the humming-bird flew in his armpit. Coyote, looked for him in vain. Then the girl said: "What shall I do? How will I make my children?" The eagle said to Coyote: "Go and marry her. She will be your wife." Then Coyote went off with this girl. He said to her: "Louse me." Then the girl found a woodtick on him. She was afraid and threw it away. Then Coyote seized her. He said: "Look for it, look for it! Take it! Eat it! Eat my louse!" Then the girl put it in her mouth. "'Swallow it, swallow it!" he said. Then she swallowed it and became pregnant. Then she was afraid. She ran away. She ran through thorns. Coyote ran after her. He called to her: "Do not run through that brush." He made a good road for her. But she said: "I do not like this road." Then Coyote made a road with flowers on each side. Perhaps the girl would stop to take a flower. She said. "I am not used to going between flowers." Then Coyote said: "There is no help for it. I cannot stop her." So she ran to the ocean. Coyote was close to her. Just as he was going to take hold of her, she threw herself into the water and the waves came up between them as she turned to a sand flea. Coyote, diving after her, struck only the sand. He said: "I wanted to clasp my wife but took hold of the sand. My wife is gone."
>
> Coyote thought he knew more than anyone; but the hummingbird knew more. Then Coyote wanted to kill him. He caught him, struck him, and mashed him

entirely. Then he went off. The hummingbird came to life, flew up, and cried: "Lakun, dead," in mockery. Coyote caught him, made a fire, and put him in. He and his people had gone only a little way when the hummingbird flew by crying: "Lakun!" Coyote said: "How shall I kill him?" They told him: "The only way is for you to eat him." Then Coyote swallowed him. The hummingbird scratched him inside. Coyote said: "What shall I do? I shall die." They said: "You must let him out by defecating." Then Coyote let him out and the hummingbird flew up crying: "Lakun!" -- Rumsien Costanoan Myth

I stand while I read it. The language is odd to me, yet kind of sublime. It somehow just...fits into this evening. It resonates. I read it again and then decide I have to get some sleep. A quick shower. As I brush my teeth I look at my faded tattoo: A hummingbird aloft, drinking from a bell-shaped flower. The color has almost gone from it, my skin wrinkled and loose from age, even on my chest, which hasn't seen much sun in my lifetime. I have always thought of the tattoo as my good-luck charm, even when looking at it made me sad, after Susan and I had called it quits. I cup my hand over it now. Maybe it will be good luck for me one more time. I climb into bed. And of course I'm suddenly awakened by the aches already starting in my body from the night's adventures. I think of The Cormorant as I drift off, and I say aloud, "Well, old lady, if you're going to give me some sort of sign, then now is the time."

15

Instead of seeing The Cormorant or the lake as I finally drift off, the first thing I dream about is The Leader. He's indoors, not the auditorium, as far as I can tell, but underground somewhere. Once again I can feel that I'm dreaming, and a vividness comes with that feeling. He's standing in an underground cavern of some sort, and scant light comes from somewhere that I can't figure out. Dream light, I guess. I think about waking myself up--I don't like this sort of thing, and I'm not sure I want to be here. But then he kneels down, and I see a body of water in front of him. An underground lake. I look around, hoping to see The Cormorant, or at least 'a Cormorant', something to tell me that I shouldn't wake myself up. Curiosity does that for me, as I see The Leader, white-robed, kneeling in the mud, digging with his fingers in the wet, slimy mulch of the lakeshore. My view gets closer, but I don't feel my body, don't see my own feet, I'm just a pinpoint of consciousness, somehow moving toward him. I see his hands are bloodied, sharp shell fragments buried in the muck he is digging through. It's him all right, I can see the deep desire in his eyes as my view shifts to somewhere over the lake, looking straight at him.

He digs, searching, as if he has lost something, but he's digging deeper and deeper, his blood mixing in with the mud and shells. Whatever he's looking for (the totem?) continues to elude him. He's groaning with effort, with frustration, until he's almost sobbing, wiping away sweat and tears from his face, leaving it both blood-stained and muddy. He begins shouting "NO!" repeatedly, until it is a chant, a benediction, his fists pounding the mud. My pinpoint is floating higher now, viewing him from above the underground lake, and I once again think that maybe I need to wake up. Before I can, the lake's surface ripples from deep below, and tendrils begin to push through the dark wetness into the dim light, slowly, moving with his chant toward him. I flit down for a closer look, and that's what it feels like now, like I'm an insect, zooming around, hovering where I want to. I like the feeling. It's freeing, and I continue to feel like I can wake myself at any moment. I get closer to him, look from behind him at the tendrils moving, gyrating toward him. They surround him, lift him onto his feet as his head is thrown back in ecstasy now, the arms holding him up off the mud a few inches. What I'm seeing is impossible, and I know it's a dream, but it doesn't feel like a dream. It feels like a memory.

He stops sobbing, stops chanting his rhythmic "No" and is quiet now, eyes open as the tendrils set him back down. I flit to his hands and see they are healed. The tendrils retreat away from him, leaving him standing, and then they join each other together, into one large, snaky arm, glistening, thick and wet. It rears up, and then plunges into his chest. He receives it like a parishioner receiving a laying on hands, his knees buckling, and it enters him, fills him. I see his skin turn smoky, his body convulse. And now he stands, feet firmly planted, his entire posture changed. He is changed. It's not him anymore, I somehow know, deeply. In this place, in the dreamtime at least, the creature he wants to bring forth has been brought forth, exists now within him, is him. He looks at his own hands, falls to his knees again and begins digging in earnest, slinging mud behind him. His hands seem stronger now, impervious to the sharp shell fragments, and he digs deep, still not finding what he's looking for. I flit in close for a moment, then back out. I feel that he's not going to find it, whatever it is, and part of me is buoyed by that feeling. He won't get the totem, and he needs it desperately.

Then, suddenly, he stops, stands, and looks straight at me. His hand shoots out, and a black tendril pours out of his palm, coming at me. I will myself awake.

I'm awake, laying in my bed, and it's still dark, still night. I get up, move into my office and take a look out the window to make sure my police protection is still out there. I see him sitting in his car, his face lit up by his phone screen. I'm still tired, so I go back to my rooms, locking the door behind me, and crawl back into bed. I think of Susan, hoping that will somehow protect me, and I sleep soundly through the night.

***

I wake up to the sounds of Darya in the office. I can tell she's trying to be quiet, and I listen to her not-being-loud for a while before I get up. It brings me back to normal, again, hearing the normal sounds of her getting her laptop set up on her desk, making tea in the microwave (catching it before it beeps so as not to wake me), mumbling to herself a few times, and then I hear keys clicking on her keyboard, mouse-clicks. I can pretend for a few minutes that we're just working on our normal cases, tracking down some missing money, a missing person, some missing marital fidelity. I toy with the idea of staying in bed today. I haven't done my normal morning walk around the lake in days, but I've been busier than I have been in a long time, which I've got mixed feelings about.

Force of habit moves my body, and I'm swinging my feet onto the floor before I even realize it. I want my walk, I want my morning chai. I want to see the people walking by the lake, heading to work, oblivious to the beauty surrounding them. And hopefully oblivious to the danger we might all be in. I even want to see the damn joggers. I want it back to normal, whatever that is. I'm uncomfortable with the way the last few days have progressed, that's certain. I guess that's part of what I've loved about the lake, about Oakland, about my life here. Sure, it's changed over time. The past ten years it's changed more than the previous thirty. But it's still recognizable change, some sort of gradual change. People slowly started moving back toward downtown, and now downtown is booming, the lake is all dolled up, but I could see it happen.

This, this sort of thing is kicking my worldview around, beating it up, bruising it. I don't like it. I'm averse to change, sure. It's something that sometimes comes with age, but I've always been this way. I've worked at having just a little flexibility. Hell, my job used to be about finding people in the real world, and now I find their virtual ghosts, their data trails, long before I see them in person. I've grown accustomed to that, even grateful for it, because it has allowed me to do this work into my seventies. But dream birds and magic totems? It's too much. I need to get a handle on it, and to get a handle on it, I have to actually admit something not natural is happening. I don't want to.

I sigh, get dressed, cleaned up a little, and head out into the office. I'm grateful for Darya keeping up the facade of normalcy for a few more minutes at least. She says a quiet "hey" as I shuffle out to make my chai (which she has replenished for me this morning), then look out at the lake for a few minutes.

"Let's go for a walk," I say, breaking the normalcy spell. I usually do my morning walk alone. "Walk and talk with Walt," I say, trying to keep it light.

"That sounds like the worst reality show of all time," Darya responds. "You sure you're up for it?"

"Yes."

"You sure we should be walking around the lake with….with all of this going on?"

I do hesitate, but just for a moment. "Well, if we can't walk around the lake in the morning light, then what's the point in all of this. Let's go. We'll talk outside."

"You think it's safe?" she asks.

"Probably not. But we'll bring Officer Babysitter with us if we have to. Or he can follow us. What are they going to do, mass hypnotize the whole city? I think the joggers are more than a match for some random KKK Wizard."

"OK, I'm in. Let me grab my coffee."

***

And then we do walk and talk, sipping our drinks. We talk like we haven't been through the past few days, even though we do have a new plainclothes cop following behind us, thanks to Harks. I'll have to get Harks a gift card to Caffe 817, her favorite little local place down by the police station. If we survive. Darya and I talk about the ridiculous little electric scooter things that have been popping up around Oakland, things you rent by the hour to zip out into traffic and knock over old people having their morning walk. We talk about how beautiful the lake looks when it's just this depth, when the water has risen enough to cover the rocks on the shore, but not so much that it looks like it will break its banks. She tells me how upset her girlfriend is at her long nights, and she doesn't even know the danger Darya is in at the moment. She blames me, I'm sure; she was never happy with Darya taking this job, even though she's always been nice to me in person. That brings me some solace, because it means I might have a chance at convincing Darya to stay on after I'm gone, do the work that I can't do much longer. If her partner is worried about her staying on, maybe it means she will stay on. Of course, after all of this, she may change her mind. If we all survive.

"Why do you keep the worst of it from her?" I ask. "You think you're protecting her from worrying?"

"I'm not sure. No. It's more selfish than that, I guess," Darya says. "Part of it is that I don't want to worry her, part of it is that I don't want to deal with her reactions." She takes a sip of her coffee and looks out at the lake. The pelicans are returning now, doing their dives into the lake. It's pretty spectacular. Almost nobody is watching them. "I think I like having this as my thing, too. Something I don't share with her, or with my classmates. My thesis committee doesn't need to know that I stole a magic totem last night." We both laugh.

"I'm not even sure I want to know that," I can't help but saying. "But I hear you. Yeah, it's your thing. Your thesis, even, you get that thing edited to death by your partner, your committee, all that. This is something that is mostly yours. I get that."

As we make our way around the lake, I'm glad we did this walk together. I make my move: "I haven't talked about this much, but I guess it's as good a time as any. I won't be around forever. In fact, if things go south in the next few days, I may not be here long."

"Shut up, Walt. You're talking crazy."

"You have a magic elixir to make me young again?"

"Who knows? Maybe your Cormorant savior bird will grant you three wishes."

"Funny. You're a funny lady. Anybody ever tell you that?," and before she can respond, "Didn't think so."

"Especially the 'lady' part."

"Especially that, yes. Just listen for a second. You think I like this? But I have to talk about it. I know that you're going to go off when you finish and corrupt the youth with your crazy ideas about race and class and all of that, but you might think about it before you do."

"Think about what?" she says. I can't tell if she knows where I'm going or not. That poker face style of listening will do her well.

"Maybe before you go to teaching, maybe you work here in Oakland, doing P.I. stuff for a while."

"You old dog. You can't live without me?"

"I did for a long, long time, and I certainly can. Thing is, I wonder if Oakland can."

"Is this your 'Oakland needs you' speech? It's kind of weak, given that you've been here forever and you're not really going anywhere."

"Yeah, but I am. I will be. It's a fact. And I think you should take over the business."

"You're serious."

Now it's my turn to be taken aback. I didn't expect such a quick rejection, I guess. I should have eased into it more.

"Serious. You'll know it when I'm joking, because you'll be laughing."

"Well, I am laughing. Don't worry Walt. I've got you."

"What does that mean, exactly. You understand where I'm coming from?"

"No, it means I'll do it. Been thinking about it for a while. Just waiting for you to bring it up. Keep you on at twenty-five percent as a consultant, and I'll take over the business. I come to you if I need to, but you can take it a little more easy. I already do your books, I see how you're doing. I can do pretty well on seventy-five percent. I don't want to move in to your apartment though. You can take that. But you'll have to pay the rent on it. We'll work it out."

Now it's my turn to laugh. "I see you've thought this through. What if I want to negotiate?"

"You negotiate all you want. We'll still come back to my terms, and you'll take them. But sure, you have that sort of time to negotiate. You'll be semi-retired soon."

"And what about Nathalie? She won't like it."

"No, no she won't. I'll cross that bridge when we get there."

"And what about your thesis?"

"I'll finish up my degree this semester, as planned. I just won't start looking for an academic job yet. We'll see. I don't have to plan my life out with you right this moment, do I?"

"No, no. You don't. But I have lots of ideas about what you should do."

"And I can pretend to listen, if that makes you feel better."

"Well, you sure did make this one easy on me. I've been dreading this conversation for months."

"I know. I like to see you squirm."

"Sadist."

"You don't know the half. I love this place, Walt. I will probably have to move if I get a placement anywhere in my field. This way, I get to enjoy Oakland for a bit more time, take a break from writing, and maybe save the world."

16

We continue walking, about half way now. At my pace, by the time we finish we will see a lot fewer people, all of the commuters having already walked to BART to go into San Francisco. I think about what Darya has said--only half in jest--about saving the world. That's what Susan has always been about, ever since I met her, saving the world. I was mostly content with helping individual people, carving out a place for myself. There's a privilege involved in my kind of life. I've always been aware of that, but the older I get, the more starkly it's shown to me. I got to choose who to fight for, to choose the clients I took on or didn't take on. In some ways, Susan and Eddi have had those choices made for them--Darya has to fight certain fights as a Black woman cop, Eddi probably fights battles as somebody who isn't a man and isn't a woman, battles I can't conceive of. Neither Darya nor Eddi can easily opt out of some of the battles there' in the way that I can. In the ways that I *have*. Because I have. Susan and I might have lasted if I had picked my battles differently.

And yet, even though they had fewer options in whatever ways, they also have chosen to fight for everybody, to fight for Oakland, for the lake, for everybody here. This fight, this...whatever we're up against, it's not just after them, or their people. It feels like it's here to take us all on, to beat us all down, into a pulp, until there is nothing left. How is it that some of the most oppressed folks, Ohlone Natives, and the people of this new super-secret group of Black Panthers, how is it that they end up doing all the dirty work yet again, while "my" people end up being either in the way, or actively aiding the bad guys. Not that I'm in the Klan or anything, but still, the lines are drawn, and it's disheartening.

"What are you thinking about?" Darya asks, interrupting my pity party.

"Oh. Thinking about how far up this all goes. I forgot to talk to Harks about who was blocking things up at the top, keeping them from going into the auditorium."

"I asked Nathalie to keep her ears open on that. She did say that there have been some super-secret meetings around city hall, but those happen kind of frequently anyway. She'll let us know if she hears anything relevant." Nathalie is a lawyer working in some capacity for Oakland, I never really asked how she fit in there. I didn't want to intrude, didn't want Darya to think I would ask that of her, ask her to get us a spy in city hall.

"That's good. Thank you. Good."

"There's something else, Walt. What is it? You already regretting handing over the business to me?"

"Handing over seventy-five percent of the business. And I haven't signed anything yet, so don't get cocky."

"Then just tell me. You regretting time lost with Susan? You've got some weird look on your face."

"I was sort of thinking about Susan, yes. Which reminds me, how did it go with Harks last night? Did you manage to get home without her having to cuff you or anything?"

"She wishes she could cuff me. She flirted, but I resisted."

"Right. She flirted. I saw how much you were resisting her, even in the middle of us almost dying."

"I like to enjoy life. Harks was quiet, actually. She's not happy with all of this, with going behind her supervisor's back, even though he kind of knows she is. She's used to avoiding her partner, but this is different for her. But I guess that's how it works there, when bullshit orders come down. About time that cop culture worked in our favor. She mostly was freaked out by the Klan Ghosts, as she called them."

"Understandably."

"You still think it was a mass hallucination?"

"I don't know what the hell it was. What I do know is that I trust Susan, and Susan trusts Eddi, and Sii, and I'll go with it."

"Whatever, Mr. Hummingbird tattoo. Dr. Spiritual."

"You're going to turn my business into a crunchy hippie spiritual thing, aren't you?"

"I mean, we'll do séances and stuff, sure," she laughs. "Really, Walt, I don't believe in this stuff either. I believe in facts--statistics, research. But I also believe in lived experience, you know? And we definitely lived some experience last night."

"I don't relish being deeply involved in things I don't understand," I sigh.

"So you don't like being alive?" Darya laughs.

"Some days, Darya, some days. This I understand," I point to a cormorant, "even him, I thought I understood. And now I'm having dreams about his god or something."

"You remember that really old horror movie? It had the guy with wolverine claws or something, he was all burned up?"

"Nightmare on Elm Street?"

"That's the one! You're my dream warrior, Walt!" she cackles with laughter now.

"Every joke like that gets you further from seventy-five percent of the business. You're down to seventy percent."

"You'll be lucky if I let you consult, Dream Warrior!" We continue our walk as she scares people with her laughter.

***

As we round the last bend before the auditorium, I slow down. Darya asks in mock seriousness, "Think we should turn around, go back the other way?"

"No, this is just where Stoney used to set up his tent. I'll miss him."

"Yeah, he's a good guy. And he kept his eyes open. Maybe he'll come back. I think Eddi will have a way to get in touch with him."

"This is where the body was found, too," I say, pointing to the shore. In just a few days, the reeds and grass have recovered, and there's no sign that a dead body had been found here.

"At least we know who it was now." Darya sips her coffee. "I don't think I knew Frank."

"Me either. But those fuckers killed him." I can see the auditorium from here.

"Or that thing controlling those tentacles," Darya echoes.

"Same thing, I guess," I say, drifting over to the spot where the body had laid. "The lake feels different now, and I can't tell if it's just because I know what's going on with these people, like it's my imagination, or if it really is different. Something is off."

"No, I felt it too, even before the body," Darya says. "I thought it was just nerves for finishing my paper, waiting for you to pop the question."

I see gulls, and cormorants, and herons, a few ducks, geese. And a pelican. All from where I'm standing. And then it hits me, something missing. Something wrong. It's subtle, for sure, but

I think back over the past few weeks and there it is, the difference. Feels like I've been followed around for a while by somebody that I can't quite catch following me, and now I've finally turned around quickly enough to spot them. It's like a missing constellation, little pinpricks of light that you don't even really see most of the time, but something in you would notice, deep down, that they are gone. I'll have to ask Susan what it might mean. Hopefully she knows. I think she knows.

"Walt, you've got that look on your face like you've figured something out. I know that look. What is it?"

"Where are all the hummingbirds?"

***

We don't talk more about it until we're back at the office, having passed by the auditorium without any trouble, or any extra information. The camera is gone, of course, and the parking lot is empty. We kept moving, keeping aware of what lay behind us.

Now I'm sitting in my office chair, she's checking email nearby, and I'm thinking. I knew there was something off about the lake, for a bit, but I couldn't put my finger on it. And then I chalked it up to the bodies that started showing up, which I can forgive myself for. I try to think back to my recent walks--I almost always see a hummingbird or two, even when it's not spring. Or if I don't see them, I hear one, a low-pitched buzz that doesn't really have a comparison. Nothing quite like that sound. And I love watching them, mostly because they look impossible on a so many levels. Their colors, the way they hover, their impossibly small bodies, their speed. Years ago I found a dead hummingbird on the sidewalk, so dead it had dried out and flattened, and yet it was still beautiful. Some of its iridescence still shone through the rest of its dusty feathers. Poor little guy's body had been so flattened and dead for so long, that I flattened it between the pages of a book. Still have that, somewhere. Some of them are so, so small.

"Hey Walt, maybe we should take a look at all of this from a different angle," Darya's voice yanks me out of my hummingbird reverie.

"I'm open to new angles, if you got one."

"Did I ever tell you that Nathalie loves astrology?"

"I don't think so."

"Like, to the point that we have shelves of books about it. She ruminates on it, looks through its lens at things about work, friendship...even love."

"Are you compatible signs?"

"Apparently, or I think she wouldn't have even dated me. I don't really hold that much to it, but I have learned about it because the love of my life enjoys it so much. She knows I don't 'really' believe in it all, but I do enjoy the lens, if you see what I mean. It lets me look at my life from different directions, even if I don't believe in it."

"Kind of like Bahá'í beliefs?" I say, continuing our long teasing conversation about religion.

"Har, har, you heathen," she says, then reconsiders, "but sure, let's use that for a second. You know I believe in it, and I know you don't believe in...well, in much." She's teasing back, but continues: "And yet you know it informs my worldview, the decisions I make, much like your...heathenism...informs yours, pushes you to make this or that choice. It is a lens, too, yes. Maybe it's like when you call Susan to get her take on something regarding the biology of the

95

lake--her belief system includes all sorts of knowledge you don't have, and you value that knowledge, enough to look through her lens for a bit."

"Because it pays off," I add.

"Because it pays off," Darya agrees. "And I'd say we're in over our heads here with this supernatural stuff. But maybe we should look at it as though looking through another lens we're not used to."

"The batshit crazy magic sorcerer Klan lens?"

"When are you retiring again? Anytime soon, smartass? No. But there's obviously something going on we don't get. And we can maybe piece together what we don't get if we let go of our worldviews for a second."

"I'm game, Darya. Let's try it."

"What have we got?" She goes to the whiteboard on one wall, by my apartment door. As she talks, she draws little shapes, arrows and the like. "We have the walking dead body, covered in crustaceans. We've got the seagull attack here in the office you told me about. We've got that totem that looks like an octopus fucked a pit-bull. The cormorant, your little dream-bird." She's drawing each around the board in a circle as she talks. "We've got the Little Red, who is also somehow the Leader guy, maybe. He loves that little totem very much, enough to try to kill for it, I'd say." She draws a line from him to the totem. And we've got you, let's be honest," she draws a frowny-face to represent me.

"That's me?"

She looks at the drawing, back at me, holding a thumb up for reference."It's a reasonable facsimile. Actually a pretty good likeness." Smiling, she continues: "We've got a lack of hummingbirds," she draws a little hummingbird off in the corner of the board, "and we've got you with a hummingbird tattoo, Mr. Tough Guy," drawing a line between me and the hummingbird.

We stand back from the drawing, and it's like looking at modern art for me. I want to see something, but I'm not sure I do.

After thirty seconds, Darya laughs, "Well, it was worth a try. Maybe you should call Susan."

"Wait," I say, taking another look. "You have given me an idea with all of this, even though I don't want to be on your team for pictionary." I get a snort from her for that one. "These are all pieces to the puzzle. We'd add Susan and Eddi, I think, and maybe some vague feelings I've had, and some things from my dreams, but I see what you were saying about different lenses. If there is magic crap going on, and I can't really say there isn't any more, not without ignoring things that have happened, then these are all pieces. And the hummingbirds being gone says something important. We just have to figure out what it is. So I will call Susan, but this helps," I pull a fresh cigar out of my desk drawer, stick it in my mouth, chew on it for a minute, still staring at the drawings. I look from object to object, letting it all sink in. I am drawn over and over back to the Leader and his place in all of this. And that's when it hits me, where I think I've seen him before. But that's crazy. Crazier than the things I've seen recently? It's unclear. I've lost my bearings on crazy.

"Darya, let me use your laptop for second," I say, drifting over to her desk.

"You've got your own computer three feet away! Are you going to be like this when you are consulting?"

"Worse," I say, opening up a browser and then going through her history.

"Hey! That's private!" she is only half-playing, trying to stop me.

"As of today, you still work for me. No privacy," I say, and go down to a link from her browsing history, clicking on it. Up pops a picture that she showed me just two days ago. I click on it, zooming in on one person, somebody not in the main picture, but in the background. "That's him. That's the Leader."

"Walt, that's impossible. Our guy is about the same age as this guy. This guy has got to be dead by now." But then she looks closer. "There is a remarkable resemblance, though," she admits. "Maybe they are related?

"Darya. Look through this other lens you've given us. Our guy was disguised, somehow, as a woman who looked nothing like him. He does mind-control chanting. I say he can live longer than other people too, that's no big deal compared to bringing the dead back to life with mussels."

She looks again, closer. "I think you're right. My logical brain says no way, but my magic brain says there's no way it isn't."

We stare at the grainy black-and-white photo, pixels from the scanned newsprint getting larger as we try to zoom in more. "Who is this guy?" I ask the air. The Klansmen stare back at us.

17

This was the sort of creepy lead that Darya loved, so I let her dig into it while I do some busywork. I tell her to search for "time-traveling-Klansman", because why the hell not, with all of this magic stuff, why don't we throw time-travelers into the mix. She starts to laugh at that, but then shrugs her shoulders in a 'why-not?' gesture and continues to research. I do some emailing, and then decide to give Susan a call from my apartment, more to give Darya some privacy than for my own concerns. Darya is hard at work, clicking away at the computer, little grumbles coming from her throat, with an exclamation or two coming out from time to time. "What?" "Fuck." "You are shitting me." She definitely speaks my language, sometimes. I leave her to her fun and frustration, and dial Susan, who picks up on the second ring.

"Hello Walter. Are you ok?" She's calm and collected, as always, but there is an edge to her voice that I haven't heard often, so I know she's worrying.

"Not bad, considering. Darya and I had a lovely walk around the lake this morning. No dead bodies, no attacks by wizards, so I'm counting blessings."

"I like your new positive take on the world, Walter. It's a good look for you."

"You can't even see me, Susan."

"You're not the only one with spy cameras, Mr. Private Investigator."

"Right. You've probably got Sii watching me with her third eye or something."

Susan pauses just a bit, and then: "Funny you should say that. We were just talking about you."

"My ears weren't even burning. You know I don't like to be objectified unless you tell me about it."

"Well, we were also talking about an object, but don't get your hopes up. We were talking about you and the totem, and how you were able to trick the Leader and get away with it. Sii thinks that was even more amazing than we might have thought."

"What do you mean?"

"She thinks that the totem and this man are linked in a way that he should have known that you still had it, even as you pretended to throw it away."

"Well, he had a lot on his plate at that second."

"Sure, yes. But this link isn't even a conscious thing. It's almost as if part of his soul is in there, so he should have known exactly where it was, unless something was blocking it, like how Sii is blocking it now."

"I wasn't doing anything, I swear. It was just in my pocket. I cast no spells."

"And that's just what we were talking about. There's maybe something about you, about you, your body, your mind, your soul, that protected the totem, protected you."

"I'm just really charming, Susan, you know that. It's probably the protective power of charisma."

"That's as likely as it being the protective power of your stinky cigars."

"Or that."

"But that's not why you called me. We're making plans for Saturday--is that what you wanted to talk about?"

"No, I had a biology question for you."

"I see. What would you like to ask?"

"There are usually hummingbirds around the lake," I begin, but she gently cuts me off.

"Yes, you've noticed there haven't been hummingbirds in the past month or so?"

"Exactly. Took me a month to notice, I guess."

"We've been keeping an eye on that, too. It's more than odd, but I didn't think of it as in relation to these...things we've been dealing with until recently. I thought it was merely an ecological problem," I hear somebody in the background near Susan say something. "Sii thinks I am short-sighted in that regard," she continues, and I hear the Susan I fell in love with once again, a sardonic lilt in her voice, gently mocking Sii's youthful opinions. "Perhaps she's right, but these things are all very complex," she says more to Sii than to me.

"So what do you think is going on now, with the hummingbirds?"

"We don't know. I don't think it's purely ecological. Anything regarding the ecology of the lake would affect other birds, and the bees as well, and other pollinating creatures. As far as I can tell, there's nobody else missing, ecologically. In fact, the lake is more alive than ever."

"So alive that bodies crawl out of it."

"Well, yes, there is that. And you're joking, Walt, but the new life in the lake may be related somehow to that body. We haven't sussed out all of the connections yet."

"I have a hummingbird tattoo."

"Yes, I know. I was there when you got it." I can hear the smile of recollection in her voice.

"That's a weird coincidence, don't you think?"

"I don't think. Sii thinks you might be some sort of hummingbird spirit, though she shakes her head when she talks about it. You don't have a drop of Ohlone blood in you, but she still thinks you are somehow here to help the lake survive, but with some help from Ohlone ancestors. I'm not shy to tell you it sort of pisses her off, honestly. I'm pretty sure she wants to be the lake's savior, not you," this last is for Sii, who is obviously still listening in the background.

"Well you can tell her I'd rather she be the savior too. I'm nobody's savior. Not even my own. My last "saving" almost got me killed and I had to be rescued. "

"But you got the totem."

"Nope, not even that, really. Darya got the totem, I just got it out of there. By misdirection. Hardly hummingbird behavior, I'd say."

"Shows what you know--for some Ohlone, hummingbird was the smart one, smarter than the crafty coyote, who was always trying to kill hummingbird. Hummingbird always outsmarted him though. Also attacked with his sharp beak when he had to. That sounds like you to me," a gentle laugh tells me she means it, even as she jokes about it.

"Darya says I've always tried to be a White Savior, so maybe you're right."

"I don't think that means what you think it means, Walter."

"Oh, I know it's not a nice thing. But here I am working on it, and now you're telling me that I'm somehow here to save the lake."

"No, that's not it. You're a piece of the puzzle though, in ways you are resisting."

"So the hummingbirds left because of me?"

"Hmmmm. I hadn't thought of that. Maybe something like that, maybe. And like Sii told you last night, there may be something here about sacrifice, which is why I asked if you were ok. It's not clear, but you may be asked to sacrifice more than anybody with this thing, Walt."

"I don't love the sound of that now anymore than I did last night."

"I don't either. But I know you'll do the right thing. That was never your problem, the acting on things. Getting to what is right, that is where we differed."

"How can we get the hummingbirds to come back? Maybe that would help somehow?"

"Wow. My Walter, thinking like a shaman!"

"Darya's got me thinking outside of the box today. So what do you think? Industrial sized hummingbird feeders?"

"I'd say you should sleep on it, see if the Cormorant has anything more to say. Think 'hummingbird' when you take a nap today."

"That's ridiculous, and I'll still try it, in the spirit of trying anything I can. How are you coming with the plans for Saturday? Ready to fill me in on them yet? I don't see the value of having me in the dark."

"This from the man who says he was hypnotized by the Leader, almost twice hypnotized. No, it's for your safety and the lake's safety that you only know what you need to know. And you don't need to know yet."

"Can you at least tell me where and when?"

"Nope."

"You're a hard woman, Susan," I say, sighing.

"It's true. For your own good though, this time. Love you Walt. I'll call you later."

I'm taken aback for a moment. "You too, Susan, you too." It feels more familial than romantic, but it's good to hear those words from her. We hang up, and I call out to Darya. "I'm going to lay down for a bit," I say, and she responds with a 'go way leave me alone' noise, so I lay down on the bed, thinking of hummingbirds and cormorants, of the lake, and our walk, of the day when I can "advise" more than "run" investigations. Seems I'm already doing that a little-- just a pawn in the larger game, going to be sacrificed at some point soon. And I'm ok with that. I sleep.

***

I quickly find myself in another dream-that's-not-quite-a-dream. I'm starting to get the hang of this, I guess. Still frustrated that I'm finding so many answers by falling asleep. Goes against my grain. Trying to keep an open mind though, like Darya encouraged me to do. My dream self is standing on the lake's edge again, over by where the body was found. Susan is standing next to me; she's her age now but dressed as she often had been back when we first met, in her sandals and overalls, her "study outfit" she called it then, just a t-shirt, overalls, not much makeup, her hair tied back with a bandana. She smiles at me wordlessly, and points out to the middle of the lake. The moonlight is bright tonight, but I look around and can't see the moon at all. I'm starting to enjoy some of this dreamscape stuff. I follow her pointing, and see a figure out in the middle of the lake. Standing on the water--it's the Leader, I'm sure of it, though I can't make out his features. I suppose his features don't matter much, given he can change them the way he does. He's wearing a white robe though, a dirty silver color in the light of the absent moon.

I look again and Susan is gone, and my perspective changes again. I'm up in the air a few stories, looking down at the Leader, who is still standing on the lake. I move toward him now, buzzing quickly, impossibly to just a few feet away from him, just above him. This perspective shift happened before. I was able to move around in dreams this same way, and I'm almost comfortable with it already, which startles me a little. The Leader is holding the totem in front of him in both hands, like an offering, but the totem is different--less solid, even in the shade of night, and larger somehow, too. And I can hear the low chanting the Leader is making, or rather I feel it pulsing, as the totem pulses too. But this is wrong, he doesn't have the totem in waking life. And even in my last dream he was digging for it. Does he have a backup? I would. I flit closer, but then back off, as I see (and feel?) movement beneath the water, directly beneath his feet. He is rising up, on slick mussel-covered stone, a small hill rising up out of the lake.

But not a hill. It's moving, not just up and out of the water, but undulating slightly, the shells rubbing against each other with a horrid nails on a chalkboard screech. It's a wet sound too, as the thing raises itself out of the muck. He's riding it, on the creature's neck just behind his head, and the monster rises impossibly out of the water, showing its face now, as the Leader disappears behind the bulk of It. The night is almost silent, but for the sound of this thing pulling itself out of the mud and grime at the bottom of the lake. It's covered in mussels, its head is huge, with six, seven, maybe eight alien eyes randomly dancing around its face. Instead of a mouth, shell-encrusted tendrils hang, it's hard to know how many as they move around slowly, but wildly--eight at least, but it doesn't matter. As It stands up, I see two arms, two legs, a large, muscular body, almost mammalian. I can feel the pulsing of power pushing out from its head, and I flit around It, trying to see the Leader again.

But the creature has seen me, and its gaze follows my flight, turning its head and body to follow me now. I'm directly in front of that briny smelling face, the silvery eyes dripping saltwater. Pupil-less, they look right at me, and through me, and I feel them trying to look right through my dream self into the real world. I'm not going away this time though. Tired of running, at least in my dreams. I call out to It: "You are one ugly bastard, aren't you. You look like a pro-wrestler fucked a squid." If it hears me, it ignores that, bringing Its gargantuan hand up to swat me. But I'm faster than It is, and I zoom around to the back of Its head, seeing the Leader again, holding on Its back for dear life, one of his hands grasping the totem, the other holding on to the shell-encrusted back of the creature. I go the Leader's his eyes, zooming in, poking with my little beak, because of course that's what my dream-self is, a wily little hummingbird who is tired of this crap. He is surprised by my move toward him, and tries to swat me away, but loses his grip and falls down the back of the creature, down into the dark water. When he does the totem falls too, and the creature screams out into the night, its tentacles writhing in pain. It's being pulled back down, quickly, as the lake itself opens up for him, like Moses was hanging around with his staff, and I briefly see the lake bottom, covered in detritus, shells, and algae, but with a silvery black hole at its center, into which the creature is being pulled, impossibly, because he's larger than the...portal itself. And then he's gone, the water splashes down and the night is quiet again. All I can see is the lake, and all I can hear is the buzzing whine of my own wings.

It's pretty cool. I feel safe here. I'm fast, and young.

I fly around for a little while, visiting my favorite parts of the lake, flying over by Eddi's building, then I buzz a family of pelicans sleeping quietly on a little patch of land. It's exhilarating. I feel not only young, but other. It's the feeling you feel when you can control your dreams and really fly, that feeling of quitting a job you hate, of finding a love of loves, everything rolled into one glorious moment. I fly to my office, look in my window as see myself napping, and then I wake up.

***

I laugh to myself, out loud. That was actually fun. For the first time in days, I feel like I have a handle on things a little better, which is crazy, since it's really only a dream. I'll take what I can get though, at this point. I rub my face, grab my cigar from the side table, and head into the office. Darya is still there, standing at her desk now, and looks up when I come in.

"What are you all happy about? I know you love your naps, but you look like you had a wet dream," Darya says, sipping her coffee.

"That's harassment. Now that I'm a contractor, I won't stand for it. And I kind of did. I dreamed of the lake again. It's wet."

"Mhmmm. Keep the details to yourself, employee. Hey, you want to know what I found out?"

She's at her most charming when she's figured out something that I wouldn't be able to, or haven't been able to, and I love it. I roll my chair to her desk and say, "I absolutely do. Let's see what you have."

"His name is Max Wessen," she says, "Probably pronounced like 'Vessen'. I'm going to pronounce it that way, since he's a dirty Klansman anyway." I tracked him down not because of the picture, really, but because he used to be heavily involved in Oakland politics."

"He was? I don't remember him at all."

"That's because it was before even your time," she snarks.

"You mean back when dinosaurs roamed city hall?"

"Kind of. It was back when the KKK took over Oakland briefly, back in the twenties. You know about that, I assume."

I look at her, gauging how I should respond. "I know that after the earthquake, Oakland grew by leaps and bounds, and it had a kind of political machine not unlike Chicago, where quid pro quo ruled the day. And didn't the Klan capitalize on that?"

"That's right. It was happening all across the country, but here in Oakland it was moderately successful, at least briefly. The Klan campaigned against that machine, which they said was run by Italians, Jews and other 'unsavories', including of course Black people, who really didn't have much power in city hall in those days. Anyway, the Klan moved up in the world in the early 1920's gaining a lot of power in the city, with city hall listening to them, appointing them to committees. Well, Max Wessen had a hand in that. He organized, raised money, ran one of the Klan groups in the area to that end."

"Ok, great. This is good information. Does it say anywhere in there how this guy has lived to be 120 years old? Or how he appears as a woman with a completely different face and body? Show me that part."

"You know I can't, but what I can show you is that Max's 'son' is part owner of the auditorium." She pauses for a moment, and then pretends to play the piano, with a "dun-dun-duuuuunnnnnn" sound. Only we know it's not his son, it's him. And guess what, he's a big donor to the mayor, and several of the city council members.

"So how did you crack that? Before you said it was impenetrable."

"It helped to have a name, once I had that, it was easier," and again she pauses. "Nathalie helped a little."

"I knew it. You got your girlfriend to figure it out. Again."

102

"She's in city hall. Like literally. She has access to things I don't, like I don't know, the fucking mayor herself."

"She got the mayor to talk about this guy?"

"Kind of. She brought up the auditorium and the body, and the mayor, well the mayor is chatty with insiders. It's kind of her thing. So. What do we do with this?"

"You're the boss."

"Not yet, I'm not. I did the work, you tell me what's next. You're the consultant. So consult."

I chew thoughtfully on my cigar. "I think we go to Eddi with the information. They've got all of these connections, and we know they were looking for the higher-up connections to the auditorium. And I suspect they will be delighted to know a Klansman from the twenties is somehow still operating in Oakland. What do you think?"

"I like it. But I don't want to give Eddi too much for their plate--they've already got one person dead, Walt. And they were all pretty freaked out after last night."

"Even more reason to tell them we've officially connected the Klan not only to their dead compatriot, but to city hall. Give them some ammunition for this fight. If they are anything like the Panthers of my day, they'll be attacking this on every level."

"I'll give them a call," Darya says, picking up her phone and placing a call. "You need another nap?"

"Very funny. No, I have some research to do."

"On what?"

"On noneya."

"You're a hilarious old man."

"No, on hummingbirds."

"Look, if you don't want to tell me, just say so," she says. Then: "Hey Eddi. It's Darya..."

18

Some days I feel like I'm tired of learning things. Not like I know everything already, but more of an apathy seeping in. There are always more facts to know, always more ignorance to vanquish. That used to only make me feel more and more curious. When life isn't crisis management, that curiosity is one good reason for being alive. These days I don't feel that as often. I learn amazing new things, like about how important hummingbirds are to the lake's ecosystem (and that along with hummingbirds, bats also play a huge role in pollination and spreading plant seeds), and it should make me feel a sense of wonder. Today I'm not feeling the wonder. I want to crawl back into my nap dream today, and flit around like a hummingbird, rather than learn more about them. Or I want to go see Susan, and tell her all of the times I've missed her over the years, all of the kisses I've longed for from her. Or I want to just sit out by the lake, in the shade on a cool spring day, and let the beauty of it permeate me.

I'm tired.

But as I daydream about being a hummingbird, I realize that I can't unhear that message: My brain, my subconscious, or, lord forbid, the spirit of the lake, want me to do something. A part of me has been convinced that I can do something. And it's not the normal thing that I do, investigating, digging out facts, connecting details and people in various ways--although I suppose I've also done that, a bit, over the past few days. There is something I can do, and it's weird, it's odd, it's not going to feel comfortable, but I'm going to do it anyway. Maybe I'm losing it. It's possible my brain is failing, and would I know it if it were? Don't know. But I have two days until the vigil, two days until Susan and Sii's plan kicks in, and suddenly I know exactly what I need to do.

Darya is done with her call to Eddi. "Darya, I'm going to go home for a bit. Unless it's an emergency...hold my calls," and then I add, "I've always wanted to say that."

"Yeah, we don't have a landline, Walt, so you'll have to hold your own calls. But I won't bother you. You want to know what Eddi said?"

"In broad strokes."

"They thanked us, and they were practically salivating with the news. They're going to put something into action on their end, something about zoning and who can own the auditorium, maybe pull the rug out from under that guy and his cultists from a civic angle. Almost like getting a gangster on tax evasion, but whatever works."

"I like it."

"What should I be working on while you go hibernate?" she asks.

"Don't you have a thesis to finish?"

"Seems like a small thing with all of this going on, but yes."

"So stop procrastinating. Finish it. You want to get it done before the world ends Saturday anyway, right?"

"That doesn't make sense, really, but yes, I do. Just some finishing touches. Ok, I'll be here in the office, but I will do some work on it while you take five more naps. Must be nice to be old."

"It is decidedly not nice, mostly, and the saving grace is that I think you'll live long enough to discover that on your own," I say, and head into my apartment, closing the door behind me.

I go to my closet, open the door, and pull out one of my little memento boxes. I think I still have a few, but I'm not sure--ah yes, there they are. Small 'blanks' of wood intended for whittling, which I used to do a lot of. I'm not sure why I stopped. It had something to do with the ridiculous image that me whittling conveyed to those around me, I think, like I grew up on a farm instead of in a city. Part of it was just pain, as my hands became a little arthritic, and I lost some confidence with the knife. That's when you start cutting yourself, when you're distracted, have a dull knife, or lose your confidence. My knife is sharp, even if I'm out of practice, and for my purposes these things don't have to be pretty. I start with the hummingbird, and I'll get to the other thing tomorrow. I can't help but let a smile sneak onto my face, even though I'm feeling uncomfortable as hell with this, whatever it is. Carving some totems, I guess, I have to admit it to myself. Through the discomfort though, I feel that curiosity about life, about everything around me, has flooded back in, and I don't question it. I get to work.

***

Over the next few days Darya and I wrap up our regular clients' cases, as well as turning away a few new cases. We want to stay focused on the task at hand, even if we're not quite clear on just what that task is. I do my work in my apartment, cutting myself only twice, and not too deeply. I finish a rough hew of the hummingbird the first day, and begin on the other even before I give the first one some more detail. Darya raises her eyebrows at the two band-aids on my hands, gives me her patented "I'm not gonna ask" head shake. It reminds me of my mother, if I'm honest. It feels weird to think of Darya as a kind of mother figure, but in a way she is that, in addition to being a friend, a workmate, and more. That's something else I've been thinking about as I've been whittling: How my relationships to others, instead of calcifying into some sort of harsh categories as I get older, insist on being muddled, spread out, the kids today might say "on a spectrum". I'm older than her father, but she reminds me of my mother. What a strange life.

In the meantime, Susan and Sii have been planning, and keeping me almost completely out of the plans. There has been no attempt by The Leader to retrieve his totem from them, as far as I know, which was my chief worry. Eddi and their group, too, has been moving forward, and Nathalie lets us know that the protection from the mayor and some of the city council is vanishing, as it becomes known that our buddy Max is the 'son' of a Klansman. It's looking like he'll be shut down next week in any case, though nobody is sure where his silent partner, the tech billionaire Victor Immack fits in with all of this. I run the fact that Max is getting shut down by city hall soon past Susan and suggest maybe all the things we're doing might be superfluous.

"That will just corner him, I think," Susan says after some thought. "It will force his hand. Which isn't a bad thing--it's what we want, actually. But I think he had planned on making his move Saturday anyway, which is why we're countering him then."

"You have to let me in on it, at least a little, Susan. Please. You know I hate being in the dark."

"I think you can figure it out if you let yourself. You're a smart man. With a newly opened mind, right?" she's teasing me, but also encouraging me.

"If I had to guess, I'd say he's going to try to use that night as some sort of power source," I say. I hadn't yet told her about my most recent dream. For some reason I am embarrassed by it. Doesn't make sense, but I am embarrassed nonetheless.

"I think you're right. He needs to tap into something bigger than his people, than that thing in the auditorium."

"Didn't his totem do that? And we've got that now."

She pauses for a few beats. "Yes, that's right, we think. But it's more complex than that. The totem doesn't have its own power. It's a focus, a locus for him to put his will into. Kind of like you and your cigar butts."

"My cigar butts never brought demons from the lake."

"As far as you know," she jokes with me. "It's an example. They are your totem in a way. You chew on them to think more clearly, you focus your energy on it, and it helps you come up with answers. This is similar."

"I'm trying, Susan, I really am. I hope you're right about that. The focus thing."

"I hope I am too. So tomorrow is Saturday. The vigil is at 7 p.m. You're going to meet us at six, on the lake. We'll tell you where just before. Won't take you long to get there."

"Again, why the secrecy?"

"We're not sure how he knows what he knows. We don't want to show our hand."

"You think Darya is a spy for evil or something?"

"No, not that, not at all. But there are other ways of knowing."

"He doesn't have mics here, I promise you."

"Just trust me, Walt. He may be listening, despite what you think. You trust me." It's not a question, but a reminder. It makes me want to kiss her.

"I do. I'll see you tomorrow. Around six. Somewhere." Laughing, we hang up.

Darya peeks in from the office. "You laughing to yourself? Hold it together."

"Talking to Susan."

"Ah good. Six tomorrow, yes?"

"Always the last to know," I say, mostly to myself.

"I'm going home to make love to my wife," she says, quoting one of her favorite movies.

"You know," I say, "I should have known you'd make a great P.I. when you started quoting 'Clue'."

"It's the best. I may watch it again tonight. After the lovemaking."

"All right, enough, enough. Keep the details to yourself."

"A lady never tells," she smiles, heading back out into the office.

"You're no lady," I shout, belatedly, when she's almost out the office door.

"You got that right!" she shouts back.

I pick up the hummingbird and start carving again. Lose myself in it, until it's dark and I'm tired and I look at my handiwork in a conscious way for the first time in, what, in hours. My hands hurt. It looks good. Can't capture any of the beautiful iridescence that hummingbirds have because I'm working in wood, but I like what I see. Pretty little fella. Like a child, I put him under my pillow when I go to bed, but even though he's there, I have a blissfully dreamless night's sleep.

***

And then Saturday is here. I feel oddly comfortable with the feeling of stillness and quiet in the office without Darya there. She texted early, before I woke, to let me know that she was working with Susan and Eddi on preparations for tonight. What am I supposed to do, I texted back, just wait around? She acknowledged that doing 'nothing' would be the most difficult for me, but that's exactly what I should be doing, according to Sii. Resting. Relaxing. Tonight would be difficult in various ways, Sii's message was passed along to me--it would be taxing on all of us physically, mentally, spiritually. I don't know what it might be like to be tired spiritually, but I have experience with the others in spades. In a different time, just waiting would be tough for me--but I've grown more comfortable with taking it easy lately. Some of that is just forced on you, as your body slows down, and as it takes more work to keep your mind on track, to remember what you need to remember. Some of it is just experience, too, knowing that you have to have some down time or you don't keep your edge. Lately there's been another aspect though, an aspect of simply appreciating what I've had. I'm not ready to die or anything, but I am ready to look back and appreciate it all, even the bad times, and find myself grateful for it all. Not nostalgic, that's not this feeling. Nostalgia feels a little indulgent. This is just gratitude. And it feels good. I think about all of this while I put the finishing touches on my other woodworking project. I no longer feel so opposed to being the sacrifice. Maybe it's time.

I get a feeling sometimes when I'm carving, I suppose people who sculpt, or paint or whatever feel it too, where the thing just comes out of me. That's how the hummingbird felt, as if the movements of the knife with the wood were predestined, somehow, releasing the bird from the wood rather than carving an image into it. This other totem I'm carving, it also comes out of me, but if feels like it has to be pulled out by me. It feels more like work. I worry more about cutting myself, and do get a few more nicks. With the hummingbird carving, I thought about Oakland, about the loves of my life, about friendships that have sustained me for over seventy years. The house I grew up in over in East Oakland. School over on Broadway. Working with my father for years in his auto shop, and learning almost nothing about cars, but a lot about how to work with machines, and with people. I thought a lot about Susan while carving, and about the other descendents of Ohlone folks that I met through her.

But with this other totem, none of those thoughts will stay with me. The poisons of my life pour into it. That one time I pushed a girlfriend in a fit of rage, and she looked at me aghast. The anger and shame I felt around getting pulled over, drunk driving. The bar fights, way back when I still drank too much. Disappointed looks from my parents when I decided to not go on to college. Even more disappointment when I joined the army, and was discharged too early for it to be really honorable. The mistakes, the failures, the harm I've caused in the world. Once I started engraving all of that in the newer totem, I felt like I couldn't stop until it was done. I don't know how I would know when it was done, but eventually I was finished. I was sweating, and maybe crying a bit. If this is spiritual, then I don't want anything to do with it.

When I felt done, though, it was a relief. I had a fair copy of The Leader's totem, there in my hand. Somehow I had found that creature, in that little block of wood, darkened by my sweat and a bit of blood from nicking myself. Not sure what drove me to do this one, or to do the hummingbird, really, either. Just felt right. I do sometimes go with my gut; though that's not always the best strategy, sometimes it's all you have. This felt like one of those times. I'm definitely in over my head. The only thing keeping me from panic about that is the web of people supporting me. I trust them. Even Eddi and Sii, who I don't know well at all--I feel supported by them as much as by Darya and Harks, who I suppose are two of my closest friends at this point.

I hold the creature totem in one hand, and the hummingbird in the other. They balance, somehow, in ways that I just don't understand. But it feels right. I don't think I could have done justice to the hummingbird without also...pulling out...the creature totem. And it's an ugly bastard. Too many eyes, distributed unevenly over its face, tentacles where a mouth should be, flowing down like a fucked up beard. It's beautiful in its own way, too, I suppose. I like looking at it as I rub some wood oil into it, giving in a cooler texture. Not sure why I want to make it so that it lasts, but I do. Hummingbird too, I decide, though I try to keep the original wood coloring shining through on that one. They're so different. One feels natural, the other not so much. But they're both part of me, I suppose. Simple truth. I like that.

I take a nap in the early afternoon, worn out from carving, and I dream of the hummingbird and the creature, but they're regular dreams, not the seemingly real ones I had almost become used to. They're stress dreams, I guess, thinking about what is to come tonight.

And what is to come tonight? The vigil is has become an annual event in Oakland. It had started out as a vigil for Oscar Grant, a young man murdered by police at a BART station. Tragically, it had grown into a yearly event where the names of others were added. Young black men and women killed by police happens too much in and around Oakland. In and around our entire country. Sahleem Tindle, Oscar Grant, Alan Blueford, Stephon Clark. The vigil has changed to reflect many names, many deaths, many injustices. It's become something needed here, as change is slow, and that moral arc of the universe doesn't feel like it's bending in the right direction some days. It's needed because we are a community, and we have to grieve as a community for these people, for ourselves, for the injustice as well. People bring candles, or candle apps on their phones, and encircle the lake completely, to a greater or lesser degree. They meet at dusk, and as the sun goes down, they light the candles, sing songs, talk with one another, grieve. I have been to a few. I feel out of place sometimes, more part of the problem than any solution. I suppose I grieve in other ways. Even Harks goes sometimes. That woman has a complex moral compass, though we've not talked about it. The vigil is powerful. People cry, sing, laugh. There is some anger, and it's channeled into the crying, the talking. Whatever Susan and Sii have planned, whatever the Leader has planned, I can sort of see why tonight would be a good night to do it. Lots of people will be out, so it's easier to do things out in the open, with many people about. I won't pretend to understand the shamanistic stuff, but if even an old atheist like me can feel the power of the vigil, it makes sense that evil people might want to hijack that power.

And then the day is almost done. It's cooling off, and I can hear people begin to gather outside by the lake in greater numbers. I look out the window and see Darya coming up the walk. "Hey Walt. You ready?"

"Let me just grab my coat, in case," and do just that, putting a totem in each pocket. I make sure I have my phone, my wallet, keys. I look around the office, wondering if I'll be back. I definitely feel the possibility that I won't encroaching into my mind. Could this be it? It's a ridiculous thought, but then again, this whole thing is a farce, really, making fun of most of what I've known to be true about the world. I wonder for a moment if I'm already gone, and this is a death dream of some sort, a kind of purgatory, though I never believed in that either.

"Walt, you ok?" Darya is concerned. Apparently I drifted for a moment. I hold the hummingbird in my left hand, leaving it in my pocket. I feel it in my hand, feeling it's edges, the few feathers I inscribed, the sharp beak, the soft finish of the wood. It does help me focus. Huh. Maybe I'm getting the hang of this.

"Yes. I'm here. I'm ready. Where are we going?"

"Not far," Darya says, and we walk. People are milling about, some just cleaning up from a day at the lakeside, some getting ready for the vigil, people all talking softly, almost respectfully. Even the children, who I can usually hear crying about not wanting to go home, or not wanting to be here at the lake, are mostly quiet. Darya keeps her own counsel about where we're going, and we walk north along the lakeside, until we round onto Grand Avenue and it's suddenly hits me where I think we're going, where we must be going.

"We're going to Fairyland, aren't we?" I ask, though I know the answer.

"Yep. Children's Fairyland."

I hold the hummingbird in one hand, and slip my other hand into the other pocket of my jacket, holding the creature tight.

"That makes sense," I say, palming the totems, "and I brought my toys."

19

Kids seem to really love Children's Fairyland, which I suppose is appropriate. It's a lovely jewel in the set of gems that is the park around the lake. Most of it is hidden away from casual viewing by trees, shrubs, and other landscaping. You could miss it completely when walking around the outside of the lake, except for the large, colorful "CHILDREN'S FAIRYLAND" sign on a prominent little lakeside hill. My favorite part of Fairyland, aside from the fact that it's called 'Fairyland', is that it's based on fairy tales that are public domain. Little old woman who lives in the shoe, Alice In Wonderland, Peter Rabbit, things like that. Also random pieces like "The Happy Dragon" and "Willie the Whale" that make me think that the original designer may have been involved with medical marijuana before it was cool. It's a little mini theme park, for very little kids, and there's nobody hawking t-shirts or freaking mouse-ears or anything, which endears it to me further. Oh, and there's a little train, because of course kids love trains, never having had to ride one across the country. The place has been here since the early fifties, and for young kids I'd bet they enjoy it just as much as they enjoy Disneyland.

I'll be honest, I like kids, but only for about ten minutes. They're fine for some people, and I guess I'm glad people have them. I have been an honorary uncle, and that's fine. You hang out with the kid, teach them something their parents might not teach them, and then hand them back. It's just not for me, so I'm not bothered by the fact that Fairyland doesn't let adults in unless accompanied by a kid. I'm guessing that Susan and Sii have some sort of exception in place for tonight. Still, as we approach the entrance it does feel odd going in to Fairyland as dusk begins, since it's almost always closed at night, and it is weird to not hear kids laughing, crying and screaming right around the first few little attractions. Darya walks us in like she owns the place, which tells me she's already been here today. There is a Fairyland employee manning the gate, and she waves us through without a word or a smile when she recognizes Darya.

"This way," Darya says, and heads toward the little outdoor puppet theater. It's set up like a mini outdoor auditorium, only the stage is full of adults sitting on its edge. For a moment the people onstage look like puppets to me, just because of the setting, and I wonder if maybe I didn't get enough rest today after all. The group is made up of ten or so women, sitting on the stage, legs dangling down, and they are quietly singing in a language I don't understand. Two men are there as well, standing on the edges of the stage, eyes closed in...meditation? Electric lanterns dot the stage and on the first few rows of the low benches which serve as seating. I spot Susan sitting in the front row, talking to another small group of people, including Sii, who is watching us come in as if she's been watching us since we left the office. Sii's gaze unnerves me, and I reach for my cigar, but it's not there. Instead, I feel the creature-totem again, and it has a calming effect on me. Susan was right with the cigar-as-focus thing. It's hard knowing that I'm so easy to understand. Ah well. I smile at Sii and she nods at me, opens her hand and gestures for me to join them. I notice she holds a small wooden box, adorned with symbols I don't recognize. She doesn't have to tell me--I know she's got the Leader's totem in that box, and that somehow it's keeping him from accessing it. But why bring it here? I join them and Darya walks over to Harks, who I now see is standing to one side at the back of all of the benches, with Eddi and a few others, whispering conspiratorially. When I get to Sii and Susan, the few other women around them look at me for a moment, give some forced smiles, and head off, and into the larger park.

"I feel like I crashed the party," I say, indicating the quick escape the women had made.

"Always the colonizer," Susan chuckles at me. "Or are you our white savior?"

"Maybe I should just go home," I say, looking around, listening to the singers change their tone slightly, their voices an odd soundtrack to the growing darkness.

"Too late for that, Walt. You're almost on," Sii says, putting her hand on my shoulder. For the first time since I walked in, I feel welcome.

"Ok, then. Tell me what to do," I say to them. "I napped all day, so I guess I'm ready for anything, but I'd like to buy a fucking vowel if I can and get some idea what's happening here."

"Show us what's in your pockets," Sii says. She's serious, though it's a hilarious request to me, and I let out a stifled laugh.

"You want to see my wallet?"

"Just show us, Walter," Susan says, mischief in her eyes.

"This is just weird," I say, and pull out a totem from each pocket, holding them out for Sii and Susan to see. When Sii reaches out to touch the creature-totem, I reflexively close my hand over it, pulling it back from her.

"Look but don't touch?" Sii asks.

"I worked hard on these. But yeah, if you want them, here you go." I'm bewildered by my own possessiveness, and consciously hold them out for the taking, opening my hand again. "I didn't mean to all "my precious" with them, sorry."

Sii gently closes my hand over the creature-totem again. "No, your impulse is good, Mr. Denin. Go with your impulses tonight, if you can. I just wanted to see you handiwork."

"That's some nice work," Susan says. "You maybe have a backup profession if P.I. doesn't work out for you."

"I'm thinking shamanism as my backup," I joke. Nobody laughs but me.

I am distracted by the low singing of the Ohlone women, which draws my ear and my eye back to them. It's so low as to be barely audible, but it's entrancing, low tones I hear not only with my ears, but with the base of my spine. I've seen a few of their faces before, when Susan and I would go to events, but I don't know any of them. I find myself unconsciously edging toward them. Susan touches my arm and brings me back. When she does I still hear the music, but I now also hear people in the distance, the crowd gathering for the vigil around this part of the lake, not far from the entrance to Fairyland. I'm sure it's my nerves, but I feel something, some sort of energy growing, like a big game is about to begin, or when election results begin pouring in. Or like the house lights going down: The play is about to begin.

"So, we have a goal tonight, Walt. Want to hear the plan?"

I sigh. "Lordy yes."

"We believe the Leader is going to attempt to use the people attending the vigil as a kind of engine for opening a rift for his...creature to come through."

"Much like he did, apparently, decades ago with Klan members," Sii says, as Eddi, Darya and Harks approach us.

"Did someone say 'Klan'?" Darya says, chuckling.

"You can joke right now?" I ask.

"I can't help but joke right now, my dream-warrior consultant," she pretends to chide me. "And besides, I love this place. Lots of good memories here. Nice pick, Susan," she adds.

"It was Sii's idea," Susan says.

Sii responds, "It was the will of the group, actually." She points to the singers, who I note are growing ever-so-slightly louder. Again I find myself drawn into it, the language I can't understand, the rhythm that feels undeniably understandable.

"You'll have to explain that one to me later," I say to Sii, "when the world isn't in danger. I mean, why would a group of Ohlone want to do this smack in the middle of a bunch of dead white people's fairy tales? I don't get it."

"Yes, explaining may come later, but let's just say it's a combination of a dearth of options, and of the universality of the joy of children," Sii says.

"Well that clears that up," Harks chimes in under her breath, and we all laugh, including, reluctantly, Sii. The tension is broken for a moment.

"So yeah," I say, "please tell me what the plan is. What I should do in particular."

Sii tells me, as if we're in a room alone: "You already know, or you wouldn't have been invited."

"I really don't."

"You don't? Then why do we have to keep pulling you back from the singers to listen to us?" She is serious, but a hint of a smile plays in her eyes.

"What can I say. I don't know art but I know what I like," and my mind drifts toward the voices again, my hands in my pockets now, holding my totems, one in each hand.

Susan takes over, and leads me toward the stage. "You'll hang out here with the singers. You'll stand there, behind them, and listen to the music. From there, Sii will guide you, and, if all goes well, your Cormorant will too."

"That's the plan? For me to take a hypnotized nap?"

Darya and Sii follow along, and Darya adds, "That sounds like the perfect plan for you, old man. What, are you complaining that it's too difficult?" Part of me recognizes that Eddi and Harks are heading toward the entrance, and now they have some people with them. The "New Panthers" and police working together. Well, the Panthers and *some* police, I guess. More and more I don't understand any of this. Things I thought I knew are falling by the wayside moment to moment. I try to go with it.

The Ohlone man near the stage moves to let us up the couple of stairs to the stage, and nods at me. The look on his face makes me think I've just stumbled into my own funeral, and it's possible I have. In fact, I see that everybody here who I don't know has kind of been treating me that way, as if I'm about to jump into a volcano. "Susan, just how dangerous is this?" I ask, fear welling up inside me.

She nods to Sii and Darya who leave the stage the way we came up. Darya uncharacteristically gives me a peck on the cheek. "See you in a bit, Walt," she says. I hear the singing more strongly now--I'm closer to the singers, but they are again getting louder. Sii says as she goes back down: "It's dangerous. There are many unknowns."

"I'll say. I feel like it's all unknowns right now."

"Not true," Susan says, touching her hand to my face. "I know that you're a person to be trusted. And that you're going to kick the Leader's ass." She looks at the singers, and adds, "Spiritually speaking, of course."

"I'd feel more comfortable doing it without the spirituality."

"I know. This is hard for you. But look at your carvings. There's something in you that believes."

"I don't think so."

"That's ok. You brought the carvings, you're here, and you're surrounded by friends and people who believe in you. That's what will keep you safe. That, and your stubbornness."

"I hope you're right. I'm counting on some sort of spiritual placebo effect," I say, partly to myself. I feel the pull of the singing building. My memories of past vigils around the lake fuel images flashing through my mind, images of lovers of justice standing around the lake, candles lit, sometimes hands held. "I feel like somebody spiked my drink, Susan."

I glance down and see that Sii is sitting in the first row, hands in her lap holding the small box I noticed before. She is getting ready to open it, to release the power of the Leader's totem for some reason. I give myself over to trusting her. I hope she knows what she's doing.

"Look at me, Walt. I love you. Feel the sounds, feel the love we have for you. And go kick his ass."

***

I stand behind the singers, keeping my knees bent slightly, holding a totem in each hand. I can feel the details of each of them, a few feathers on the hummingbird, its beak, little tail; the tentacles and eyes of the creature-totem. As I dissolve into the music, the rhythm of my heartbeat syncs up with the singing, and I feel a calm flow through my body, as if warm light from the vigil's candles is flowing through my veins. Or like a shot of tequila. On an impulse I move to my knees, and then lay down on the little stage--maybe I should be on my feet for any sort of fight, but I'm not sure how long this will go on, and I don't want to collapse. I grin at the idea that there's a right way to do this crazy stuff. I'm going on pure instinct now, and on the support of those close to me. I'm sure they'll course-correct me if need be. Sii told me to trust my gut.

Once I feel the stage against my back, I let my arms lay out, and splay my legs, like I'm making a snow-angel. A dust-angel. Why am I suddenly feeling giddy? It's the music, must be, or the sheer oddness of it all, the oddness of my week. My hands open, the totems resting in my palms, my fingers playing along their details a few moments here, a few moments there. In this state I imagine I can almost feel actual feathers on the hummingbird, and the creature-totem feels wet, slick, almost slimy. Another impulse: To stop all of this, to open my eyes, chuck these totems, walk away from all of this, all of these people. This is ridiculous. I have let myself get caught up in some sort of 'magic' bullshit. The impulse is strong. So strong, in fact, that I am immediately skeptical of it. It feels...like a foreign body in my brain. I keep my eyes closed, gripping both totems now, and push the thoughts away. They leave me like I've shut a window during a storm.

That fucker. This isn't self-doubt. This was that bastard, the Leader or his creature, somehow in my brain. That will not do.

I think of the dead body, that eye snapping open. I think of the 'ghost-Klansmen' blocking our exit from the auditorium. I think of my more-real-than-real dreams, and of my hummingbird tattoo, of my deep love for Susan, and my love for my friend Darya. I think of Oakland, through

113

turbulent times, coming like waves for the whole time I've been alive. I think of the Ohlone people right here next to me, fighting a fight I could never understand completely, supporting me for some unknown reason. An image of Stoney comes to mind, our many conversations over many years, his laughter, the joy and sadness radiating from him, sometimes at the same time. And I think of the lake, the center of all of this to me for so long. There's no way I'm going to let this guy harm this lake, my world, the people I love. I picture him, first from the old photograph, and then from just a few days ago, and I grip my totems, and suddenly, I'm gone.

My eyes snap open, but I'm in darkness for a few moments, for forever. I don't feel the stage beneath my body, but rather the ground, rocky and even muddy. I see stars, literal stars above me, the milky way brighter than it's ever been in my lifetime, impossibly bright. Other stars feel intensified as well, clear and cold and sharp moments of light, pulsing. I can still hear the singers, can still feel, somehow, the generational strength of them buoying me up, supporting my mind. I know I'm not really here, that I'm back in Fairyland, but I am also here. In creature-land, maybe. I sit up, feeling a totem in each hand. As I stand up, I slip them back into my pockets, dust myself off. Strangely, I find an old cigar butt in one pocket, and pop it absentmindedly between my lips. Maybe that's all the totem I really needed, after all? I can't help but chuckle, still feeling the giddiness of...what? Of adventure? Maybe. Of danger? Definitely. I feel my fight-or-flight reflexes kicked in, dialed up to eleven. No way I'm running.

Looking around, I see I'm at the spot where the body was found, the lake dark, but reflecting the galaxy's starlight from the sky. On the lake's surface, a second sky, as deep as the universe. I feel the mud between my toes, realizing I'm barefoot, somehow. Dream logic is dirty, I guess. Before I see him, I feel him, coming around the bend from the direction of the auditorium--we're alone on the dream-lake. He wears his white robes, no hood, and holds out some object in his hand, like a lantern guiding him to me.

"There you are, Walt. I probably should have guessed you'd be right here, right where I need to be. Not sure how you're doing that, honestly. I've worked for a hundred years to get my power, and here you are, stepping right into my realm with little idea what you're doing, or even how you got here," he shakes his head.

"Jealous?"

"Of course I am. But that will all be moot in a few minutes. You don't know what you're doing, so you will lose. I am going to kill you, and take the power of the fools standing around the lake right now, and bring It here, finally, where I may serve It for eternity," at this last his eyes sort of glaze over and he stops walking toward me, just a few feet away now. He is feeling an ecstasy that may be something like my giddiness. He sounds like a preacher who is enjoying the loss of his own mind. In the background I can still hear the singers, growing louder, and, looking around me now, I see little lights around the lake, and nearby ghost-like images of the people at the vigil. It's clear to me that the Leader neither sees them or hears what I'm hearing, and that feels right.

"I don't know if your mother didn't love you enough, 'Max', or if you are just an asshole or what, but you're an idiot if you think that thing you're worshipping is going to make you King of the World. Fuck, man, haven't you ever read Faust? Frankenstein? Didn't you at least see the Evil Dead movies? You're playing with things you don't understand, and your hubris is glaring. You're going down, and your little godlet isn't getting anywhere near my lake."

114

The Leader's laughter starts low and builds quickly, maniacally, like a cliché of the bad guy in a B-movie. Maybe he has seen Evil Dead? He really can't seem to keep himself from laughing. "Me? *I* am playing with things I don't understand? You have no idea what the hell you're doing!" He's bending over laughing now. "You have my totem and you aren't even using it! Even worse, I can sense it now, so some idiot has brought it to the lake--not you, no, but somebody in your group. They must not understand that I don't need to fucking hold it to use it. I could have done what I need to do without it, but now it will be oh so easy. Amateurs." And I feel it, the power building in him somehow, as he comes right up to me, the mud caking the bottom of his robe. He looks through me now, as if I have become insignificant to him, and he points to the center of the lake, all the while looking straight through me.

"That," he says, "is your new world. Get used to it." As he does the lake begins to ripple, and through the reflected starlight I see the creature from my previous dream, rising from the center of the lake, the shells encrusting its hide grating against each other, so many shells as if it's been there at the bottom of the lake the whole time, which isn't possible. It's larger than the lake is deep. It's eyes are blacker than the night around us, tunnels of darkness trying to suck us in, rather than globes for looking out at us. The Leader laughs again, right in my face. I think of the Cormorant from my dream, and then she's there, flying in. I can hear her wings, can feel the wind they make as she approaches us, flying low. I sense she's going to pass us by and go out to meet the creature, and my spirits rise.

But then: The Leader reaches out as she flies by us, snagging her right out of the air. She's the dream-cormorant one moment, impossibly large, strong, black, and then, the next moment, he has her, and she is a normal cormorant, his hand around her neck. "I hate this dream logic bullshit," I can't help but say under my breath, as I cry out, feeling rage as he breaks her neck.

"Thank you for bringing her, Walt!" the Leader says joyfully. "My master will love this tribute," he says, tossing her body into the lake. The creature is rising up still, a humanoid body, two arms, two legs, with an impossible head, all eyes and tentacles. It's standing ankle-deep in the lake now, growing in size every moment. The sounds it makes are as if it is still underwater, roaring from deep below the surface, and I think that perhaps that sound is coming from the actual world, not my dream world. I can't let it drown out the singing I'm still hearing. I know that. I have to do something.

He's still laughing, standing right in front of me, so I do the first thing that comes to mind. The thing I have wanted to do for a while now: I haul off and knock him in the jaw. It hurts my hand, but it catches him off guard, and he's landed on his ass in the mud. Out of the corner of my eye I think I see the creature turn toward us now, curious.

The Leader rubs his jaw thoughtfully, still smiling. "Nice one, Walt. But it does nothing. Nothing! He's coming now, and you have lost. Your pitiful god-bird is dead, your people will be dead soon. And I will rule this world for my master!" And I feel it. We're on the edge of a precipice now, a precipice of power. Gotta do it now, whatever the hell that is. And he's right, I don't know what I'm doing, but really, that hasn't ever stopped me from trying. The Cormorant is gone. What do I have left?

As he begins to get up, I grip the hummingbird totem hard. I imagine I can feel the blood that went into making it coursing through it now. When I pull it out of my pocket, it's a living little hummingbird, looking around from the nest of my palm. I show it to him, sitting in my open palm. I take my cigar out of my mouth with the other hand, pointing at him with it. "You Klan people were always a wee bit overconfident, don't you think? Overcompensating with the robes and burning crosses and all of that shit." I take a breath, hear the song from the Ohlone singers, see the ghost-images of the vigil-makers, and I toss the hummingbird, into the air, watching him take flight.

20

The Leader is bent on one knee, still getting up, when my little hummingbird friend zooms away, toward the monster in the lake. The creature itself has begun a slow walk, wading ankle-deep in the water now, still growing in size. Its body is like that of a muscular human, almost, but covered in mussel shells everywhere, even on the mass of tentacles coming from where a mouth should be. I hear a grumbling roar building up from the creature as the hummingbird approaches it. I shouldn't be able to see my little friend anymore--he's so very small, still small enough to fit in the palm of my hand, but somehow in the dream-world, I can. The creature plants its feet, flexes its muscles. I can see and hear the shells coming off of it as he does, scraping against each other. Its eyes look wildly in all directions, eyes sprouting up all over its massive head, and I get the sense it sees the hummingbird coming.

The Leader speaks, standing up, looking at the spectacle with me: "What the hell have you done? You think that will somehow stop Him, even for a moment?" He looks at me, for the first time not in a threatening way, but incredulous. "That's your master plan, another fucking bird?"

Laughing, I say, "Never had a plan. You've planned for what, over a hundred years? And that's going to get you exactly squat." I move like I'm going to hit him again, and he flinches. I laugh. "Bullies are all the same," I say. "Really just cowards in the end. You're afraid of an old man. Though I guess you're technically older than me."

We watch the creature and the hummingbird. We're at a kind of impasse, I guess, fighting by proxy. The hummingbird zooms close to the creature now, who finally rears back its head, makes fists, and screams an inhuman scream, like elephants trumpeting, like reality breaking, a sound that I feel in my spine as much as hear through my ears. I cover my ears but keep my eyes on the scene in front of me. The sounds of the Ohlone singers rises up once again, in answer to this creature's yell. I see the tentacles on its face part, and a gaping maw opening up underneath them, a mouth of a sort, with sharp shells instead of teeth, and it snaps it's face forward, engulfing the hummingbird, who flies directly in the path of the creature's mouth. The creature turns and heads toward us slowly.

The Leader drops back down to his knees, his once-white robes now mostly covered in slimy mud. He is prostrating himself before his God, writhing in ecstasy in the mud. My hand slips into my other pocket, holding tight to my creature-totem, finding it warm and...pulsing, as if it, too, may come alive.

"You see!" The Leader looks at me for a moment, then back to the monster he has summoned. "That is perfect! That is how He will swallow the world you know, Walter Denin, with one snap of his jaws. And I will be with him for eternity!" The Leader is screaming his words in ecstasy now. I take a deep breath as the creature approaches us. The Leader reaches out one hand toward his god, fingers splayed, afraid but wanting nothing more than to receive His blessings. The creature roars again, and the Ohlone song rising up again to meet it. It's something of a beautiful cacophony, dueling celestial orchestras.

And then the creature stops his slow move toward us, his entire body frozen for a moment. I think I know what's happening--I read the Ohlone folk tales after Susan and Sii talked about my hummingbird tattoo--and I ready myself for...something, I'm not sure what. I know the hummingbird meant to fly into the creature's mouth, and just like Hummingbird from the story, he won't be there for long. The creature's hands move to its own body, and I'm reminded

117

comically of a person making sure they haven't forgotten their wallet, their keys. The creature bends over from its human-like waist, obviously in pain, and groans the groan of a god, which sends waves through the lake.

"What...?" The Leader stammers, his reverie broken. Then he looks at me, "What have you done? You. You!" He stays on his knees, but closes his eyes. I can feel him connecting to his totem again, the one in the real world, the one that Sii has offered back up to him. For a moment I feel my real body, my waking body, the stage beneath my back, the Ohlone music coursing through me, and then I will myself back into this dream world, and take out the creature-totem, keeping it closed in my fist. It is alive now as well, of course, it's little tentacles writhing around my fingers, leaking cold, wet, slime into my fist. I focus on it, try to use it as a...what did Susan call it? ...a locus of power or some such. It's easy to focus on it, a living thing in my hand, but part of me doesn't want to hold it at all. It's warm, slimy, like picking up a handful of slugs.

Meanwhile, the creature has begun to shrink. He is buckled over, on his knees now too, the three of us like some sort of obscene triangle. He tries to move toward us, but now the water is up to his chest, and with every movement the hummingbird is banging away at his insides. This god feels pain, and that realization gives me some strength. I can feel the power struggle, as the Leader tries to hold the creature here, and I try to push the creature back into the center of the lake. For a few seconds, The Leader is winning. He has more experience at this, I know, and that's paying off during this last round. The singers are very loud now though, channeling their power to me, and the ghost-images of the people holding their vigil are almost solid now. I feel the power of Oakland, the tragedy and the joy that makes up our community. I feel the power of resistance, of the art of living a life, the spirit of a place that refuses to give up or back down, refuses to succumb to the harsher angels of our nature, a place that thirsts for justice. I spit out my cigar, take a breath, and send out a wish for Sii to close off his channel to the totem. Now would be great, I think, gritting my teeth as the creature, now only a bit larger than a man, is almost to shore.

And Sii closes the box. I can feel it. There is a rubber-banding of power, and the Leader falls back as if kicked, and now I can feel the creature is under my control, my creature-totem like a game controller in my hand, controlling the madness that is the diminishing elder god. He stands almost before me now, reaching out with his tentacles, but I hold him back with my will and with my totem, pushing him back. He's struggling against some invisible force that I am providing energy for, a force pulling him back toward the portal in the center of the lake. I give in to the flow of energy, knowing it may very well take me with it. I have to beat him now. He's without the Leader's power, but it's still a dream-scape, and I can feel that he has power here.

His chest bursts open and black bile flies forth, my little hummingbird friend zooming out, clean and unscathed. The creature can't even scream now, as I push him back into the center of the lake. He's struggling, but it's over now. He has lost, and his minion here on our planet is out cold (can you be unconscious in a dream world?). He is moving back to the center on his own now, but I keep pushing until he's under water, and I can feel him move back through the portal he came from. One more big push, and it closes, knocking me back this time. He is gone.

The creature totem has stopped moving in my hand, back now to its wooden form. The hummingbird flits about, stopping by a few flowers to take a drink, then hovers back in front of my face. Without thinking, I hold out my hand, and it lands there. I feel soft feathers shift into hard wood, and I look around the lake, listen to the singers voices still resonating into my dream, see the vigil-makers with their candles and phone-candles shuffling their feet, some heads bowed, some looking around. For a moment, they seem to see me too, pointing at me, talking to each other with words I can't hear.

***

And then I'm awake, on my back, looking up at a dark, cloudy sky and at the concerned faces around me. Roosting above me on the top of the puppet theater's little building, is a large cormorant, looking down on us. As the clarity of wakefulness seeps into my mind I look at her, and she looks back at me with one black eye. Her wings spread wide, though she doesn't take to flight. She stands there, wings spread, just as cormorants do to soak in the sun, and to appear larger to possible predators. I can't help but feel she's saying something to me, to all of us, a thank you, a nod-and-wink. After a few moments, she flies away, her heavy wings thumping through the air until she is quickly gone.

Looking up, there's Susan, and Sii, and some of the others who I don't know yet, who guided me through my dream. "Nice job, Mr. Denin," Sii says, a hard smile on her lips. "You made it."

"You seem surprised."

"A little."

I look at Susan, "And you?"

"Not surprised at all. Relieved, though. Can you sit up?"

It's only then that I realize that I'm drenched in sweat, and exhausted. Looking at my own body, I can't help but mutter, "...I was only there for a few minutes. How?"

Sii answers, "You worked hard, Mr. Denin. I'll spare you the details, but whatever you were doing in there, you're going to need some time to recover. It seems that perhaps your sacrifice is still in the future."

I do sit up, and start to stand, with some help from the others. Why does this feel more like a dream than the dream? The others around me are quietly celebrating our victory, embracing each other, softly laughing, a few shaking my hand. I look for Darya, but don't see her. Before I can ask where she might be, there is a commotion at the entrance, and I see a mix of a few white-robed men and Eddi's people. A shout above the din: "Where is he? Where is he? I'm going to fucking kill him!" It's The Leader and a few of his men, but he is a pitiful shell of himself now, his formerly deep, melodious voice bereft of any force now. He is hoarse from screaming. "Let him through," Sii commands her people. "But just him." The Leader's men seem relieved to be held back, as The Leader walks up to the stage, stumbling on his own white robe. As he gets closer, he, too is noticeably weary and worn, his anger the only thing keeping him up. He stands there alone, and I look around, surrounded by a community, a web of communities, really, as I note Eddi's folks at the gate, the Ohlone folks here, and now Darya, walking calmly past Eddi's people, smiling when she sees me standing. Harks is with her, and I see her gun is out in one hand, her other hand resting on some restraints, ready near her belt.

The Leader stops short of the stage, as if suddenly realizing there are people between him and me, as if realizing he wouldn't be allowed to just walk up to me.

"I am going to kill you, old man. And all of these...friends of yours," he gestures weakly around.

"What, and our little dog, too?" I say mockingly, but then defer to Sii and Susan with a glance. I feel like my fight has been fought, and I don't have much left. The Leader reaches out his open hand, and then makes a fist. Like in my dream, I can tell he is trying to draw on the power of his totem again, to focus any power he has left through it, even though he has been blocked from it already. Sii steps toward the edge of the stage, toward the Leader.

"Looking for this?" she says, opening the box. She picks up the totem and tosses it to him, to my amazement and fear. But even from this far I can see that it is just a piece of wood now, and cracked, broken. It falls at his feet, he stoops to pick it up, and he begins to shriek; no words come from him, just unnatural noises. He tries to draw power again with a yell, but this time it's not the totem he aims for, it is all of us. And we feel it, all of us, like a punch in the gut. A few people fall to their knees, and I find myself among them. "How…?" I start to say, and then I feel Sii rifling through my jacket pockets. "Sorry Mr. Denin, but I need to borrow this," she says, finding what she's looking for, holding up my hummingbird. "I'll give it back, I promise." she adds, holding it in both hands." Susan is on her knees too, her head next to mine. Through gritted teeth, Susan whispers, "I don't think we knew he could do that." I look up, past Sii, past The Leader, and see Harks raise her gun. I shout "Harks, wait!" and she hesitates.

The Leader shouts again, a primal noise, and again a wave of something washes over us. No, not a wave, but what comes after a wave, the receding of the water back into the ocean, that's what it feels like, pulling something out of us, toward him. But Sii is still on her feet, her hands together around the hummingbird totem. For a moment I wonder if I'm dreaming again, because this sure does feel unreal, frightening in the way that dreams can be. Sii is saying something quietly in an Ohlone language, saying it to herself, or whispering it to the totem. I feel The Leader winding up for another round of sucking life from us, and then some small thing falls from the sky, directly onto his head, distracting him. He turns and looks around, and up, looking for what has hit him, and where it came from. We all seem to feel released from the connection he had to us, a connection lost in his distraction. And then another thing flies at him, hitting him in the chest, and flying off. And another. Like a hailstorm escalating quickly, he is soon smacked from all sides by hummingbirds. The hummingbirds have returned to the lake, pummeling his body with their small little bodies before flying off again. We watch in horror, all except Sii, who has her eyes closed, continuing to whisper to the totem. Now there are a hundred of them, landing on him now, driving him to his knees. He tries to swat them away, but they are too quick, too small to easily hit them. He falls onto his back, trying to cover his face, but still they come, now in the hundreds. It's the sound of them that will stay with me, I know, the small zip-zip they usually make amplified a thousand fold, a churning sound turning over and over as more and more fly into him. They peck at him, and soon he is actually bleeding, and they are in a frenzy. His screams have stopped, and his robe is dotted with spreading spots of blood. There is blood covering the birds now, all his blood, and their zip-zip sounds continue, with an added note of wet, smacking blood.. A few more moments of this, and he has stopped moving altogether, and Sii gives a deep sigh, letting her hands drop, the totem held gently in one.

Like a shot, all of the birds fly away in all directions, leaving the bloody body in the dirt of the theater floor. Susan stands and comes up behind Sii, supporting her. Sii holds out my hummingbird totem. "Thank you, Mr. Denin," she says, and rests her head in her hands, Susan and the others holding her, gently supporting her.

I approach the edge of the stage, noticing The Leader's men have been held fast by Eddi's people. Harks steps forward with Darya to the Leader's body, looking down at it. Harks checks for a pulse, stands up slowly, shaking her head, her fingers bloody from touching his neck.

"Well," says Darya with a wry smile, "thank god you didn't let Harks shoot him."

I can't help it. I laugh, and then so does Darya. The people around us do not join in.

Darya climbs onto the stage and gives me a big hug. "Glad you're ok, boss." Then, indicating The Leader's body, she adds, whispering to me, almost giggling: "I do not think he will be walking out of the morgue."

Epilogue

A few months later, Darya and I take a walk to go meet up with Harks for coffee. She's going to fill us in on how things played out with the mayor, and with the people from the cult who were arrested. Loose ends around the tech billionaire funding and the like. A phone call probably would have worked just as well, but it's nice to catch up with her, and of course Darya is always willing to hang out and flirt with Harks.

It's early still, but the sun is shining brightly, reflecting off of the lake. We walk back to where Stoney used to stay, but of course he's not there. Eddi says Stoney's doing ok living with his brother, offered to put me in contact with him, but I tell them that's ok, let Stoney be. I don't want to remind him of what he went through. "Just tell him he's missed," I say. Eddi understands, which is why I haven't been to see them much either in the past two weeks. Eddi's folks are still grieving their loss. I want to tell them that maybe somehow their Frank lives on through the lake, but that's not my place. Let them grieve however they want.

I thought I would be grieving too, grieving the life I am leaving behind, my business, and Darya as my employee, but that's not how it's shaping up. I try to stay out of her hair, but she bounces ideas off of me more often than not, telling me that I need to 'earn my consulting fee'. She doesn't really need advice, of course, but it can always help to throw something out and see what another person sees in it. I mostly do what I had been doing for the past year, walking the lake, drinking my chai, talking with friends and acquaintances. I only rested after my ordeal for a few days. Turns out I'm more resilient than maybe I thought. In the liminal time between my head hitting the pillow and my dreams coming, I feel guilty, a little bit. It's almost as if The Leader and his mad plans gave me a bit more life, in the end. Not just the will to make a change, but...actual life. I still don't really believe in all of that spiritual stuff, my mind can't help but look at what happened as some sort of mass hypnosis or some such, but there is no doubt that I have a bit more spring in my step these days, and it feels somehow connected to the Leader's death. Strange stuff, magic, if it exists. When I broached the subject with Sii, she gave me too much information, talked about how everything has a price. She's still surprised I survived the ordeal. I was meant to be more of a sacrificial lamb of some sort, which I sensed going in, and I was ok with. That it didn't turn out that way may be a problem, Sii says, always with a confused look on her face. So be it. I'm feeling great, and those near to me are safer than they were a few months ago.

Of course, that spring in my step might have something to do with reconnecting with Susan. It's not romantic, really, except in that it will always be romantic between us. It's friendly, which is more than enough, and I'm grateful for it. We spend a bit of time together, talking, laughing. We've hit the point where we talk more about our lives now, day-to-day, than about the past, which is nice. There's lots going on these days with the Ohlone folks--they are getting another step closer to getting recognized officially by the government, they're gaining more support from the larger community regarding sacred spots. Part of that support is from Eddi and their folks, I'm told. Also, Harks is now a kind of informal liaison between Eddi's Panthers and police. We'll see how that plays out. Historically, that sort of thing just wouldn't happen, but what the hell, I'm feeling optimistic.

"What do you think of the Gonzales case? Did you read my email?" Darya stirs me out of my thoughts.

"Oh, yeah, I read it. I need something to help me get to sleep at night."

"Funny man."

"You know what you should try in your reports?"

"What."

"Verbs. More verbs. Throw in an adjective or two once in a while."

"I'm all about the facts, Walt."

"I think you made the right choice with the Gonzales case."

"You think?" she sounds genuinely surprised.

"I do. Abuse is abuse. And we both know calling in police in this case wasn't a good option. Now it's up to him, I guess. Either he'll learn or..."

"Or he won't, right. That's what I was thinking. I'll keep an eye on him. Ok. Thanks, that puts it in a good light for me. Appreciate it."

"Just earning my money."

"Just....barely."

"We should probably have Harks pay for coffee. At least she's in a union."

"I'm with you on that one."

We walk. The lake smells a little briny this morning, low tide probably. I see my seagull friend Frank up ahead, working on a mussel right in our path. "Howdy Frank," I say, tipping an imaginary hat. He looks up at me, turns his head so one eye peeks out from under feathers at me. He makes a sound, "craw!" warning me to stay away from his food. "Don't worry, man, I'm not that hungry today," I say, guiding Darya a little to the left, out of Frank's way.

"You going Dr. Doolittle in your semi-retirement?" she asks.

"He's an old friend," I say. Darya looks at me for a moment, but leaves it at that.

Before we turn the corner I look out at the lake. The birds are busy. The people are hustling about, heading to work mostly, though a few souls are here looking around, looking at the water, the birds, the trees, and soaking it in. Enjoying it. I take a breath, smelling the brine, even enjoying it a bit, if only because of the familiarity. We saved this lake, I think. And who knows, maybe the Town. Maybe the world. I reach into my pocket for a cigar and feel my hummingbird totem for a moment. It calms me down to feel it there, so I keep it around. Popping the cigar into my mouth, I feel around in my pocket for the other totem, the creature-totem. I want to make sure it's there. I feel the warmth of the wood, and part of me is making sure it still is wood, that there's nothing cold and wet in it, wanting out.

Acknowledgements

Much gratitude to my mother, aunt, and grandmother, who encouraged my love of reading with both their words and their actions. Thank you to Amanda, Sara and Charlie for such generous help in making this book. I hope y'all know you're signed on to do this for life now. And thank you to Lauren, who, when they finished the first draft, immediately asked me when the next book was coming out. Love you.

About the Author

Jeff Pollet adores Lovecraft but hates racism. He lives in Oakland with a human (Lauren), a cat (Isabella), and a dog (Snowflake).

www.jeffpollet.com

Made in the USA
Lexington, KY
27 August 2019